Also by Tom Turner

Charlie Crawford Mysteries
Palm Beach Nasty
Palm Beach Poison
Palm Beach Deadly
Palm Beach Bones
Palm Beach Pretenders
Palm Beach Predator
Palm Beach Broke
Palm Beach Bedlam
Palm Beach Blues
Palm Beach Taboo
Palm Beach Piranha
Palm Beach Perfidious
Palm Beach Betrayers
Palm Beach Schemers
Palm Beach Scavengers
Palm Beach Psycho
Palm Beach Rogues
The Battle of Palm Beach
Palm Beach Shooter

Nick Janzek Charleston Mysteries
Killing Time in Charleston
Charleston Buzz Kill
Charleston Noir

Savannah Sleuth Sisters Murder Mysteries
The Savannah Madam
Savannah Road Kill
Dying for a Cocktail

Matt Braddock Delray Beach Series
Delray Deadly

Broken House
Dead in the Water
Killers on the Doorstep

Copyright © 2025 by Tom Turner. All rights reserved.
Published by Tribeca Press
This book is a work of fiction.
Similarities to actual events, places, persons or other entities are coincidental.
www.tomturnerbooks.com.
ISBN 9798262841011

PALM BEACH SHOOTER

CHARLIE CRAWFORD PALM BEACH MYSTERIES BOOK 19

TOM TURNER

TRIBECA PRESS

JOIN TOM'S AUTHOR NEWSLETTER

Get the latest news on Tom's upcoming novels when you sign up for his free author newsletter at
tomturnerbooks.com/news

ACKNOWLEDGMENTS

Thanks go to Heidi Rosenberg and Bill McKissock.
Love goes to Serena, Georgie, Teddy and
new-born Cameron.

ONE

Dominica McCarthy walked into Charlie Crawford's office at the Palm Beach Police station looking, as usual, bright, fresh, and exceedingly beautiful. He had complimented her on these qualities many times in the past.

"Got a minute?" she asked, waiting to be asked to have a seat in one of the two chairs facing him. She knew which was his partner's, Mort Ott, and which was hers. Ott's was well-worn and had sunk much lower than hers.

"For you…I have an eternity," he said, holding out his hand to the two chairs.

"You've used that line before, Charlie," she said, sitting.

"It was true then and it's true now," he said, leaning back in his pseudo-leather chair. Naugahyde to be exact.

"So I figured I could ask you a favor now that you're not busy," she said.

"Ask away," he said with a smile.

"It's about Rose," she said, meaning their mutual friend, Rose Clarke, who it just so happened had been Crawford's friend with benefits until Dominica came along. She had come after a sexy art dealer, who turned out to be a crooked art dealer, named Lil Fonseca and right before Dominica. "I don't know if you're up to speed on her love life, but she's been going out with a guy named Alastair Christopher."

"All guys with the name of Alastair are pompous limeys," he said with a straight face.

She laughed. "Well, you're right about the limey thing. I'm not sure about the pompous part. He's a tall, handsome Brit."

"Go on. What else?"

"Well, I just met him one time. Rose and I were at LoLa, and he stopped by and joined us for a drink," she said. "He looked like the perfect package: as I said, tall, handsome, nice smile, well-dressed, well, except for the blue sweater around his shoulders."

"You have a thing against blue sweaters?" he asked, putting one foot up on his desk.

"No, I have a thing about sweaters on guys' shoulders," she clarified.

"I happen to agree with you on that," he said, bringing his other foot up.

She looked at his shoes. "Are those new?"

"Yes, as a matter of fact, Skechers' finest," he said of his dull green slip-ons that set him back $41.95. He didn't buy much of anything in the clothing department that wasn't on sale. TJ Maxx was his favorite store.

"Yeah, I like 'em," she said. "They look really comfortable."

"Hey, if they're good enough for Tony Romo, they're good enough for me."

She looked blank.

"Tony Romo, the ex-football quarterback…Cowboys? Ring a bell?"

"Vaguely," she said. "So as I was saying—"

"Yeah, you got sidetracked," he said. "First, the sweater, then my shoes."

"Anyway, the guy, Alastair, was witty and, you know, pretty well-spoken, and, of course, a British accent goes a long way with us girls. But there was something…I don't know."

"Well, give me a clue, what?"

"He kept, um, scanning the room at LoLa. You know, checking out everyone there, especially the women. No, only the women. It wasn't like it was really obvious, but just something I noticed. I don't know if Rose was even aware of it because he also spent a lot of time looking at her. Smiling and laughing, being pretty charming."

"So far I'm not seeing the problem," he admitted.

"I don't know, maybe I'm just not explaining it well."

"I mean, based on what you've told me so far, he sounds fine. Well, except the sweater thing," he said. "I mean, I got news for you, all guys check out women *all the time*. It's not like he's doing something weird."

"I know, I know," she said, "but you don't."

"Are you crazy? Of course, I do."

"Well, not in such an obvious way."

"Maybe because I've got you to look at. It doesn't get any better than that in the checking-out-women department."

"Thank you, that's very sweet," she said, and reached out and patted one of his new Skechers shoes.

"And true," he said. "So what else do you know about this guy?"

"Well, not all that much. Just that he's not working at the moment. According to Rose, he used to be in finance in London, then was up in New York for a while. I'm not sure whether he was working up there or not."

"Where's he live?" he asked.

"Supposedly he's staying with a friend on the island while he looks for a place. That's a little bit murky."

"Why?"

"Because, as I understand it, he's been staying at the friend's place for almost four months."

"Well, maybe he's paying rent or something."

"I don't think so," she said, raising her hand. "Oh, that's another thing. When we got the check at LoLa, guess who paid."

"Um, I'm gonna guess, Rose."

"Bingo. I got the impression she always did when they went out for drinks or dinner."

"Okay, anything else?" he asked.

"Nah, that's about it," she said, giving him a shooing motion. "But hey, you're a detective, so come on, time to *detect*."

"All right, all right, I'm not quite sure how I'm gonna do it, but I'll look into him. The reality is, as you know, there're a lot of people in Palm Beach that look like they have money but don't. Which is all right, as far as I'm concerned, as long as you're not a total mooch, you know? Sounds like you haven't seen this guy long enough to know whether he fits that category or not."

Dominica nodded. "I just don't want her to go through what she just went through with that jerk Pierre."

"The married guy?"

She nodded.

"Well, for one thing, any guy whose name is Pierre and is American you gotta wonder about. Better yet, run from immediately. I mean, wasn't his last name Smith or Jones or something?"

"Brown."

"I rest my case. Pierre Brown. It would help if Rose's antennae were working a little better. I mean here she is, the most successful real estate agent in Palm Beach, making a bloody fortune, and beautiful to boot, and she falls for some dude named…Pierre Brown. Come on, girl."

She laughed.

"What?"

She pointed at him and smiled. "Hey, she also fell for you."

He laughed. "Well, there you go, case closed, she's clearly got suspect judgment."

Dominica patted his right Skechers shoe then stood up. "Okay, well, let me know if you find out anything."

"Will do. Hey, how about dinner on Wednesday?" he asked. "Are you free?"

"Just so happens I am. Where were you thinking?"

"Let's see…we haven't been to Rocco's Tacos in a while, how's that sound?"

"Yum," she said. "A couple of their Añejo margaritas would really hit the spot. And they've got some of the best people-watching around."

Rocco's Tacos was on Clematis Street and had many tables on the sidewalk.

"Okay, so pick you up at six thirty? Is that good?"

"Yup, then you can tell me what you've found out about Alastair. I hope it's good and juicy."

TWO

That dinner at Rocco's Tacos never took place because Crawford and Dominica were both at the scene of a triple homicide at the Ocean Club on North Ocean Boulevard instead. Murders in Palm Beach were rare enough, but a triple homicide was a first-time-ever event.

A 911 call came into the Palm Beach Police station at three fifteen on Wednesday afternoon. It was a woman, clearly distraught: "A man just shot a bunch of people here at the Ocean Club," she said. "There's blood everywhere."

Bettina, the station receptionist, fielded the call. "Is the shooter still active, do you know, ma'am?"

"I don't know. He may have ran off. Come quick, please."

"We will," Bettina clicked off and rang Crawford who was in his office. "Shooter at the Ocean Club. Woman there reported 'blood everywhere.'"

Crawford grabbed his coat and ran out his door picking up Mort Ott at his cubicle on the way and relaying the information.

Bettina immediately called the ER at Good Samaritan Hospital in West Palm Beach which was just over the north bridge and not far from the Ocean Club, then Emergency Management in Palm Beach. Then she phoned the crime scene techs on duty: Dominica McCarthy and Candy Tamposi. They left for the Ocean Club immediately.

Crawford and Ott made the two-mile drive in less than two minutes.

Chaos was the only word to describe the scene at the Ocean Club, though a close second would have been carnage. As Crawford and Ott pulled up, the first thing they saw was a woman in a bikini in front of the Ocean Club screaming like the woman in the famous Edvard Munch painting. Her hands were at the sides of her lipsticked mouth and though Crawford and Ott couldn't hear her—at first anyway—they were sure other people around her certainly could. Looking closer, Crawford, in the passenger seat, noticed a spatter of blood on the side of her bikini bottom.

To her left they saw two men with tennis rackets rushing toward the club from the courts across the street. At the same time they saw a horde of people dressed in everything from shorts and collared shirts to more formal dresses and sports jackets pouring out of the club, looking fearful for their lives. As Ott roared up to the front entrance, Crawford looked up and saw a helicopter hovering in place above the club; then it angled away and landed on a patch of grass a hundred yards from the building. The ALS team, he assumed. Ott adeptly pulled up to a nearby handicap space and skidded to a stop at the side of the club entrance.

He and Crawford jumped out of the Ford Interceptor vehicle and started running to the front entrance, firearms in one hand, ID in the other.

"Police!" Crawford shouted as they ducked through the double-door front entrance of the club. A man in a white shirt and a black tie spotted them and raced up to them.

"Detectives Crawford and Ott," Crawford told the man. "Where'd it happen?"

"Delbert Roth," the man said. "The manager here. Over there, at the outside bar."

Crawford and Ott ran to where the man was pointing and that was the moment when they saw three blood-stained bodies lying on the floor and several others sitting, in crouches, or bent over, Good Samaritans trying to minister to the wounded.

Ott, seeing a uniform cop who had gotten there before them, turned to Crawford. "I'm gonna go talk to Linetti, see what he knows."

Crawford nodded. There was more blood than he'd seen anywhere except at a deadly four-car crash on I-95, which had resulted in five casualties. Some of the injured were being aided by Ocean Club employees or friends, who, Crawford guessed, had been here when the bullets started flying. As he surveyed the scene, a trio of first responders rushed in, dressed in white and carrying their heavy kits.

"What the hell happened?" one of them yelled at Crawford.

"Don't know exactly, at least one shooter, maybe more," Crawford said, as the man knelt down next to a woman who looked like she had been hit in her stomach or chest, or possibly both.

She was wearing tennis whites and sneakers and, Crawford guessed, was around sixty. He also guessed she might be in shock because she was remarkably calm and not hysterical the way other people around them were.

"You okay, ma'am?" the first responder asked.

"No, goddammit, I'm not okay," the woman rasped. "I've been shot."

"I know," said the first responder as he prepared to give her an injection to ease her pain, "but we're gonna fix you right up."

"You better, 'cause I'm hosting a dinner party tonight," she said, then suddenly she winced in pain.

The first responder looked up at Crawford and smiled as if to say, *tough old broad.*

The manager had walked away but now he was back, looking at the injured people and appearing helpless that he was unable to do anything.

Crawford gave the manager a wave and he walked over.

"What can you tell me about what happened?"

"Aw, man, it's just a blur," Roth said. "I didn't see it but best I can piece it together is a guy came in, dressed in tennis whites carrying one of those big tennis bags and pulled out an AR-15 or something like that and just started shooting."

"Any eyewitnesses, anyone get a look at his face?"

"That's the thing, this man who saw the whole thing said the guy had one of those big floppy tennis hats and sunglasses with blue lenses. Told me all he could really see was his nose and his mouth."

"That doesn't help much. Anyone else see him?"

"A woman, but she was pretty hysterical. She left, I think."

"Do you know her name," Crawford asked taking out his hand recorder.

"Mrs. Dunn. Ellie Dunn. Like I said, I'm pretty sure she left."

"Anyone else?" Crawford asked.

Roth looked around and pointed. "Oh yeah, that man over there. Mr. Lombard."

"Thanks," Crawford said and walked over to the man. On his way he saw the three bodies, now covered with large white beach towels. Someone had the presence of mind to cover them.

"Mr. Lombard?" Crawford said.

The man nodded and took a long drag on a cigarette.

"Detective Crawford, Palm Beach Homicide. I understand you were here when the shootings took place. Are you okay if I ask you a few questions?" Crawford asked, not waiting for an answer. "Did you see what happened?"

The man nodded and took a long sip of his drink that had dark brown liquid in it.

"Guy came in and just started shooting," Lombard said with a shrug.

"Can you describe him and tell me exactly what you saw?" Crawford asked, holding up his pocket recorder.

"Had on whites like he just got off the tennis court," Lombard said. "Had this big red bag that said Wilson. Pulled out this automatic rifle, I guess it was, and just started shooting. Seemed like he was never gonna stop."

"How big was he, would you say?"

"Tall, like about your height, six two, six three." He took another long sip, more like a gulp, and drained it.

"And did you get a look at his face? I know he was wearing a hat and sunglasses."

"Yeah, no, I was too busy diving for cover to notice his face. I mean, Christ man, I was just trying to stay alive."

"Understood. After he stopped shooting, did you see where he went?"

"Yeah, out back, maybe ran down the beach, I don't know. I wasn't in a big hurry to go after him and find out," Lombard said, looking down at his empty glass. "Hey, Detective, I've gotta go make another drink. It's not every day you're a few feet away from a mass shooting."

Crawford nodded. "Can you give me your number, please? I might want to call you back, ask you some more questions."

Lombard gave him his cell number then walked toward the bar.

Crawford turned and saw the crime scene techs, Dominica McCarthy and Candy Tamposi, squatting next to what looked like dozens of shell casings. He walked over to them.

Dominica looked up and saw him. "Horrible, huh?" she said, shaking her head.

"Hey, Charlie," Tamposi said grimly.

"Hey," Crawford said, pointing at the shell casings, "how many?"

"Forty-two," Dominica said. "Might've missed a few."

"You know what caliber?" he asked. "Not that it really matters at this moment."

Dominica picked one up. "Looks like 5.56x45mm. Standard for an AR-15, right?"

He nodded. "Same as a .223 Remington, I think."

"How could this happen here?" Dominica asked, her head shaking again. "I mean…"

"Suspect was a guy, six two or three, dressed in tennis whites and sneakers. Walked in with a big Wilson tennis bag—"

"With the AR in it?"

Crawford nodded. "And a hat and sunglasses to cover his face."

"So where do we go from here?" Dominica asked.

"That's a damn good question."

THREE

The man in the tennis whites and the red Wilson bag ran south on the beach, looking back several times to see if anyone was chasing him, though he figured no one would be so foolish. Even if a cop gave chase, he still had at least a five-minute jump on them.

The house where he was staying was only two houses south of the Ocean Club. The home between his and the club was owned by a couple from Philadelphia who had already gone north at the end of the season.

He made it to his house unseen; inside, he stripped down in the living room. Then he took the semiautomatic rifle out of the Wilson bag and shoved it under a sofa along with his sunglasses. In his bedroom, he put on his new Vilebrequin bathing suit and a collared, short sleeve Lacoste shirt and flip-flops. Then he went back out to the living room gathered up his tennis whites, sneakers, and floppy hat and went outside and threw the clothes and the Wilson bag on top of the smokeless copper fire pit and ignited it. It only took a few minutes until it was all just black ashes.

Then he turned off the fire pit and walked down the beach to the Ocean Club.

He walked into the club from the beach and went up to a short, balding man who had an air of authority about him and a black leather notepad out, having just interviewed one of the bartenders.

"'Scuse me," the man said, "what exactly happened, I was walking on the beach and saw the helicopter and heard all the noise."

"Are you a member here, sir?" Mort Ott asked.

"No, I live nearby."

Ott's eyes locked onto the man's eyes and he said in a staccato tone: "A man shot a lot of people, three are deceased, and there were a lot of injuries, too." Ott looked at his clothes. "By any chance, did you see a man dressed in tennis whites carrying a big red Wilson tennis bag on your way here? We think he might have run out onto the beach."

"No, definitely not, I would have noticed that."

Ott nodded. "And were you walking north or south?"

"South. I went pretty far down. I'd say halfway to the Breakers. It's my regular walk," he said.

"Okay, well thank you, sir," Ott said. "I'm going to have to ask you to leave now. This is an active crime scene."

"Got it," the man said. He made a motion to leave but turned back. "Good luck. I hope you catch the guy."

FOUR

Neither Crawford nor Dominica mentioned their dinner scheduled for that night. They didn't need to because they both knew it was off. Not only that, but they'd be in no mood to eat, drink and laugh after what they'd witnessed at the Ocean Club.

It turned out that, in addition to the three dead, there were six injured, ranging from the grave and serious to a lucky man whose shoulder had been grazed by a bullet. Crawford and Ott didn't leave until a little after seven-thirty that night, then went straight to Crawford's office at the Palm Beach Police station, while the techs preceded them by forty-five minutes. But the reality was, there wasn't that much for them to do. There was no dusting for fingerprints, no DNA samples, nothing except the shell casings. Though no one claimed to have seen it happen, they guessed the killer slid that automatic weapon back into his red Wilson tennis bag and fled with it.

Most though not all of the grisly scene had been captured on two security cameras in the Ocean Club, one close to the primary location where the killer mounted his attack and shot at people in the pool area and those seated at the bar. Crawford and Ott quickly ruled out an AR-15 as the murder weapon because the killer's firearm had a distinctive design quite unlike an AR. It also had other unique features, namely a white stock and a black barrel and an elaborate black scope, which of course the killer had not needed. Crawford planned to go to an in-house gun expert and see if he could ID the murder weapon.

As for the man himself, his identity was effectively concealed on the club's footage.

Crawford and Ott had, of course, no answer to their biggest question: Had this been a random attack by a deranged madman or was there a specific target, or targets, and the rest of those killed or injured were collateral damage? There was, of course, no way of knowing at this point but Crawford and Ott discussed this at length: because there had been many mass shootings where the targets were random and others where the shooter singled out specific victims. Or in other cases, which fell somewhere in between, where members of certain races or religions were singled out. Like where Jews were the target in the Tree of Life synagogue attack in Pittsburgh and where Blacks were the targets in a Buffalo supermarket and at the Mother Emanuel church in the Charleston slaughters.

At just past eight, Crawford got a call on his cell phone. He didn't recognize the 305 number.

"Hello?"

"Detective Crawford?"

"Yes, who's this?"

"Agent Saperstein, FBI. I called your station asking about the mass shooting. Pretty bad scene, huh?"

"Yeah, sure was," Crawford said, clicking the speakerphone on so Ott could hear. "Where are you located?"

"Down in Miami. Well, Miramar, actually," Saperstein said. "Hey listen, man, we're not trying to horn in, just thought we could help out."

"So what exactly did you have in mind?" Crawford asked.

Crawford's experience with the FBI was, nine out of ten times, that's exactly what they did, *horn in*.

"Whatever you need. Send up an Evidence Response Team or guys from Victim Services Division. You know, help out with interviews, get our behavioral analysis people on it."

"We got all that, but without the fancy names," Crawford said and Ott shot him a thumbs-up.

"Hey, I didn't mean to get you all riled, just trying to be helpful," Saperstein said. "Obviously, the shooter violated state and local criminal laws, so it's your jurisdiction, not ours. Just—"

"Trying to help out," Crawford said. "And I appreciate it. So I got your number and I'll get back to you if we need you."

"Okay, Charlie, sounds good…it is Charlie, isn't it?"

"Yup. And you?"

"Neil."

"Okay, Neil, thanks for the call," Crawford said, and clicked off.

Ott clapped his hands. "Nicely done."

"I had one experience with those guys up in New York," Crawford said. "Talk about horning in."

"Yeah, and remember when that gallery on Worth Avenue had all those fake paintings, they moved right in on that with their fancy little unit."

Crawford nodded. "The Art Crime Team," he said. "That guy seemed okay, though, not too pushy."

"Yeah, but once they got a foot in the door," Ott said, "look out."

"Hey, I'm going to go show the footage to Nick Boone"—Palm Beach Police's foremost firearm expert—"see if he can ID the murder weapon."

"Good idea," Ott said. "I bet he can."

Ott was right.

"No question, man," Boone said, as Crawford played back the tape a second time, "that's the best bullpup ever made, an Austrian-made Steyr AUG A3 assault semiautomatic."

"Bullpup? What the hell's that?"

"Meaning its action and magazine are positioned behind the trigger and grip, so it's got a shorter length."

"Shorter, you mean compared to a conventional rifle?"

"Yeah, exactly. I recognize it because of its scope. Distinctive as hell. And its white stock."

"Hey, thanks a lot, man, I knew you were the guy to come to," Crawford said.

"Anytime, Charlie."

Crawford and Ott talked long into the night at the police station about other mass shootings as well as the one that had happened that afternoon under their watch. One of the things they speculated about was, would the shooter take his own life the way past shooters often had? Maybe he already had, Ott suggested. This led to a long discussion about how, it seemed to Crawford anyway, that mass shootings were a selfish way of committing suicide. Where the shooter insisted on taking out a lot of completely innocent people with him. Or in other cases—what was known as "suicide by cop"—where the shooter fully expected, and, in fact, hoped he (because it was almost always a he) would be slain by a cop's bullet.

As they left the station for the night, the reality was they had nothing. No evidence from the scene, no good description of the suspect, no apparent motive, no nothing. Just a strong sense of sadness and sorrow for the victims and their families. Along with a disbelief that this could happen in their own backyard. It was surreal. The only solace they took was that they had been in this position before and had somehow managed to solve the crime. But unless the killer killed himself or stumbled badly, they had a long way to go.

FIVE

At nine o'clock the next morning, Crawford and Ott were seated in Chief Norm Rutledge's office for a meeting hastily scheduled the night before.

Rutledge, who was never shy about making bold statements, led it off. "This is the single most catastrophic thing that's ever happened in Palm Beach. We gotta catch this guy and fry his ass," Rutledge said presumably meaning sit him down in the electric chair and shock him with two thousand volts and seven to twelve amps. Only problem was "the chair" had not been used in Florida since 1999.

"No argument there," Crawford said. "How do you want to proceed on it?"

"Well, for starters I want everyone in the department on it," Rutledge said, which was not even remotely feasible because how were motorcycle cops and meter maids supposed to catch a dangerous killer?

Ott glanced over at Crawford, caught his eye, rolled his own for a split second, then looked up at Rutledge.

"Norm, with all due respect we've gone down this road before and it didn't work so well," Ott said.

"What road is *that*, Ott?"

"The clusterfuck road. Getting everyone out there so we fall all over each other," Ott said calmly.

"But you're the boss," Crawford said. "We'll play it any way you want, we just think it's too early for all hands on deck. We should see where we are in a few days."

Rutledge pounded the top of his desk. "A few days? We gotta solve this sumbitch now before everyone either cancels their reservations down here or gets the hell out of town because they're afraid for their lives. I mean, this is serious shit, Crawford."

"Trust me, I'm aware of that," Crawford said, "and I'm not trying to downplay it, but we can't go charging off in all directions at once."

Rutledge emitted a deep sigh, then threw up his hands. "Okay, what's your first move then? We got three dead people and six injured, two serious. What are you geniuses gonna do after you walk out of here?"

"What we always do in murder cases," Crawford said, "check out the sheets for anyone with a conviction for using any kind of firearm or weapon along with everyone ever arrested for possession of one, then go interview everyone who was there at the crime scene but left before we got there. We have a pretty long list, from the manager to all the guests who were there, in addition to the employees."

"At the same time we're going to look into the background of the vics and talk to members of their families," Ott said. "See if any of them had any history of bad blood, serious disputes, or altercations with anyone."

"Meaning the shooter might've had a specific target, rather than it being a random thing?" Rutledge asked.

"Exactly," Ott said. "Who knows, maybe what looks like randomness was actually disguising a hit on one guy."

"Yeah, maybe," Rutledge said, skeptically.

"So far we're getting the same description from eyewitnesses—"

"Tennis whites, a floppy white hat and blue shades, right?" Rutledge interrupted Ott.

"Yeah, around six two or three," Ott finished.

"Also, Norm, the other thing we're going to do—maybe the most important thing—is put a list together of all the gun shops within a twenty-to-twenty-five-mile radius from here, take around photos of the gun used, and see if we can find where it was sold. We get a hit there and good chance we got our shooter."

"That's asking for a lot," Rutledge said, shaking his head.

"Not really, the gun used is pretty rare. It's a Steyr AUG A3," Crawford said.

"What's so rare about that?" Rutledge said. "I know what Steyr AUG A3s are. I've seen 'em around."

"But I'll bet not ones with a white stock and a black barrel and a special scope," Crawford said.

Rutledge nodded. "Well, maybe not exactly. You need manpower to go around to those gun shops, let me know."

"Yeah, we probably will," Ott said. "We'll probably be stretched pretty thin."

"So, Norm," Crawford said, "we don't have much, admittedly, but it's not the first time that's been the case. You know what I bet happens? We'll get calls from random people saying you should look into so-and-so for those murders or my neighbor owns an AR, you should talk to him, he's got anger-management issues. You know, anonymous or otherwise."

"I hope you're right. We need all the help we can get. You think we should put something in the *Post*?" Rutledge said referring to Palm Beach's newspaper.

"You mean something like, 'If you know anything about the recent shootings at the Ocean Club in Palm Beach, call our special tip line'? Something like that?" Ott asked.

Crawford glanced at Ott, who shrugged. "You know, that's not a bad idea in this case. I always thought those tips never went anywhere or were a big waste of time, but maybe not here. You want to take care of that, Norm?"

Rutledge nodded. "Yeah, I'll take care of it. What else?"

"I had a call from an FBI agent," Crawford said matter-of-factly.

Rutledge leaned halfway across his desk. "No shit? They trying to horn in?"

Crawford and Ott laughed.

"What's so funny?" Rutledge said, frowning.

"That's exactly what Agent Neil Saperstein said he was *not* going to do," Ott said. "In those exact words."

"Yeah, you can trust those guys as far as you can throw 'em," Rutledge, the cliché king, observed.

"We're just telling you. We politely said, 'thanks but no thanks.' Well, that about covers it," Crawford said, getting up out of his chair.

"All right, boys, get the killer off the street," Rutledge said. "Dead or alive."

"Yes, boss," said Ott, saluting Rutledge, "we're on it."

They walked back to Crawford's office and sat down.

"Well, I was a little surprised," Crawford said.

"What about?"

"I don't know, he wasn't as hysterical as I expected him to be."

Ott nodded. "I agree. Or as we've seen him in the past for much lesser shit."

"Maybe we got an older and wiser Norm."

Ott shook his head slowly. "You're dreaming, my friend."

SIX

At the end of the day, Crawford and Ott had compiled a long and varied list of men they wanted to interview. They ranged from a West Palm Beach resident who had just been released from prison for shooting his live-in girlfriend to a Wellington man who'd killed a horse with an AR-15 while target shooting to an ex-con who'd robbed the Palm Beach Tiffany's at gunpoint. But Crawford admitted to Ott that his gut told him none of these guys seemed the type to commit mass murder.

They also had interviewed six members of the Ocean Club and only gotten confirmation of the killer's basic physical description.

The murder victims were Roland Embry, Jeffrey Fisk, and Lauren Faircloth, all members of the Ocean Club. Embry was a sixty-seven-year-old retired banker who spent a lot of time at the club, primarily doing laps in the pool or playing backgammon inside the club.

Fisk was a forty-five-year-old hedge fund manager who had met with several prospective investors at the club for a late lunch and who had stuck around for a swim in the ocean, then a shower, then a swim in the pool. His potential investors, not members of the club, had left an hour before the shooting began.

Ott had discovered this by calling Fisk's office on Royal Palm Way. Fisk's distraught assistant told him about the late lunch meeting and he pieced together the rest in a phone call with the lifeguard.

The slain woman Lauren Faircloth, thirty-eight, had taken a lesson with the Ocean Club tennis pro across the street earlier in the afternoon, then stuck around for a massage followed by a sauna and shower afterward. The assistant manager confirmed that Lauren came to the club several times a week to either take tennis lessons or play with friends, followed by a massage.

Scheduled for tomorrow was an appointment with Mrs. Embry and Lauren Faircloth's husband then the next day with Mrs. Fisk along with a partner of Fisk's. Crawford and Ott hoped that a suspect or two might emerge from these interviews, unless—as remained entirely possible—the shooter had randomly decided on a club instead of a school or a church upon which to unleash his deadly violence.

Another thing that Crawford and Ott had done was recruit three uniform cops to make a list of all gun shops within a twenty-five-mile radius of Palm Beach and, along with photos of the Steyr AUG semiautomatic, see if the murder weapon had been sold at one of their shops.

Crawford and Ott were in Crawford's office at eight o'clock the night after the murders, wolfing down a large pizza they'd had delivered from Mellow Mushroom in West Palm Beach.

"You saw Numb Nuts's email, right?" Ott said, putting down a crusty end of a slice. *Numb Nuts* was Ott's nickname for Rutledge.

"No, what did it say?"

"Nine thirty meeting with Mal, which we knew was coming. But also a cast of thousands," Ott said, referring to the mayor, Mal Chase.

"What do you mean?"

"Well, people from the Chamber of Commerce plus something called The Association."

"What the hell's that?"

"All the muck-a-mucks who own and run the stores on Worth Avenue."

Crawford nodded. "I get it. They're all going to come in and piss and moan about how a triple murder is gonna turn Palm Beach into a ghost town and kill business for them up and down Worth Avenue."

Ott picked up a fresh slice. "That would be my guess. And since we've seen this movie before, I'm guessing Numb Nuts will be there joining in the chorus." He sighed, then smiled. "Though I do remember that one time when he stood up for us. Said how we were the two best homicide cops in the whole state of Florida or some shit. Then a week later totally denied ever having said it."

"Yeah, but the other ten times he said, 'what the hell are you guys doing, it's been three days and you don't have anyone in jail yet, let alone any suspects,'" Crawford nodded. "I'm guessing that's the Numb Nuts we'll see on display tomorrow."

"Probably right," Ott said, washing down a bite with a pull from his Coke. "I also heard they closed down the Ocean Club for the time being."

"Oh yeah, why?" Crawford asked.

"Well, if I wasn't the sensitive guy I am, I'd say something like 'it takes a while to clean up all the blood,'" Ott said, "but I think it's probably more about the fact that the place is overrun with the press. I heard they've got cameramen and reporters all over the place. From England and France and Italy and even Japan."

"One of the uniforms told me he saw like three or four helicopters hovering a hundred feet above the Ocean Club at the same time. Media guys, I guess. So my guess is the powers that be at the club decided it was a safety issue and shut it down."

"Plus all that publicity," Ott said shaking his head. "Christ, the club really doesn't need that."

"Yeah, I know. I feel bad for them," Crawford said. "So it's a day later, what's your gut telling you at this point?"

"No clue. Absolutely no clue," Ott said. "Those guys with sheets—the guy who shot his ex, the dude who held up Tiffany's, I just don't see any of 'em as the doer. I mean, right now I'm leaning to it being a random act. I mean, talk about a soft target. If you're mentally disturbed or fucked up in the head you couldn't ask for an easier kill location."

"I agree," Crawford said, followed by a long slow sigh. "I just keep saying the same thing over and over to myself: If you're not safe from something like this in Palm Beach, where the hell *are* you safe?"

SEVEN

There were eight men and three women crammed into Norm Rutledge's office.

None of them were smiling. In fact, frowns were the order of the day. Mal Chase, the Palm Beach mayor, led off.

"All right, thank you all for coming," Chase said. "We're all, of course, grieving over the terrible tragedy at the Ocean Club two days ago and hope our exemplary chief and his detectives can bring the killer to justice soon. Having said that, I'll give you the floor, Jake, since you were the one who requested this meeting."

Chase sat as Jake Kaufman, the owner of the oldest men's store on Worth Avenue, stood. "Thanks, Mal. Well, to me that was the darkest day in the long, splendid history of our beloved town and we mourn the loss of our three citizens and hope for the best for those who sustained serious injuries." He turned to Rutledge and raised his hand for emphasis: "Chief Rutledge, you gotta get this lunatic. I don't need to tell you, this has already done irreparable harm to the town's reputation and our own businesses." Six heads nodded in agreement. "My store, for example, had exactly eleven customers in it yesterday and several were from out of town and somehow did not know about the awful tragedy. What about you all? I'm guessing it was the same with you?"

A woman shook her fist. "You were lucky, Jake, I had three people come through my gallery yesterday. And not one sale." She turned to Crawford and Ott with an accusatory look." I know you fellas are supposedly the best around, but are you anywhere close to catching the man who did this?"

Crawford glanced at Rutledge. "Do you want me to answer that, Chief, or do you?"

Rutledge, shaking his head, clearly wanting no part of the question. "You go ahead, you're on the front line," he said to Crawford.

"Okay, well, as much as we'd have liked to bring in the killer right after it happened, he obviously got away," Crawford said. "We're presently pursuing all leads and are working around the clock to capture the killer."

A tall, bald man with a substantial paunch, wearing khaki pants and a pink and white shirt spoke next. "Sounds to me like you got a big, fat *nada*. Sounds to me like we need to bring the FBI or the CIA into this."

Crawford knew he was the head of the Chamber of Commerce and his name was Fred Somebody.

"Sir, with all due respect, this is out of the jurisdiction of the CIA, but we have been in contact with FBI operatives, though their primary duties have to do with national security threats."

"However, Fred," Rutledge said, "I can personally assure you we will cooperate with any regulatory body in order to solve this heinous crime as quick as we possibly can."

"Easy for you to say," said Fred, "but we need this thing solved…like yesterday. I mean, how can somebody just walk into a club, kill three people, and injure six others and just disappear?"

"Mister…I'm sorry, I don't know your last name?" Crawford began.

"Burgess. Fred Burgess."

"Mr. Burgess, within fifteen minutes of these murders taking place, we had police stationed at all three bridges checking every car or truck, one by one, to see if they were in possession of an assault weapon, in this case a Steyr AUG A3. Not only that—"

"What about South Ocean Boulevard? He could get away by just driving south," another man spoke up.

"I was just getting to that," Crawford said. "We had police stationed at just above the par three golf course also checking every vehicle heading south."

"So you're saying the killer didn't leave Palm Beach?" a woman seated next to Chase asked.

"We believe that to be the case," Crawford said., "but it's impossible to guarantee it."

"But maybe he could have escaped by boat or even a helicopter," Fred Burgess piped up.

Ott stepped in. "Look, we're working the case, and there's only so much we can do. I mean, hypothetically, he could have escaped by submarine."

Crawford did his damnedest not to laugh.

"And you are?" Burgess asked, frown firmly dug in on his face.

"Mort Ott," he said. "Detective Crawford and I are running the investigation."

"Running it into the ground," Burgess muttered.

Rutledge shot Ott a look that said, *Not another word out of you.*

"You know what scares the hell out of me"—it was Jake Kaufman again—"is that this killer is still here. I mean, free as a bird, walking down the street or in a house next door to mine."

"I agree," said the woman next to Chase. "Makes me want to go inside and lock my door 'til you find this maniac."

Rutledge put up a hand. "I certainly understand your concern," he said, "and I can assure you we have every man and woman in the police force on the lookout, scouring the town twenty-four hours a day."

"Well, are there any other thoughts…comments?" the mayor asked, clearly hoping there were not.

"So there are no suspects at all at this point?" a woman in a green paisley dress and a pageboy haircut asked.

"I'd like to tell you otherwise," Crawford said, "but the answer is no."

"However," Rutledge said, "the detectives are interrogating a number of possible suspects later today. Not to mention, the spouses of the three deceased victims and others that we expect might shed light on the, ah, shooter's identity."

Crawford gave a quick glance around the room. Nobody looked happy.

Mal Chase smiled optimistically. "Well, thank you all for coming and if you all would like we can have another meeting later in the week and give you all an update."

"What would be even better," Fred Burgess said, "is that you tell us the guy's dead. That one of you put one between his eyes."

That was a bit of a showstopper and no one said anything for a few moments.

"Well, thanks again," Chase said. "Let's hope we can soon get things back to normal and get all your businesses thriving again."

"Can't get any worse," Burgess said, slowly getting to his feet.

There were more than a few nods to that as the eleven people wordlessly walked out of Rutledge's office.

Crawford and Ott met at Ott's cubicle.

"Well, that went—"

Crawford held up a hand. "Don't say it."

"Shittily."

*****

Jeff Fisk's partner had changed the appointment and Crawford was now meeting him before the husband of Lauren Faircloth. Fisk's office was not far from the Palm Beach Police station on County Road. Meanwhile, Ott was heading down to Lake Worth to meet with the man that had shot his wife.

Crawford parked behind the office building and took an elevator up to the top floor. He was greeted by a receptionist with a bright smile and a black dress.

"You're here to see Mr. Zoller, sir?" she asked.

"Yes, I'm Detective Crawford."

She nodded. "I'll tell him you're here."

"Thanks," he said and sat down.

The magazine selection was meager. *Hedge Funds Monthly*, *Trusts & Estates* and *Golf*. He, of course, picked *Golf* and turned to an article, "How to Chip like Jordan Spieth." Chipping was the bane of his existence on the golf course so he dived right into the illustrated article. Just as it was getting instructional, he heard a voice.

"Detective Crawford?"

He looked up and saw a man—early fifties, he guessed—wearing a bow tie and a dour expression.

He stood. "Yeah, hi Mr. Zoller, Detective Crawford," he said, "my condolences about your partner."

"Tragic," John Zoller said. "Jeff was in his prime. We're all going to miss him very much."

The receptionist nodded her agreement as Zoller led Crawford back.

He followed him into a small conference room that had grey-tinted glass walls, where Zoller directed Crawford to sit. They sat facing each other and Crawford launched right in.

"Well, at this stage, we're looking for as much information as we can accumulate on the unfortunate victims of the shootings in an effort to determine whether one of them may have been an intended victim."

"Oh my God, who would ever want to kill Jeff? The man was the salt of the earth and had a million friends," Zoller said.

"And no enemies that you're aware of?"

"My immediate answer would be no, but everybody I know has, once upon a time, rubbed somebody the wrong way. But *enemy*? No, that's way too strong a word."

"Well, can you tell me who Mr. Fisk might have 'rubbed the wrong way,' then?"

"Okay, well in this business you have rivals that aren't unhappy to see you fail or investors who aren't always satisfied with how you're doing. Jeff had a man, a client, who bad-mouthed him a lot. Even sued him once, but I could never see him resorting to what happened at the Ocean Club. Inconceivable"—he shook his head—"never, not in a million years."

"Can you give me the man's name, please?" Crawford asked taking out a pad

"Sure, Henry Brusca. Lives here in town, somewhere up north in the summer."

"B-r-u-s-k-a?"

"B-r-u-s-c-a."

"And can you describe him, please?"

"Sure. I'd say around six feet tall, maybe a little taller, mostly bald, kind of stoop-shouldered."

"Anyone else?"

Zoller tapped the conference room table a few times. "Um, this goes back a ways...a man named Harding Leitner. Jeff had an affair with his wife...ended up marrying her. I don't think Harding was too happy about that."

"But he lives in Palm Beach?"

"Oh yeah, you see him on the society page in the *Shiny Sheet* all the time," Zoller said and chuckled. "But I'm guessing maybe you don't read it?"

Crawford smiled. "Not much," he said. "Anybody else you can think of? Or anybody else you think I should talk to? Besides Mr. Fisk's wife, I mean?"

"Nah, I don't think so. I knew him about as well as anyone. Most people wouldn't even know about those two I gave you."

Crawford stood and shook Zoller's hand. "I appreciate your time, Mr. Zoller," he said. "How's Mrs. Fisk doing, do you know?"

"I stopped by and saw her once," Zoller said. "I don't think she's doing too well."

"Sorry to hear that. She lives down on Jungle, right?"

Zoller nodded.

"Okay, well, I'll see myself out."

"Good luck finding that lunatic, Detective."

*****

Ott usually did better with the hard cases than Crawford, so Crawford was happy to let him interrogate them. Ott liked questioning tough guys, and sometimes badgering them, because he could relate to them better than he could the smoother, slicker Palm Beachers, whom he generally found to be a little dull.

Oxnard Rennie was definitely a hard case. Ott had looked at his sheet before going to his house in West Palm Beach and found that before shooting his live-in girlfriend he had two arrests for assault and another one for reckless and drunk driving. He was a big man and barely fit within the door frame of his small ranch-style house. Ott had called him after the meeting with the worried merchants of Worth Avenue and had gotten the man to reluctantly agree to meet him.

"What's this all about?" Rennie had demanded on the phone.

"I'll tell you when I get there," Ott said, then hung up.

Rennie asked the same question when he answered the door. He was big, probably close to three hundred pounds and close to six and a half feet tall.

Ott ignored the question. "I assume they call you Ox," he began.

Rennie chuckled. "And I assume they call you Ott."

"Yeah, but you can call me Detective," Ott said. "I don't even need to come in 'cause I can see you're too big."

"Too big for what?" Rennie said.

"Never mind," Ott said, turning to go. "Nice to meet you, Ox. You can go back to watching lady wrestling on the tube."

He walked back to his car. It had been a forty-five-minute waste of time, and boy, did Ott hate wasting time.

*****

Lauren Faircloth lived on Golfview Road in Palm Beach, named for its commanding views of the Poinciana Club golf course.

Crawford had called the number, which Bettina had gotten for him. He called the night before and the man who answered identified himself as Warren Faircloth. He sounded a little old, or maybe a little crotchety to Crawford…or maybe his was the fragile voice of a man in mourning.

The man who came to the door after Crawford rang it was indeed old. Crawford would need a little back-and-forth between them to determine whether he was crotchety. His wife, Lauren Faircloth, had been thirty-eight at the time of her death; this man had to be closing in on seventy. An age gap, Crawford had noted over the years, that was not uncommon in Palm Beach.

"I'm Detective Crawford, sir," Crawford said. "Thanks for seeing me, Mr. Faircloth. I'm sorry about your loss and having to meet with you under these circumstances."

"Thank you, Detective," Faircloth said, making no effort to shake Crawford's hand. "Come on in."

Crawford followed Faircloth through the foyer into a living room that looked like the antithesis of Faircloth himself. If Faircloth was wizened, thin and musty-looking, the living room was bursting with brightly colored paintings, decorations and furniture.

"Beautiful room, sir," Crawford said, by way of a conversation starter.

"Thanks, my wife's creation," he said, "one of her many."

Crawford wasn't quite sure what that meant.

"Speaking of her, and again my condolences," Crawford said, "I'm one of the detectives investigating the tragic shootings at the Ocean Club, as I mentioned on the phone, and anything you can tell me about her that might help apprehend her murderer would be very much appreciated."

Faircloth put his left hand to his throat, temporarily obscuring what some referred to a part of the anatomy known as a *turkey neck*. Then he sighed. "Oh, Lauren. God, I miss her so much. I still can't get over it. I still can't get over it. I still can't—"

"Mr. Faircloth, what we're trying to ascertain, or rule out, is whether the murderer had an actual—well, for lack of better word—target, when he went to the Ocean Club."

Faircloth nodded slowly. "Oh, I see what you mean. You mean, if the man in the tennis clothes was out to kill either Lauren or one of the men who died."

Crawford nodded. "Yes, sir, or possibly one of the injured."

"But, do you really think so? My understanding was that it was a random act. Like those ones in Texas and places like that."

"Well, it might have been. We're not ruling that out, we're just trying to narrow it all down, as I'm sure you can appreciate. Now, to the best of your knowledge, Mr. Faircloth, did Mrs. Faircloth have any, well, enemies might be too strong a word, but any people who might have wished to do her harm?"

"Good God, no," Faircloth said, frowning so hard Crawford could barely see his eyes. "Everybody loved Lauren. She was never one to say a bad word about anyone and always went out of her way to be nice and considerate to everyone she met…even, no especially, to people of lowborn status."

Crawford wondered if that's how Lauren would have categorized him.

"She was just a peach of a girl, an absolute peach."

What more could Crawford ask him after that? It was apparent he had gotten all he was going to get.

He thanked the grieving widower and let himself out.

*****

After Ox, Ott had an interview scheduled in Riviera Beach with the convicted armed robber who had held up the Tiffany store on Worth Avenue.

On his drive up, he felt that it was a long shot at best, and almost called the guy simply to ask how tall he was. If the man said six three or above, like Ox, or five eight or below, like Ott himself, he wouldn't have bothered with the interview since it was a one in a million anyway. But he went anyway, figuring…well, figuring you never knew what might come out of a Q&A with a felon. His past experience was that every once in a while a worthwhile nugget might just fall out of the sky.

The man actually lived in a very nice house, much nicer than Ott's. Maybe the result of a few robberies for which he had never been caught.

He knocked on the door and a few moments later a six-foot man opened it.

"I'm Detective Ott, Glen," Ott said. The man's name was Glen Matusek.

"Yeah, so you said. You got some questions?" he asked, not inviting Ott in.

"I'll make this quick. Where were you this past Friday late afternoon, say between three and four?"

"Workin' at an auto body shop in Lake Park. Why?"

"What's the name of the place?" he asked taking out his ancient leather-bound notebook.

"Gerber Collision on Old Dixie."

"And someone there can confirm that you were there at that time."

"Yup. Punched out at five."

"You don't own a semiautomatic assault rifle, by any chance?"

"Matter of fact, I don't own a gun of any kind."

"You used to."

Matusek nodded. "You're talkin' ancient history. I did ten years for that and the Glock got confiscated. I never got another one."

"You go to Palm Beach a lot?"

Matusek scratched his chest, then smiled. "Oh Christ, this is about that mass murder down there, huh?"

Ott just stared him down and didn't answer.

"How is it you make a connection between a guy who held up a jewelry store twelve years ago and went straight after that to a wacko who guns down a bunch of rich dudes?" Matusek said, shaking his head.

It was a fair question.

Ten minutes later Ott was on his way back to the station. Another waste of time.

He made a note to call Gerber Collision, even though he was 99 percent certain Matusek was not his man.

EIGHT

After leaving Warren Faircloth's house on Golfview, Crawford decided, spur-of-the-moment, to go back up to the Ocean Club and have a another look around. He dialed the cell number the manager, Delbert Roth, had given him, figuring he would probably be there even though the club was closed. He struck Crawford as a conscientious steward of the club. Turned out he was there and said he'd be happy to meet with Crawford. He met him at the outside entrance under the porte cochere.

They shook hands.

"Just a few more questions, Delbert," Crawford said.

"As many as you want," Roth said. "Want to go inside?"

"Yes," Crawford said and followed him in. They went into Roth's office, cluttered yet neat. The man was a tidy stacker.

"My first question is, did Ms. Faircloth, Mr. Fisk and Mr. Embry have anything in common that you can think of? And, also, were they friends?"

Roth laced his hands together. "Um, not that I can think of. Mr. Embry played croquet, so did Mrs. Faircloth. Mr. Fisk and Mrs. Faircloth were both tennis players, but I can't really remember them playing together or of the three having dinner together or anything. Or even having a drink together. They probably knew each other, at least by sight, but as far as being friends…no, I don't think so."

"How many members are there here?" Crawford asked.

"A little less than five hundred…496, to be exact."

Crawford nodded. "In the two days since the shootings, I'm sure you must have received calls from members. Have you had any calls from anyone speculating who might have been responsible for the shootings?"

"Well, as you can imagine, most of the calls are from members asking when the club is going to reopen, but others…well, one actually was kind of strange."

Crawford leaned forward. "How so?"

"Let's see, what's the best way to describe it? Well, it was from one of the wait staff, Linda Forchelli's her name. I remember her words were something like 'you should tell the police about Alain.' See, Alain Fournier was the chef here for years, a very good one too, but he also had a reputation for harassing—sexually harassing—waitresses and kitchen workers alike. Which I didn't find out about until later. He had a hot temper too. Kind of a volatile guy. One of the waitresses was actually the niece of a member and she told her aunt about it. Well, long story short the aunt reported it to me and I had a long talk with Alain. Basically told him if I ever heard anything again, I'd fire him. So six months later, there was another incident, and not I, but the head of the Board of Governors, fired him."

"Describe Fournier, will you please?"

"Um, around six feet tall or more, I'd say, shaved head, blue eyes, I think—"

"Skinny, fat, average, or what?"

"I'd say about average."

"And when you say he had a hot temper and was volatile, can you give me an example?"

"Okay, how about throwing a knife at one of the sous-chefs. Or screaming at the top of his lungs at a male waiter, then shoving him really hard."

Crawford shook his head. "He actually threw a knife at someone?"

"Yes, all this came out after he was fired," Roth said. "I can assure you I would have fired him long before if I knew about any of that."

"Do you think, can you possibly imagine, this man being capable of coming back here in disguise and shooting all those people?"

Roth thought that over for a few moments. "You know, I've read about people cracking. Over something bad happening in their lives. Or even nothing at all. One thing I do know is that Alain hasn't worked in six months or so. Part of the reason, I'm guessing, is that he's got a big gap in his résumé since no one here would ever give him a good recommendation. I mean, who knows? It seems like kind of big leap, though, or I would have called you already."

"Could you give me his address and cell phone, please? And landline if you have it."

"Sure," Roth said, turning to an old Rolodex on his desk.

He wrote the information for Crawford.

"Thanks," Crawford said. "Anything else?"

"Nope, not that I can think of. But if I think of anything I'll certainly give you a call."

"Please do," Crawford said. "When Alain was fired by the head of the Board of Governors, did he say anything to him? You know, have any kind of reaction?"

"Oh yeah, he sure did. Cussed him out and said it was all made-up bullshit and how the club was quote, unquote, 'a shitty place to work, worse than McDonald's,' calling the head of the Board an 'asshole,' you know, the guy totally lost it," Roth said. "I oughta know…I was just outside the room here taking it all in. It got really ugly in there."

NINE

Crawford was eager to report his conversation with Delbert Roth to Ott, but first he stopped at Melanie Embry's house on Dunbar Road. She was Roland Embry's widow and had called him back after he left his phone message the night before. The meeting was set for two o'clock and he was fifteen minutes late after listening to Roth's story about chef Alain Fournier.

Mrs. Embry opened the front door at her house on Dunbar. It was brown and big and not particularly distinguished architecturally.

"Hello, Detective," she said. "Come on in."

"Hi, Mrs. Embry, sorry I'm late," Crawford said. "And, as I said, I'm very sorry for your loss."

"Thank you for that," she said. "I'm sure you've been very busy."

Crawford followed her inside the brown house. The living room was dominated by brown furniture, leading Crawford to guess that Melanie's late husband must have drunk brown whiskey.

"Would you like something to drink, Detective?"

"Ah, no thanks, I'm fine."

They sat and Melanie smoothed out her dress.

"So what questions do you have for me?"

"Well, first, I just want to say I'm appreciative of your time at this, no doubt, very difficult time," he said.

"I want you to catch that terrible man, Detective, so, of course, I'll do everything I can to help."

"Thank you for that," Crawford said. "Some of the questions I'm about to ask you might be difficult, may even hit a nerve, so I apologize in advance, but I hope you understand."

"I do. I know it's your job and it's necessary to get at the truth," she said with a faint smile.

"What I'm trying to do is either rule out whether the shots that killed your husband were meant to, ah, cause his death or were random. So my question is, did your husband have any enemies who you think might have intended to do him harm?"

"Oh my God, no," she said without hesitation. "I can't conceive of anyone wanting to do something like that to Roland. I mean, he was just a banker. The worst thing he could have ever done to anybody was deny a loan or a mortgage. And in his private life he was a husband, a father and a grandfather, and I might say, a damned good one." She was starting to tear up.

"Take your time, Mrs. Embry, I'm in no rush at all."

"Well, that's about all there was to it," she said. "He was a pretty simple man, and since he retired he spent a fair amount of time at the Ocean Club. He liked to play backgammon with friends there and swam in the pool because he was kind of a nut about staying in shape and being healthy."

Crawford nodded. "That's a good kind of a nut."

"Yes, but look where it got him," she said, her eyes downcast. "But if you were to ask me to name one enemy Roland had, I couldn't come up with a single one."

"Even going back ten or twenty years, or more?"

She shook her head. "Not one."

"That's very helpful, ma'am. See, if the family and loved ones of the other victims answer the same way you have, it will lead us to the conclusion that it was most likely a random violent act."

She nodded. "I understand. But does that mean it will get you any closer to catching this despicable human being."

"Well, that's hard to say," Crawford said as his cell phone rang.

He looked down at the display. It read *Ocean Club*.

"Oh, do you mind if I take this quickly? It may be important."

"No, no, go right ahead."

"Hello?"

"Detective, it's Delbert Roth again."

"Oh, hi, Delbert, what's up?"

"Well, just a couple of things I thought you'd want to know," Roth said. "I had a long talk with one of my bartenders who was on duty when the shooting started and he told me it was his sense that the shooter seemed to target the people who were shot."

"Really? He thought that?"

"Yes, he said the guy was going from right to left and seemed to be skipping over certain people but targeting others. So, in other words, he wasn't spraying everyone in sight with bullets, you know, without any rhyme or reason to it."

"I didn't speak to this man, the bartender, and I don't think my partner did either. Did he leave before we got there?"

"Yes, he took off right after it happened, the way quite a few others did. Both members and employees. Can't blame them, they were scared for their lives," Roth said.

"Could you give me his name and cell number please?"

"Sure," and Roth did.

"Something else, too," Roth said. "You asked me if any of the members who were killed had anything in common, and I said I didn't think so. Well, I was wrong. For what it's worth, Mrs. Faircloth and Mr. Fisk were on the club's Membership Committee."

"And what do they do? Interview prospective candidates for membership and basically let people in or deny them admission?"

"Exactly."

"How many members are there on that committee?"

"Eight."

"Do me a favor, will you email me their names and contact information? I gave you my email, right?"

"Yup, got it right here."

"Okay, great. Thanks for the call, I'm actually in the middle of an interview right now."

"Oh, sorry for interrupting you."

"No problem, that's good intel, thanks again," Crawford said, and clicked off. "That was Delbert Roth at the Ocean Club," he told her. "He had some helpful information for me."

"Oh, that's good."

Crawford cocked his head. "Mrs. Embry, do you know if there are a lot of people who apply for membership at the Ocean Club and are turned down every year?"

"Um, I don't really know. Roland used to be on Membership there and he wasn't supposed to talk about it. You know, about who was turned down. I think it can be kind of, well, awkward."

"Understand," Crawford said. "Okay, well, I think that does it, Mrs. Embry. I really appreciate your time."

"Oh, you're welcome," she said, glancing at her watch. "I have my son and his wife coming here pretty soon. They were in the middle of a trip to Africa and had to cut it short…for, well, the obvious reason."

Crawford got to his feet. "Well again, thank you very much and, of course, I will keep you abreast of our investigation and let you know when we solve it."

"I like your optimistic attitude, Detective."

"Oh, we'll solve it. We definitely will. It's just a matter of when."

As he walked out to his car, he was consumed by one thought: Could being turned down—blackballed—by an exclusive club like the Ocean Club drive a man to commit mass murder? He played it out on his drive back to the station. It was an extreme theory, but not totally out of the question. A man who counted on the social validation of becoming a member of an illustrious club, along with the business contacts and prestige that came along with it, having had the rug pulled out from under him and effectively deemed a loser, a man not worthy of walking through the mahogany doors of the Ocean Club…yes, that would sting. But transforming him into a mass murderer? That seemed like somewhat of a stretch.

But then Crawford thought about it some more: how it would be even worse if one's wife had to hang her head in shame at the public rejection and subsequent humiliation, if friends stopped readily accepting their dinner invitations, and if other men's invitations to play golf dried up all of a sudden.

Yes, it could be devastating. But to kill three people and maim a handful of others…again, Crawford thought, that would certainly be an extreme reaction. Almost unfathomably extreme.

But still, he decided, it was an angle worth pursuing. He'd had much more far-fetched theories in the past that turned out to be true.

TEN

It was 7:00 p.m. Crawford and Ott were facing each other in Crawford's office.

"Okay, here's the big news I just got from the Ocean Club manager, Delbert Roth: he told me the bartender on duty at the time of the shootings thought the shooter was targeting his victims, that it wasn't random."

"No shit, really?"

Yeah, like he was skipping over some of them and singling out others," Crawford said. "I got a call into the guy, haven't heard back yet."

"Wow, that is huge."

"I know. The other thing is I checked with the uniforms going around to the gun shops and no luck."

"No black and white Steyr AUG, huh?"

"No, but they're not done yet." Then Crawford told Ott about his membership rejection theory.

"Come on, man, that's crazy," Ott said, on hearing it. "You're sayin' some dude got into a murderous rampage just 'cause some hoity-toity club says, 'We don't want ya…go play in someone else's sandbox'?"

"I was pretty sure that's the way you'd react but listen to this: David Balfour told me once when we were out on a golf course a year or so back about these two couples who moved down here from New

York expecting they'd be shoo-ins to get into either the Poinciana or the T & C or both."

Balfour had become a friend of Crawford's through their mutual friend, Rose Clarke, despite them inhabiting entirely different universes. Balfour was the ultimate club and society man-about-town; Crawford was… a cop. But the two hit it off right away and when things were slow for Crawford the two played golf together.

"Wait, what's the T & C stand for again?"

"Tennis and Croquet."

Ott laughed. "Croquet? Like that's a real sport."

Crawford put up his hands. "I know, I know, but trust me, some people take it very seriously," he said. "So let me finish."

"Go on."

"Anyway, because a million people moved down here during COVID and everyone was trying to get into one of the clubs, Balfour told me, both of these couples got shot down."

Ott laughed again. "*Oh, no, my life is over.*"

"You laugh, but both of 'em ended up selling the houses they had just bought and limped back to New York. Completely humiliated. And one of the wives divorced her husband because she said they got shot down because he had a reputation for being too pushy in business."

Ott's mouth was wide open. "Balfour told you this? Sounds like complete bullshit to me."

"Not only is it a true story, but supposedly all the clubs down here have three-to-five-year waiting lists to get in. So some guy who's a big golfer up in New York finds himself playing at one of the public courses or the Par 3 on South Ocean."

"Oh my God, the horror of it. The disgrace, the shame," Ott said. "I'm just glad my bowling alley will let anyone in…grifters, psychos, felons, you name it."

Crawford laughed. "Look, I'm just telling you not to rule it out until you got something better. You got something better?"

"Anything's better than that."

"All right, well, I'm gonna look into it anyway," Crawford said. "Fact is, two of our vics were on that Membership Committee. And one had been previously. I'm looking for a common thread here, and that's what I got at this point."

Ott put his hands up. "Okay, Charlie, I'm not insulting your intelligence. I just—"

"I get it, think it's a long shot," Crawford said. "And I agree with that. I mean, chances are still good, despite what the bartender told Delbert Roth, it's a random shooter, but who the hell knows based on what we got so far."

"Hey, speaking of Balfour," Ott said, "it might be a good idea to have a little sit-down with him. He knows all the players and all the clubs and all the pink and green people. Right? Why don't we run some of this by him. He's been pretty helpful in the past."

"That's actually a really good idea," said Crawford.

"Hey, somebody's gotta have 'em."

ELEVEN

Crawford called Balfour, who told them to come on over. "I'm always up for helping you guys solve a murder, particularly in a case where I knew one of the victims."

Crawford asked him which of the victims he knew and Balfour said Jeff Fisk and described him as a man with a "few skeletons rattling around in his closet." He also said he didn't know Lauren Faircloth but had "heard a few stories about her." When Crawford asked like what, Balfour answered, "They're best told over a cocktail or two."

To which Crawford replied, "I'm not drinking much until this thing is over."

And Balfour countered, "What the hell, Charlie, one Sierra Nevada's not gonna kill you."

Then Balfour asked Crawford if they had had dinner. When Crawford said they hadn't, Balfour said, "Fine, I'll order a couple Mellow Mushroom pizzas."

"Nah," said Crawford, "we had that last night. Tell you what, I'll swing by Malakor's and pick up some Thai food."

But before he did that he called and left a message on Norm Rutledge's answering machine.

"Hey, Norm, nothing so far on the uniforms checking the gun shops. I'm thinking it might be a good idea to get Nick Boone"—the gun expert detective who IDed the Steyr AUG murder weapon—"to be the contact on that. I'll get him on it if you're good with it."

Then he and Ott picked up the Thai food and drove to Balfour's house. It was 8:55 p.m. They sat down on his back porch and started in on the Thai food.

"You may not quote a word I'm about to tell you," Balfour said. "Understood?"

"Relax," Crawford said. "We never have, so why would we start now?"

Ott nodded his agreement, putting down his fork and taking his notepad out of his jacket pocket.

"Okay, so Jeff Fisk wanted to get into the Poinciana instead of the Ocean Club, but no way that was ever going to happen."

"Why's that?" Crawford asked.

"Because there have been these rumors about his fund. That it's been on shaky ground lately and there're even some whispers about it being a Ponzi scheme."

"You mean like Madoff?" Ott asked.

"Yeah, so I've heard, but nothing's been proven that I know of, just allegations, well, really, more like rumors," Balfour said. "But I do know this, it's tanked a ton in the last month."

"What's that mean?" Ott asked.

"Lost a lot of money. On paper anyway," Balfour said. "I heard it's down close to a third. Maybe even more."

Crawford tapped on the side table next to him. "So if I'm an investor and the thing is going down the tubes and I've got all my life savings in it—"

"I see where you're going, maybe I'd want to kill the bastard?" Ott said. "Sorry, Chuck, but that strikes me as almost as extreme as someone killing him because they didn't get into the Ocean Club."

"Wait a minute, Mort," said Balfour. "If you had all your money in the fund, like a lot of Madoff investors did and whose lives were ruined for good, maybe it might cross your mind to take it out on the guy."

"Yeah, I heard there were cases of Madoff investors committing suicide 'cause they couldn't afford groceries anymore," Crawford said.

"Including one of Madoff's sons," Balfour said, "and his wife, who supposedly attempted it and then ended up living in a one-bedroom apartment for a while."

"You know, now that you mention it, when I asked Fisk's partner John Zoller whether Fisk had any enemies, he mentioned something about an investor who was…I forget his exact words, but clearly the guy was irate about losing his money. Of course, Zoller never mentioned to me the fund was tanking."

"Probably his least favorite subject," Balfour said, taking a sip of his vodka. "Drink up, Mort, your Yuengling's just sitting there getting warm."

Ott took a sip. "You know, you're a hell of a good host. Stocking Charlie's Sierra Nevada Torpedo *and* my lowly Yuengling."

"Gotta keep our local lawmen happy," Balfour said. "So you want to know a little about Lauren Faircloth, too?"

"Sure, why not?" Ott said, "While we're sitting around dishing?"

"Well, I know it's not very respectful speaking of the dead in a, uh, less than flattering way, but I'll tell you what I know. Suffice it to say, she's been around—"

"Meaning a party girl?" Ott asked.

"Yes, you could say that. A party girl with no dough until she snagged Warren Faircloth," Balfour said. "Who, by the way, is a hell of a piece of work."

"What do you mean? How so?" Crawford said. "I met him and he just struck me as kind of a doddering old gentleman."

"Well, he is that, but he's also like this obsessed Civil War reenactor guy. Fights it out with the dreaded Yankees every chance he gets."

Ott shrugged. "Hey, some guys like golf, I guess others like to fight in a war they lost 150 years ago."

Crawford shrugged. "I guess," he said. "So back to his wife, Lauren."

"Oh yeah," Balfour said. "Extramarital affairs is a phrase that comes to mind."

"Not just singular?" Crawford asked.

"Nope, once with a guy I know. Another with a mystery man. Probably others I don't even know about."

"Which doesn't strike me as that much of a rarity in Palm Beach," Crawford noted.

"True," said Balfour.

"So, David," Crawford said, "one angle I'm pursuing, which Mort said earlier he thinks is a big waste of time, is that the Ocean Club shot down the shooter for membership and it messed up his life so bad that he took it out on the people who blackballed him."

"On the Membership Committee, you mean?"

"Yeah, exactly, is that too much of a reach?"

"Guy'd have to be more than a little pissed off," Balfour said, with a shrug. "But I guess it's conceivable. Clubs are a pretty big thing to people around here. I mean, as a status symbol and it can be their whole social life. I don't know what I'd do without the Poinciana. I'm there just about every day of the week."

"Yeah, but, David, isn't that a bit of a stretch that you'd go on a killer rampage because a club turned you down."

"Depends on what the ramifications were."

"What do you mean?" Ott asked.

"Did Charlie tell you about those two couples who got shot down at the Poinciana?" Balfour asked.

"Yeah, but none of them went out and bought a semiautomatic rifle," Ott said.

"True, maybe it wasn't just getting shot down by the Ocean Club but that combined with something else. You know, like a combination of bad things that drove the guy over the edge?"

Crawford nodded. "I buy that as a possibility, the combination of things." He turned to Ott. "What do you think of that?"

"Um, maybe," Ott said, nodding. "It's a world I don't live in so I guess I don't know much about it."

Balfour cuffed Ott on the shoulder. "Aw, and just when I was all set to propose you for membership at the Poinciana."

Ott laughed. "Jeffrey Epstein would have a better chance than me."

"Except he's dead," Crawford said.

"Oh yeah, I forgot."

"All right," Crawford said to Ott. "Delbert Roth, the Ocean Club manager, gave me the names of the Membership Committee members and their numbers. I'm gonna call the head of the committee tomorrow. See if I can find out exactly who they shot down."

"Good idea," Balfour said.

"Hey David, staying with the Ocean Club for a moment, have you ever gone there for dinner?"

"Yeah, I have, and they have really good food. A hell of a talented French chef, as I remember."

"No more," Crawford said. "He got fired. Apparently it was a pretty contentious parting of the ways. As matter of fact, I'm trying to track him down."

"No luck?" Balfour said.

"Not yet, I just have a phone number. He moved from the address I had for him," Crawford said.

"You're not thinking—" Balfour started.

"We're trying to expand our suspect list at this point; we'll narrow it down later."

Ott chuckled. "And a hotheaded Frog who throws a knife at a coworker *is* someone worth taking a look at."

Balfour's eyes got big. "He actually did that?"

Crawford nodded. "By the way, David," he said, "any information we give you is not for publication."

"Yeah definitely, like I said before, that goes both ways."

Crawford glanced at his watch. It was 10:00 p.m.

"All right," he said, getting up, "it's past our bedtime. Thanks for the drinks and intel. I'm sure we'll check back with you and if you hear anything that might be useful, please let us know."

"Will do, and thanks for the Thai food," Balfour said. "And good luck on the case. Are all the international media and reporters and cameramen getting in your way at all?"

Crawford rolled his eyes. "We're kind of getting used to it."

"Yeah, we've seen a lot of 'em before," Ott said.

"True," said Balfour. "Just not in a triple homicide, right?"

TWELVE

First thing the next morning Crawford called the bartender whose name and number Delbert Roth had given him and, this time, reached him. Ott was with him and Crawford had his cell phone on speaker.

"Hello, this is Bill."

"Hi Bill, it's Detective Crawford, I've been trying to reach you regarding the murders at the Ocean Club."

"I apologize. I was going to call you."

"So Delbert Roth told me you thought the shooter was targeting his victims, that it was not random?"

"Well, yes, that was my impression. I mean, I could be wrong, but that was what I thought."

"I need you to describe exactly what you saw."

"Well, it was like the guy'd aim at someone and pull the trigger, then stop, then aim at someone else, and pull the trigger again, then stop again."

"So, Bill, this is Detective Crawford's partner, are your saying that the shooter did that three times?"

"Well, yeah, kinda, but I know he also injured those six others...so, well maybe, I'm not so sure."

"But that was your overall sense, that he was aiming at specific people, not just shooting randomly?"

"Um, well, I think so, but I'm not a hundred percent positive."

Crawford glanced over at Ott, who shrugged back at him.

"Okay, Bill," Crawford said. "Well, thank you, if you have any more thoughts, get back to me, please. You got my number on your phone."

"Got it," Bill said. "Hope I was helpful."

"You were," Crawford said and clicked off.

Crawford glanced back at Ott, who was wobbling his hand. "I don't know, man, old Bill was starting to waffle on us a little there."

"Yeah, I know."

"So where are we?"

Crawford slowly shook his head. "That we can make a case for both targeted and random."

Ott chuckled. "Which is another way of saying we're totally clueless."

*****

After delivering his frustrated but entirely accurate line, Ott went back to his cubicle and Crawford put in another call to Alain Fournier.

Like the three times he had called before, he just got a recording of a man with a French accent saying: "This is Alain, thank you for ringing me up, please leave a message. *À bientôt.*"

Crawford was pretty sure from his high school French that *à bientôt* meant *see you soon* but he was beginning to wonder if he'd ever catch up with the guy.

"Mr. Fournier, it's Detective Crawford again, I need to speak to you right away," he said, in a tone decidedly lacking in warmth.

After that, he dialed the number Delbert Roth had given him of Tim Cutter, the head of the Membership Committee at the Ocean Club.

Cutter answered.

"Hello, Mr. Cutter," he said. "My name is Detective Crawford, Palm Beach Police. I'm one of the lead investigators on the Ocean

Club murders and wanted to see if I could set up a time to meet with you."

"Yes sure, I've heard your name before. I'm going to be near the police station around four today. How 'bout we make it, say, five? Is that too late?"

"No, that's fine. I'll see you then."

Then, before his appointment to see the widow of hedge fund manager, Jeff Fisk, at ten thirty, which she had changed from the previous day, he decided to go to his computer and delve into a file he had asked Bettina to create a year and a half ago. He and Ott had asked her to archive headline stories from *The Palm Beach Post, Miami Herald* and the *Sun-Sentinel,* documenting crimes in South Florida. They figured it might come in handy at some later date as a source of possible homicide suspects. Every day, Bettina perused all three papers and now had a voluminous file of crimes, including the names of hundreds of perpetrators. Twenty minutes into skimming the files, Crawford saw one that got his heart pounding. The week-old headline in the *Miami Herald* read, "West Palm Beach Slasher Escapes," and it went on to document how a man named Marlon Celestine escaped from an institution outside of Miami called the Miami Center for Mental Health and Recovery designed for people with "serious mental illnesses." The "loony bin," in Ott-speak.

Crawford remembered the original case because it occurred shortly after he moved down from New York to Palm Beach. Celestine had gone on a meth-fueled rampage in a West Palm Beach Mall called The Square (formerly City Place) and slashed and severely injured six people with a ten-inch knife. He later admitted at his trial that he was fully expecting to be shot by the cops as the final resolution but instead was tackled and handcuffed by one instead. At the trial, he was deemed to be criminally insane and was ordered to be incarcerated in one of Florida's mental institutions. But what stood out in Bettina's file, getting Crawford even more amped up, was that, during an inspection of Celestine's West Palm Beach apartment, a loaded Beretta M9 semiautomatic pistol was discovered. Okay, it wasn't a Steyr AUG semiautomatic rifle but still indicated that he had a deadly weapon back then, so why couldn't he be using an even deadlier Steyr AUG now?

Crawford immediately called Ott and asked him to come to his office.

Ott had barely taken one step in when Crawford blurted: "Hey, you gotta check this out."

Ott came around to Crawford's computer and started reading. "Holy shit, yeah, I remember that guy," he said. "Complete whack job."

"And remember after it happened they found a Beretta M9 in his apartment?"

"I don't remember the make but I remember it was a semi-auto…fully loaded," Ott said.

"Yup, like if he missed with the knife, he was going to come back and use the nine."

Ott looked up at Crawford. "So he escaped, huh? I get the feeling that some of these places can get pretty lax."

"Yeah, so now we gotta go find him," Crawford said. "This is our best lead yet. Fact that he busted out of the Miami institution two days before the Ocean Club. I want to talk to Rutledge about it."

"What for? How's he gonna be helpful?"

"Well, it's partly to show him we're making progress and every once in a blue moon he comes up with a good idea."

"Okay," Ott said with a shrug, "your call."

"Let's go now, I know he's in."

They took turns telling Rutledge the Marlon Celestine story. The more Rutledge heard, the more animated he got. He punctuated several of his reactions with the same popular two-word retort as Ott previously, and frequently, used: *Holy shit*. At the end of their presentation, he said: "Well, obviously this isn't as big a deal to the people in that Miami institution as it is to us. Just another insane inmate jumping the wall and taking off, while to us it's a possible mass murderer jumping the wall and taking off. So we gotta get the word out to every cop and law enforcement officer down there. BOLOs, APBs, photos of the guy in every squad car, you name it. Plus get a description and photo out to all the papers and blanket every square inch of South Florida."

"Yeah, you want to handle that?" Crawford said.

"Yeah, I'll take care of it."

"Even though he could be anywhere by now," said Ott.

"Could be," Rutledge said. "Tell you what, you guys should head down there right away and go after the guy. You're pretty good at tracking down killers once you get a scent and I'll organize the rest of it."

Crawford nodded his head. "All right," he said, glancing at Ott, "let's do it."

Ott stood up. "What do you think? Start at that place, the Miami Center for Mental Health and Recovery?"

"Yup," Crawford said, "2200 Northwest Seventh Avenue, Miami."

Rutledge held up his hand. "But before you go, let me ask you a couple of questions."

"Fire away," said Crawford.

"So your thinking is that after he broke out of that place in Miami he might have come up here, either already had the Steyr AUG stowed away somewhere or bought it, then went on the rampage? Is that the gist of it?"

"Uh-huh, that's basically it, though I don't know where he could have gotten the money for it after busting out," said Crawford. "Also, I'm guessing it's more likely he's in this area."

"So why start in Miami if you think he's up here?"

"I'll tell you why," said Crawford. "'Cause if he's up here, where do we start? Just drive around hoping we bump into him, get lucky and see him on the street or something?"

"See, Norm, if we go down there," Ott said, "maybe we talk to someone in the mental institution who knew him. Who he may have said something to that'll lead us to him, or at least point us in the right direction. And for all we know, if he did the job here, he may have gone back down there after."

Crawford nodded.

"Yeah, okay," Rutledge said. "Another thing I'm gonna do is contact TSA at the airports as well as authorities at the train and bus stations."

"Good idea," Crawford said. "'Course I still wonder where he'd get the money for a ticket."

"Yeah, I know, but maybe he could've scared some up," Rutledge said. "Pulled a robbery maybe."

"Okay, we're on our way," Crawford said, turning to go, Ott right behind.

"Keep me in the loop," Rutledge called after them.

Before they left for Miami, Crawford phoned Jeff Fisk's widow and said he would need to cancel their meeting and would call her back soon to reschedule it.

*****

"We shoulda brought Dominica with us to guide us around," Ott said as he pulled into the Miami Center for Mental Health and Recovery at 2200 Northwest Seventh Avenue in Miami an hour and a half later. "Plus she's good company."

Crawford was silent even though he agreed wholeheartedly. Dominica had been born and raised in Miami and her parents still lived there, along with a brood of brothers, sisters, in-laws, cousins, and other family members.

"I feel I'm getting to know the city pretty well," Crawford said, "since about half our recent cases brought us down here."

"True that," Ott said. "A lot of bad dudes seem to like hangin' in the 305."

"I like the town," Crawford said, "but I sure as hell could do without the traffic. More maniacs on the highways here than any other place I've ever been."

Crawford had phoned ahead and had made arrangements to meet with the Assistant Director of the hospital, along with a counselor who had spent lot of time with Marlon Celestine while he had been at the center.

They met in a room that seemed to double as a small conference room and a storage room, with a whole wall of file boxes stacked to the ceiling.

A woman named Andrea had been introduced as the counselor and the assistant director was Ed Suarez.

"I know Celestine's crimes, those stabbings, were committed in Palm Beach County, but that was five years ago. Why are you guys so interested in him?" Suarez asked.

Ott glanced at Crawford to decide how to answer the question. "Okay, I'll give you a straight answer," Crawford said. "As I'm sure you've read or heard about, we had a multiple murder take place in Palm Beach a few days ago and want to speak to Celestine about it."

Suarez cocked his head. "That's a pretty big leap going from a man who slashed a few people five years back to a guy who mowed down three people in cold blood with an Uzi."

"A Steyr AUG, to be exact," said Ott.

Suarez shrugged. "Whatever it was."

"You may think it's a leap," Crawford said, "but just for the record it wasn't a few, it was six people he slashed with the knife. I saw footage of it and, trust me, he was trying to kill them"—he turned to Andrea—"what is your sense? Sounds like you dealt with him on a day-to-day basis?"

"Yes, I did. And is your question do I think he could have done what happened in Palm Beach?"

Crawford nodded.

She didn't answer for a few moments. Then: "I think it's possible. Marlon is a very unpredictable, volatile man. One minute he could be calm and reserved, the next hyperactive and what I would call potentially dangerous. He was involved in several fistfights here at the center. In one he assaulted another resident with a toothbrush that he had sharpened like a blade. Cut another guy up pretty good."

"How long ago was that?" Ott asked.

"A month or two ago," Andrea said. "I mean, if he got his hands on an automatic rifle, I wouldn't rule out that he might use it."

"Really?" asked Suarez. "You really think so?"

"Yes, I have personally seen him fly into uncontrollable rages," Andrea said. "Sometimes self-directed. Like one time he was slamming his head into a cement wall. Like he wanted to kill himself. It was scary, trust me."

"I'm sure it was," Suarez said.

"So Andrea, could you describe Celestine for us physically, please?" Crawford asked.

"Sure. Pretty tall, dark hair medium length, no facial hair, no tats, um, that's about it."

"And how much would you guess he weighed?" Crawford asked.

"Um, I'd say around two hundred."

"So when you said, *pretty tall*, how tall?" Ott asked.

"Around six feet three maybe," Andrea said.

"So have your heard anything from the local police?" Ott asked. "Any sightings of him? Any incidents, you know, violent or otherwise, that he might have been involved in?"

"Not a thing," Suarez said. "Dude vanished without a trace."

"He literally climbed up over a wall?" Crawford asked.

"Well, what he did was crab-walk his way up between two walls, then got to the top and jumped down on the other side of one of 'em."

"Must have been in pretty good shape to do that?"

"Yeah, he worked out every day. He was in good shape."

"So do either of you have the names and numbers of the first-on-scene officers who came after the escape?" Ott asked.

Andrea took a piece of paper out of the breast pocket of her long-sleeved shirt. "I thought you might want that so I wrote down their names and numbers."

"Oh, thanks," Crawford said, taking the piece of paper from her.

"I also thought it might be helpful if you talked to another resident who knew Marlon pretty well and could maybe shed some light on where he might have gone when he escaped," Andrea said. "He's outside now if you'd like me to get him."

"Absolutely," Crawford said. "Yes, bring him in, please."

"I just warn you, sometimes he's a little…off."

"Understand," Crawford said. "Let's see what happens."

Andrea nodded, got up and walked out of the room.

"Do you have any other suspects?" Suarez asked Crawford and Ott.

"A few possibles, nothing solid yet," Crawford said as Andrea walked in with a man who looked to be in his mid-thirties. He had close-cropped dark hair, a long scar on his left cheek, and green eyes that blinked a lot.

"Gentlemen," said Andrea. "This is Gilbert."

"Hi, Gilbert," Crawford said.

"How ya doin'," said Ott with a nod.

Gilbert was silent.

"So Gilbert," said Suarez, as Gilbert sat down, "the detectives here want to ask you some questions about your friend, Marlon. We'd like you to try to help them."

"Okay," Gilbert said, expressionlessly. "He's gone."

"Yes, we know that," Crawford said, leaning toward him, "and we want to find him. Did he ever tell you he planned to escape or where he planned to go if he did?"

"To Lynn's house maybe," Gilbert said.

Ott leaned toward him. "And who is Lynn?"

"His sister or his mother, I forget which."

"Do you know her last name?" Ott asked.

"Just Lynn," Gilbert said. "His sister or his mother. Or maybe his shorty."

"That means girlfriend," Andrea explained.

"I know," Ott said, then to Gilbert. "Where is she…Lynn?"

"I don't know," Gilbert said. "At the airport?"

"At the airport?" Crawford said. "Does Lynn work there?"

Gilbert shrugged. "I don't know. Or at the IHOP."

"Does she work there?" Crawford asked again.

Another shrug.

"Anything else?" Andrea asked Crawford and Ott.

"Gilbert," Ott said, "did Marlon ever talk about hurting someone?"

"He beat up Sam," Gilbert said, eking out a smile. "Cocksucker deserved it."

"But anyone on the outside," Crawford said. "Did he ever say he wanted to shoot people?"

"I don't know."

"Did he ever tell you he had an automatic weapon?" Crawford asked.

"Um, maybe."

"Was it…black and white?" Ott asked.

"I don't know."

Crawford glanced at Ott, then back to Gilbert. "Well, thank you, Gilbert."

"You're welcome," he said. "Is Marlon coming back?"

"We're not sure," Crawford said.

"Come on, Gilbert, you've been good," Andrea said standing, and she led him out.

"Sorry, that wasn't more helpful," Suarez said as Andrea came back into the room.

"Well," she said. "At least you have a name"—she laughed—"though we don't know whether she's a sister, mother or girlfriend."

"Or works at the airport or IHOP," Ott said.

"Oh, one last thing," Crawford said. "What was he wearing?"

"Well, as you probably noticed, there are no prison outfits here. He was wearing dark pants and a dark T-shirt. But, of course, by now he could have changed."

Crawford nodded. "Well, I guess that does it," he said. "Thank you both for your time. We're gonna leave you our cards so if you think of anything else, or anything comes up, please give us a call."

"You got it," Suarez said, shaking Crawford's and Ott's hands.

"Good luck, finding him," Andrea told them. "And be careful, guys. He definitely can be violent."

THIRTEEN

Crawford and Ott spoke to the two first-on-scene cops next, but that didn't yield anything new or helpful. Only that a witness might have seen a man fitting Celestine's general description getting on a bus. For lack of anywhere else to turn, they Googled Lynn Celestine in the West Palm Beach area, hoping she might be Marlon Celestine's mother or sister. To their surprise they got a hit: there was a listing for a Lynn Celestine in Royal Palm Beach, fifteen miles to the west of Palm Beach. They decided to drive straight there.

On their way to Lynn Celestine's address in Royal Palm Beach, Crawford got a call. He recognized the number as one he had called several times: it was Alain Fournier.

"Hello," he answered. "This is Crawford."

"Yes, Detective, you've called me a few times, my name's Alain Fournier."

"I need to come see you, Mr. Fournier. Where are you?"

"I'm in West Palm. Why do you need to see me?"

"I'm one of the Palm Beach Police detectives looking into the murders at the Ocean Club. We're talking to past and present employees there, along with a number of members as well. How about tomorrow sometime?"

"Whoa, whoa, wait a minute. Why do you want to talk to me?"

"Like I just said, we're—"

"I've got nothing to tell you. I haven't worked there in over eight months."

"It doesn't matter. We still need—"

Click.

Ott, at the wheel, glanced over. "He hung up?"

"Yup," Crawford said. "Well, fact is, he's now in only second or third place in the suspect department."

"I know, but we still need to talk to him."

"We'll find him," Crawford said. "But first Marlon's mother, sister…or shorty."

*****

An hour and fifteen minutes later, Ott pulled up in front of Lynn Celestine's house in Royal Palm Beach. It was a small Cape Cod-style house, neatly maintained and with a colorful flower garden in front. In its driveway was a white Toyota Prius.

They got out of the Crown Vic and Ott pressed the front door buzzer.

A few moments later a woman, probably late thirties, early forties, answered the door. One mystery was solved: she was not Marlon Celestine's mother.

"Hello, Ms. Celestine," Crawford said. "My name is Detective Crawford and this is my partner, Detective Ott. We need to question Marlon Celestine. Is he your—"

"My brother. Who I have absolutely nothing to do with."

"And when did you last see your brother?" Ott asked.

"Last Tuesday or Wednesday, I don't remember exactly."

"Here?" Ott asked.

"Yes, he just showed up…like a bad penny."

"It's urgent that we find him, where is he?"

"I have no idea. See, ever since what happened—attacking those people in the shopping center—like I said, I've had nothing to do with him."

"But he came here?" Crawford asked.

"Wanting money and a place to stay?" Ott asked.

"I gave him some money, then told him to leave."

"How much did you give him?"

"About thirty dollars," she said, "then told him to leave and never come back."

"Where did he go?" Crawford asked.

"I don't know and I don't care, just away from here."

"What did he have with him? A backpack maybe? A cell phone? What did you notice?"

"Nothing. He just looked pretty bad, like he hadn't slept. Dirty, too. He said he hadn't eaten in a while so I gave him some food."

"Who else would he go see? You know, friends, or a girlfriend, maybe?"

"You'd be an idiot to be his girlfriend," she said. "Maybe a man named Jimmy Wray, I don't know. After what he did, I don't think many people wanted to have anything to do with him. He's kinda crazy, too. Jimmy, that is."

"Where does Jimmy live?" Ott asked.

"Boynton, I think."

"Do you know anything about a weapon he might own? Marlon, I mean," Crawford asked. "Or might have gotten his hands on somehow?"

"Nope. I just know about that pistol the police found after he attacked those people. It was in his old place."

Crawford took out his wallet and pulled out a card. "Ms. Celestine, it's really important that we find Marlon and talk to him. So if you hear anything or if he shows up again, please call us right away."

"Yeah," Ott said, "but don't tell him you're calling us."

Crawford and Ott handed her cards.

"Okay, but he won't be back. I made it very clear I didn't want to see him again."

"Okay, well, thanks," Crawford said and they walked back to the Vic.

They got back to the police station at a little after 4:00 p.m. Crawford had tried to locate a Jimmy or James Ray in Boynton Beach but had no luck. He walked to the station's reception desk and found Bettina.

"Hey," he said to her, "would you try to track down a Jimmy or James Ray. In Boynton, I think?"

"Sure," she said with her megawatt smile, "one of the best trackers in the business. R-a-y?"

"Yeah, I think so," he said.

He made a few calls, and as he was finishing one up, Dominica McCarthy walked in.

"You look tired," she said, then closing his door, she walked up to him, put her arms around him and they kissed.

"Um, now I'm wide awake," he said.

She pulled back. "So how's it going?"

"Slowly," he said. "Mort and I just got back from your hometown."

"Doing what?"

"Looking for a guy."

She kissed him again on the cheek. "I know how you get when you're stretched out on a case."

"What do you mean?"

"Neglect your appetite," she said. "Let me guess, Mellow Mushroom, Chipotle, and McDonald's?"

"No McDonald's…not yet anyway."

"Well, how about a nice home-cooked meal tonight, say Bolognese or Carbonara à la Dominica?"

"Oh, man, I can't think of anything better, but it'll have to be on the late side. Is that all right?"

"Sure, what time?"

"Is…eight thirty okay?"

"That's just fine. I'll have a Sierra Nevada Torpedo chilling for you."

He leaned forward and gave her a long kiss. "I can't wait."

Right after she left, Crawford got a call on his office line.

"Hey, Bettina," he said.

"Hey," she said, "I came by your office but your door was closed. Figured you were in with Norm or something."

He knew she knew he never closed the door when he was in with Norm Rutledge or Ott.

She knew.

"So I tracked down Jimmy Wray in Boynton. It's spelled W-r-a-y," she said and read Crawford the landline number, the address and a cell phone number.

"You're the best," he said. "Thanks."

Ten minutes later, Bettina called and said that his five o'clock appointment, Tim Cutter, the head of the Ocean Club Membership Committee, had just arrived and she'd bring him back to Crawford's office.

Cutter had longish white hair, a cleft chin, and a pleasant smile.

He shook Crawford's hand. "I've heard good things about you, Charlie."

"Thank you, Mr. Cutter."

"Tim, please."

"Tim…I have a question you might not want to answer, but it's very important."

Cutter's smile disappeared. "Okay, well, let's hear it."

"Over the last year, let's say, what are the names of people who you have rejected for membership of the Ocean Club?"

"Why in God's name is *that* important?" Cutter said, cocking his head and frowning.

"It just is. You'll have to trust me on this," Crawford said, not wanting the "rejected prospective member goes nuclear" theory to become public.

Cutter sighed. "Okay, I'll tell you," he said and reeled off a list of six names as Crawford wrote them down. "I remember there have been eight altogether in the past two years, so I'm forgetting two. Oh, yeah, now I remember one," he said, then named that one.

"And out of those," Crawford said, "which of them took it the hardest, getting turned down, would you say?"

"Well, none of them were pleased, of course," Cutter said. "I mean, these are people who are used to getting their way. Used to people always saying yes to them. But two in particular went really ballistic."

"Which two?"

"Rod Paul and Bob Hubbard," Cutter said. "Hubbard called me up and demanded that the committee meet again and change their decision."

"Let him in, you mean?"

"Yes, he and his wife," Cutter said. "When I said no, he said he'd make sure me and my wife didn't get into the Four Arts. See, he's on the board there and knew we had applied for membership a few months back."

Crawford shook his head. "Wow, it all gets kind of personal I can see."

Cutter's tone suddenly turned hard. "Look, it may seem petty to you but my wife is really eager to get into the Four Arts. She told all our friends that we were applying and I know she'd be humiliated if we didn't get in."

Crawford was beginning to feel that Ott was probably right in his doubt about a disgruntled prospective member suddenly turning into a crazed killer on a rampage. Even though it was becoming apparent that getting turned down would be a crushing defeat to some. But disgruntled was one thing; picturing Bob Hubbard or Rod Paul going out and buying a Steyr AUG and mowing down three and injuring six more…? Nah, Marlon Celestine was their man and they needed to track him down right away.

"Well, thanks for coming in," he said to Tim Cutter. "I really appreciate your time and you have my assurance I will never divulge that list of people you gave me."

"Yeah, please, that must be kept strictly confidential."

"It will be."

*****

Cutter was barely out of his office when Crawford started to dial the number of Jimmy Wray, the alleged friend of Marlon Celestine. Then he thought better of it, hung up and walked quickly to Ott's office.

"Hey—" he said, then realized Ott was on a call.

Ott held up a hand, then said, "Okay, thanks, I'll get back to you," and clicked off.

"What's up, bro?" Ott asked, glancing up at Crawford.

"I got the address for that guy, Jimmy Wray," Crawford said. "I'm gonna go there now. Meanwhile, I think you should try to track down the chef, Alain Fournier. Even though we both think Celestine's our guy."

"So you get the easier job, since we got no clue where Fournier is. But, turns out, I was just talking to a woman who used to go out with the guy."

"Fournier?"

"Yeah, I've been talking to a few people in the Ocean Club kitchen and one of 'em told me this chick named Stella something used to date him. So that's who I was just talking to. She told me they went out until she couldn't deal with his mood swings."

"But did she know where he lives?"

"No, just that address we already checked out. But she gave me a few other names of people who might know. Not people who worked in the kitchen with him."

Crawford looked at his watch. It was 6:35 p.m. "All right, I'm headed down to Boynton. I'll let you know if I get anything good out of Jimmy Wray."

*****

Jimmy Wray lived in a section of Boynton Beach just south of Hypoluxo, and, to the best of Crawford's memory, was a place where he'd never been before. He glanced at his watch as he pressed the buzzer at Wray's house. It was almost seven and he was hoping he could wrap up his business with Wray and get to Dominica's house by eight thirty for a dinner that his growling stomach was longing for. He and Ott had never gotten around to getting lunch.

Wray's house was on a street with several boarded-up houses and others that had shaggy, neglected front lawns. Wray's house, Crawford observed, could use a paint job, a new roof, a...well, come to think of it, it was really a teardown. But to Crawford's surprise, a man came to the door. He didn't look much better than the house...a missing front tooth, uneven hair that stood straight up—Crawford guessed he was his own barber—and a mustache narrower than Adolf Hitler's.

"Jimmy Wray?" Crawford asked.

"That's me. Who's askin'?"

Crawford showed him ID. "Detective Crawford, Palm Beach Police."

"You're little out of your territory, aren't ya, bub?"

"I'm looking for Marlon Celestine. I was told you're a friend of his."

"Lynn, huh?" Wray said, scratching the back of his head.

"Where is he, Jimmy?" Crawford said.

"Well, I can tell you where he ain't," Wray said. "He ain't here."

"I don't have forever," Crawford said, impatiently, shifting from one foot to the other. "I got a feeling you know where he is."

"I don't have a clue," Wray said. "He just showed up. No idea how he got here, just knocked on my door, said he needed a place to stay. I told him no, I got a cat and that's enough. Last thing I need in this place is a man who's one sandwich short of a picnic."

Crawford had never heard that one before and took kind of a shine to it. "Okay, but if you had to guess, where would he go? He got any other friends?"

"Hey, don't call me a friend. I just know him. My guess…he's gonna end up on the street somewhere."

"So he's got no one else?"

Wray shrugged. "No one I can think of."

Crawford reached for his wallet. "If I gave you a card with my number on it, would you contact me if he comes here again?"

"Probably not," Wray said. "Never had much of a thing for cops."

"I appreciate an honest man," Crawford said, putting his card back in his wallet and his wallet back in his pocket.

FOURTEEN

"Sounds like a real charmer," Dominica said, after Crawford told her about his recent conversation with Jimmy Wray over a glass of chardonnay and a chilly Sierra Nevada Torpedo beer.

"With hair that defied gravity and a mustache that made Hitler's look good," Crawford wrapped up his recap. "Hey, you ever heard of this saying? 'He's one sandwich short of a picnic'?"

"No, but I like it. Did that guy Jimmy come up with that?" she asked.

"All by himself."

"Sounds like something Mort would say about Rutledge."

"Believe it or not, Rutledge has actually been kind of helpful on the case…for a change."

"That's a first," she said, finishing her wine. "You ready for another Torpedo?"

"No thanks," he said. "I try to keep it to one when I'm one a case."

She nodded and poured a small glass of chardonnay. "Charlie the straight arrow. Oh hey, I need your advice on something."

"Sure. What is it?"

"Well, you remember me telling you about Rose's new squeeze, right?"

"Sure, the Brit—Alastair something."

"Alastair Christopher. Well, so I heard that right before he started going out with Rose he was hot and heavy with a really rich woman who cut him loose kind of abruptly. And, seems like anyway, glommed onto Rose right after that."

"Really? Who was the woman, not that I'd know her?"

"That's the part of the story I don't know. Who she was and why she cut him loose. I've got my spies on it. But it just makes me a little suspicious about a guy who can jump from one to the other with no time in between. Know what I mean?"

"I'd put Bettina on the case, but I need her on mine," he said. "Does makes me a little suspicious about the guy, though. Seems like he's definitely got his sights set on landing a woman with a bank account."

Dominica nodded.

"So, I take it you're not telling Rose about any of this?"

"Yeah, I wouldn't do that until I have all the facts. I don't want to warn her about something I don't know the whole story on."

"I agree."

*****

The Bolognese à la Dominica was fabulous, as Crawford knew it would be, and to top it all off, he was on his first Klondike bar of the night for dessert. Some nights he'd pig out and have two.

They decided to watch a movie with Colin Farrell on Apple TV+. Movies at her condo or his had about a fifty-fifty chance of being seen through to the end because the kissing usually began in the first half of the movie and ratcheted up to a more feverish state, culminating with them in bed together.

Crawford pulled back from Dominica on the couch. "Hey, babe, I'm gonna wimp out tonight."

"What? How come?"

"I'm just beat," he said, "I know it's a lame excuse, but I-I-I…"

She laughed. "Not only are you a wimp, but a stuttering wimp."

He laughed. "This case has got me going in circles. I wake up in the middle of the night thinking about it, not able to go back to sleep. I figure I got about three hours last night. I know that's a pathetic excuse, I just…"

She leaned into him and gave him a kiss on the cheek.

"That's all right, just don't make it a regular thing. I mean you get me all stirred up and then you douse me with cold water."

"I promise you I'll make it up to you," he said. "As soon as it's behind me, we'll have a marathon session, from sundown to sunup. I promise."

"I'm going to hold you to it," she said, then making a shooing motion, "now get out of here. Go home, get some sleep and go solve it. Shoo, shoo!"

FIFTEEN

Crawford and Ott were in Crawford's office at eight thirty with the usual assortment of Dunkin' Donuts coffee, donuts, and a so-called Wake-up Wrap for Ott, which was miraculously low on calories.

"So you're bailing on the 'someone-getting-pissed-about-getting-shot-down-by-the-Ocean-Club' theory?" Ott asked.

"Well, kind of, but not completely. I mean, threatening to get someone blackballed at the Four Arts as revenge is one thing, but…no, it's a long shot," Crawford said, shaking his head. "But I'll tell you what does make sense to me. A guy taking out a bunch of coworkers or his boss. That's happened a lot. I looked into it a little. There was one in Virginia Beach, I remember, like about five years ago. Then this truck driver in Texas who killed six people he worked with. Started out being a pay dispute…hell, too many to count."

"The only problem with that theory is that if it was Alain Fournier, he didn't shoot any of his coworkers," Ott said.

"Yeah, because his dispute was with the club people. Specifically, the head of the Board of Directors who fired him," Crawford said. "But it's almost always the case that the shooter kills himself after all the carnage."

"All right," Ott said. "Well, we gotta find 'em. Fournier and Celestine. It's got to be one or the other."

"Unless it isn't," Crawford noted.

"Why do you say that?"

"I don't know," Crawford said. "My gut's telling me maybe there's somebody else out there."

"And your gut's been pretty reliable over the years."

"But not always."

"All right, so how do you want to play it?" Ott asked. "I stay with Fournier and you Celestine?"

Crawford nodded. "Yeah, but I definitely need your help on Celestine, too."

"Hey, you know what I just thought of?" Ott said. "If it was Fournier, it's still possible he might have killed himself."

"Yeah, except, don't forget, I spoke to him."

"I know, but maybe he killed himself after that."

Crawford shook his head. "Nah, I don't buy it. That's not the usual MO. They almost always do it right after they kill a bunch of people. They're the last casualty."

"Yeah, I know," Ott said, standing. "All right, I'm out of here."

"Where you going?"

"To talk to a friend of Fournier who's a waitress at Sant Ambroeus."

"All right. We'll talk later," Crawford said as his interoffice phone rang. It said, *Rutledge*.

"Hey, Norm, what's up?" he answered.

"I wish you'd answer the phone a little bit more professionally."

"Good morning, Chief Rutledge, so nice to hear from you," Crawford said.

"Much better. You seen the *Post* today?"

"No, why?"

"There's a front-page article with the headline, 'Jeffrey Fisk's Fund Tanks.'"

"No shit. What's the article say exactly?"

"In so many words, that it was a smaller version of Madoff's fund. Another Ponzi scheme where the returns they claimed they were making were all bogus. Then in the last week or so, investors started bailing out in droves."

"Incredible," Crawford said. "I'm scheduled to interview Fisk's wife later today. That should be interesting."

"She's going to be a lot poorer today than she was a week ago," Rutledge said. "So maybe that theory of yours that Fisk was shot by a pissed-off investor who was seeing his money go down the drain has more credibility."

"Yeah maybe," Crawford said.

"How are you two coming on finding your two main suspects?" Rutledge asked.

Crawford had given him a call on his way to Jimmy Wray's house and caught him up on Marlon Celestine and Alain Fournier. Not that there was much to catch him up on with Fournier.

"They're the two we're concentrating on," Crawford said. "We don't really have any others."

"I know that," Rutledge said, peevishly. "I asked you how you're coming on finding them."

"I'll let you know at the end of the day."

"I'd like you to let me know at the end of the day that you got one or the other locked up in a jail cell."

"That would be nice," Crawford agreed.

"The other thing I wanted to tell you is the head of the Chamber of Commerce and the guy from The Association called and want to schedule another meeting to get an update from you."

Crawford groaned. "Oh, Christ, like we got time to listen to them squawk about how bad their businesses are doing."

"Hey look, these guys are taxpayers, probably some of our biggest ones, we can't just tell 'em to get lost and not bother us," Rutledge said.

"I know, I know, but why don't you meet them without us. Tell 'em Mort and I are too damn busy to listen to their bellyaching."

"Oh right, that's just what I'm gonna tell them," Rutledge said. "Then a week from now I'll be working on a goddamn sanitation truck."

Crawford sighed. "All right…but stall it for as long as you can, okay?"

"They wanted it for tomorrow, but I said we couldn't."

"No way in hell. Thanks for the heads-up about Fisk's fund…later," Crawford said.

He clicked off, maybe a little sooner than Rutledge would have liked.

His phone rang again, this time it was his cell.

"Hello," he answered. "Crawford here."

"Is this Detective Crawford?" the voice asked.

"Yes, who's this?"

"You don't know me, Detective, my name is Moira DePietro, Dr. Moira DePietro, I'm a psychiatrist, and I'm calling about those murders in Palm Beach."

"Yes, Dr. DePietro?"

"Well, I'm really going out on a limb making this call, because what I'm about to tell you could be viewed as a violation of the Hippocratic oath, no, it definitely *would* be viewed as a violation."

"Why don't you tell me why you called, Doctor."

"Okay, I saw your notice in the paper asking for any information about who might have committed those terrible murders, and that's why I called. You see, I have a patient who has voiced suicidal ideations on several occasions. First of all, before I go any further," she said, "I need to have your assurance that you will never attribute what I'm about to tell you to me."

"You have my word."

"Okay, well, at first his fantasy was to commit suicide by stepping in front of a train, then later in his car: going a hundred miles an hour and slamming into a bridge abutment on a highway or something like that. The most recent was 'taking a bunch of people along with me,' as he referred to it."

Crawford pressed his cell phone closer to his ear. "And did he spell it out, exactly what he meant by that?"

"As a matter of fact, he was very specific. He said he'd do it like that guy in Charlotte, killing four cops who showed up to issue him a warrant. The police had no choice but to kill him."

"Two questions, Doctor. Does your patient have a gun, and please describe him physically."

"Yes, to the first question, because I know he shot a deer last fall."

"Do you have any idea whether he owns an automatic firearm?" Crawford asked.

"I don't know much about guns," she said. "Tell me what an automatic firearm is exactly?"

"Well, a rifle that fires many bullets in rapid succession. An AR-15 is an example of one."

"Um, that I don't know for sure," she said. "But I do know that he's a member of the NRA, because he mentioned that before. Said how the government was trying to interfere with his Second Amendment rights. Actually kind of went into a rant about that."

"And your patient's physical description, please?" Crawford asked.

"Yes, he is right around six foot two, blue eyes, curly dirty-blond hair, a few crooked front teeth, um, a gold stud in his left ear—"

"Skinny, fat, or what?"

"Average, I'd say."

"I'm glad you called. I need to talk to your patient. What's his name, where does he live, and what are his phone numbers?"

"Jason Reardon," then she gave him his address in Lake Worth and his cell phone number.

"And does he work?"

"Yes, he's there right now. He's a letter carrier at the post office on Military Trail in West Palm."

Crawford shuddered at the thought of the numerous shootings at post offices over the years. It was so common that the phrase "going postal" had become part of the lexicon.

"Well, thank you, is there anything else you think I should know about?"

"No, that's about it," she said, "but I want you to promise again that you'll never say that I called you about him."

"Again, you have my word," Crawford said. "Oh—before you go: have you seen Jason since the shootings in Palm Beach?"

"Ah, let me think," she said. "Um, no. I last saw him right before those murders. We talked about a problem he was having with two postal workers that always harassed him and gave him a hard time."

Crawford shuddered again.

SIXTEEN

He wasted no time in calling Ott and telling him what Dr. De-Pietro the psychiatrist had just told him.

"So now we got three," Ott said. "Who's your money on now?"

"I don't know, man, could've been any of 'em," Crawford said. "Or someone else altogether."

"You keep saying that, but I gotta think it's one of the three."

"Put it this way, I sure as hell hope so. It's time to wrap this up."

"I'm with you there."

"Are you still at Sant Ambroeus?"

"No, the waitress wasn't much help. She just told me a couple places Fournier hung out at," Ott said.

"But not where he lives?"

"No, nobody seems to know where he moved to. Just that it was a one-bedroom somewhere."

"It might make sense for us to get a couple uniforms to stake out the places where he supposedly hangs out. You can't be wasting all your time waiting around just hoping he shows up."

"Yeah, I agree. Maybe I'll get Wiley to cover one and Hernandez another one," Ott said. "Want me to go to the post office on Military? Check out Jason our postal worker?"

"Yeah, because I'm gonna need to spend some time going around to homeless shelters. See if Celestine is at one of 'em."

"Are there a lot?"

"Yeah, Google it sometime. I counted at least twenty in West Palm alone," Crawford said. "A friend of Dominica's volunteers at a place call The Almighty's Place; then there's a Salvation Army one and a bunch of others."

"Plus there are places like that one up on Dixie and Twenty-second or Twenty-third. On the sidewalk or under that overhang or whatever it is," Ott said.

"Yeah, exactly. So it's gonna take me a while to cover 'em all. I'm thinking I'm gonna get some extra guys to go around at the same time I do. Just like you getting Wiley and Hernandez."

"All right, well, I'm on my way out to the PO now," Ott said. "I'll let you know what happens."

SEVENTEEN

The first thing Crawford did was call a woman named Joanne, who, as he mentioned to Ott, was a friend of Dominica's and worked at a place called The Almighty's Place on Australian Avenue in West Palm Beach. Their mission was to find housing for the homeless and they had a reputation for being dedicated and compassionate people.

A woman answered the phone and, after a long pause, connected him to Joanne.

"Charlie Crawford," she answered, "and to what do I owe the pleasure?"

"Hey, Joanne, I'm hoping you can help me," he said. "I'm looking for a man named Marlon Celestine, a homeless guy who's looking for a bed somewhere. He's around six two, dark hair medium length, no facial hair, no tats—well, as of a week ago anyway. White guy weighs around two hundred. Um, might have come by your place in the last day or so."

"Hmm, doesn't ring a bell," Joanne said, "but let me check a second. Can you hold?"

"Yeah, sure, go ahead."

She put him on hold for a couple of minutes.

"Charlie," she said, coming back to him, "sorry it took so long, but no luck. Nobody by the name or fitting that description has come in here."

"Okay, well, do me a favor, if he does, will you call me right away?" Crawford said. "And don't tell him I'm looking for him."

"Is he a bad guy?"

"He may be. So be careful," he said. "Gotta run. Thanks, Joanne."

One down, close to twenty more to go.

He decided to swing by the place on Dixie Highway in West Palm that Ott had mentioned, and where he had been before, also looking for a suspect. He had driven past it many times, usually on his way to his favorite Thai food place, further up on Twenty-fifth Street. Usually about five or six homeless people were stretched out under the overhang of an abandoned building, which provided some relief from the sun and rain. It was located across from a makeshift food kitchen that provided lunch and dinner for the homeless.

He parked on a side street and walked over to where the homeless people were. There were four men and one woman. They looked at him warily as he approached.

One of them glanced up at him and eyed him. "I remember you," the man croaked, "the detective."

"Yup," said Crawford. "How y'all doin'?"

"Could be better," said a woman, lying on top of a torn sleeping bag, her hair in crooked cornrows.

"A lot better," croaked a man missing his two front teeth.

The other four murmured agreement.

"So I wondered if a guy might've come by here," Crawford said, giving the same description he had given Joanne.

"We get a reward if we tell ya?" asked a man with yellowish, rheumy eyes and wearing jeans with holes in them. They were holes from actual wear, not ones that were designed to be stylish.

"Tell ya what, I'll give you a hundred bucks if it leads to his arrest."

He could see he had their attention. It looked like they all wanted to talk at once.

"Came by last night," one blurted.

"Ain't right in the head, that guy," said the woman with crooked cornrows.

"Didn't hang around long," said a third. "Wasn't impressed by the accommodations, I guess."

They all laughed at that.

"Did he say where he was going?" Crawford asked.

"Didn't say much of anything," the cornrow woman said. "Just seemed like a crazy white dude."

"Said it was 'worse than prison,'" the toothless one added.

"What was?" Crawford asked.

"Here," the toothless one said. "Called it *stink hole*."

"So," the cornrow woman said, "Jalen politely...asked him to leave the premises."

"Wasn't so po-lite," said a man in a wool hat that had the figure of a skier on it.

"So none of you have any idea where he might have gone?"

They all shook their heads.

"Was he carrying anything?" Crawford asked, thinking it was a long shot. "Maybe something long, in some kind of bag or something."

"Wasn't carryin' nothin'," said the one in the ski cap.

"All right, well, if he shows up again, gimme a call," Crawford said. "There's a hundred bucks in it for ya."

One of them laughed and shook his head. "One problem," he said.

"What's that?"

"None of us got phones."

Oh, yeah.

"Well, maybe go to a pay phone," Crawford said, knowing they were scarce commodities in the area. "One more question...when he left here, what direction did he go in?"

Three pointed south, two north.

EIGHTEEN

Crawford's next stop was a place called Love of Life.

Hard not to like a place with a name like that, he thought.

It was located at the south end of West Palm Beach on a side street. There was a small sign on a white, concrete-block, one-story building that said, *Love of Life. Est. 2010 with Compassion and Care in Mind.*

Crawford parked and walked inside. No one was at the desk.

"Hello," he said, then, "anyone here?"

No response.

"Hello," he said again, then he heard someone behind him opening the front door.

It was a Black woman who looked to be in her sixties and had a look of panic in her eyes.

"Help me, please!" she shouted. "Help! Help!"

Crawford took a step toward her. "What's wrong? What is it?"

"My sister! In the car! She's unconscious!"

Crawford rushed past her and saw an old, rusted-out Chevy straddling two parking spaces. He ran to it and saw a woman crumpled up in the front passenger seat. He opened the door and saw that her eyes were closed. He felt for a pulse and detected one. It felt faint.

"What happened?" he asked swinging around to the woman who had followed him out.

"She just, she just—"

Crawford opened the car door, bent down and lifted her scrawny body out of the seat and brought her outside. The woman's breaths were barely discernible. He set her down on the grass, shaded by two big flowering dogwood trees. Then he straddled her and started performing CPR, thinking she seemed to be in cardiac arrest.

"Thank you!" said the other woman. "She's my twin."

But the woman's eyes were still shut and she didn't seem to be responding. He kept giving her chest compressions, but it didn't seem to help.

Then he put his hand under her chin and lifted it up. He opened her mouth using his thumb, placed his other hand on her forehead and pinched her nose with his index finger and thumb. Then he leaned forward and covered her open mouth with his and blew into her mouth. He had performed mouth-to-mouth resuscitation once before and it had worked. But this woman was not responding and the only breathing was the heavy breathing of the woman behind him, the prostrate woman's twin.

He blew into her mouth again.

This time, her eyelashes flickered. He inhaled through his nose and breathed into her mouth again. He head footsteps behind him. Another woman had come out of the Love of Life building.

"What happened?" asked the other woman.

"My sister," said the twin sister in a low voice now, "she had a heart attack or something."

The stricken woman's eyes opened, first one, then the other. Crawford took his mouth off hers and pulled back slightly.

The woman had a confused look on her face. "Who are you?"

Crawford guessed she was around sixty-five. A Black woman with a dime-sized mole on her cheek and dark hair tinged with tufts of white. Crawford guessed she hadn't taken a bath or a shower in a while, but she had dark, expressive eyes that were taking a while to focus.

"He's the man who just saved your life, Kyra," came the sister's voice behind him.

"Are you okay?" Crawford asked.

"Yeah, what happened, Neisha?" Kyra asked her sister.

"You blacked out," Neisha said. "We were on our way here, and you blacked out."

"Where are we?" Kyra asked.

"Love of Life," said the tall, tattooed white woman who had joined them.

Crawford glanced at Kyra's twin Neisha. She was a dead ringer for her sister except she had no mole on her cheek.

"Do you want to come inside? Get something to eat or drink? Might make you feel better," the tattooed white woman asked. "My name's Christy."

Neisha looked down at her sister, still prone on the grass. "That's very nice of you," Neisha told Christy. Then to her sister. "Do you feel all right, can you get up now?"

"I think so," Kyra said.

"Do you want a hand?" Crawford asked, getting to his feet.

"Thank you," she said, looking up at Crawford quizzically. "What did you do to me?"

"Told ya," Neisha said, "that man saved your life. You were just lucky he was here and knew what to do."

"It was just CPR," Crawford said, reaching down to Kyra.

She grabbed his arm and he pulled her up.

Christy glanced at Crawford. "Was that you earlier…who came inside?"

"Yes, I'm a detective with the Palm Beach police. I'm looking for a suspect. His name is Marlon Celestine." Crawford gave the woman his description. "Did anyone who looked like that stop by here in the last few days?"

Christy rubbed her forehead and thought. "Um, I don't think so. We have a lot of people come by, as you can imagine. But I can't think of anyone who looked like that or whose name was Marlon. Marlon's a name I'd remember."

"Okay, well thanks," Crawford said, gesturing to the sisters. "Why don't you take care of these ladies now."

Kyra laughed, "First time we've ever been called ladies."

"I'll take it," Neisha said, then to Christy. "Reason we were coming here in the first place was to see if you could help us find a place to stay. We're homeless."

"Well, unless you call the back of our car home," Kyra said with a weak laugh.

Crawford smiled.

"Come on inside," Christy said. "I'll see what I can do. In the meantime, how about a nice peanut butter and jelly sandwich and some lemonade."

"Oh, that sounds great," Neisha said. "Got any chips, by any chance?"

Christy laughed. "I think I just might."

"We haven't had anything to eat since last night," Kyra said.

"Well, in that case how about two PB&Js."

The three women started to go inside. Then the sisters thanked Crawford again and after that he gave Christy a card and asked her to call him if Marlon Celestine showed up.

As he walked back to his Crown Vic he looked in the windows of the sisters' beat-up Chevy and wasn't surprised at what he saw. There were a few blankets and a ratty-looking quilt spread across the back seat. In a back wheel well was something he couldn't make out on first look, but as he leaned closer he read the label: Coleman Camp Stove. He realized it was a single cooking burner that used butane gas. On either side of it were clumps of clothes, an empty bottle of Thunderbird wine and a well-worn Bible.

NINETEEN

Crawford went to two more homeless shelters and had no luck. He looked at his watch and realized it was twenty minutes before his long-postponed interview with Jeff Fisk's widow Olive. Then he called up two other Palm Beach detectives and asked them if they could canvass other homeless shelters for Marlon Celestine. He gave them a list of ten that he hadn't gotten to yet.

Then he drove over the middle bridge to Olive Fisk's house on Jungle Road in Palm Beach. The house was a brick Georgian and like every other house on Barton was big. Crawford had gotten pretty good at sizing up houses in Palm Beach, having been in so many, albeit not as a guest but as an interrogator, that he could guess how many bedrooms a house had or what its total square footage was from a quick glance at the exterior.

He could see right away that Olive Fisk was not a typical Palm Beach wife. She was not particularly well-dressed, nor was her hair blond-streaked and stylishly wavy, nor had her house been decorated by one of the local designers who charged a thousand dollars an hour for an initial consultation. She looked to be around fifty and wore no makeup and had mousy grey hair but one of the most genuine smiles he had seen since he first laid eyes on Dominica.

They sat down in a living room that featured brown furniture outmoded thirty years ago. But it was really nice brown furniture.

Crawford offered his standard "sorry for your loss" consolation speech and apologized for having had to postpone meeting with her.

"Thank you," she said simply.

He decided, spur-of-the-moment, that he was going to get straight to the point. Skip the warm-up pleasantries.

"Mrs. Fisk, somehow you strike me as a direct woman, so I'm just going to come right out and ask a direct question: did it ever occur to you that your husband's murder was anything other than the random act of a dangerous psychopath?"

"No, but I haven't ruled anything out. Everything's been so hard to fathom lately—that's a mild way to put it—that I just don't know. I'm sure you know about my husband's company, it was all over the news."

Crawford just nodded.

"I mean, I knew that was coming, Jeffrey warned me it was going to go from bad to worse. Then all the investors were calling at all hours of the night. There were threats and Jeffrey was always shouting on the phone with God knows who." She took a long breath. "You can imagine that it didn't make for a tranquil home life."

"Tell me about the threats, please?" Crawford asked.

"One in particular. A man named Henry Brusca. Jeffrey told me right after he let him into the fund, he had doubts. Especially about whether Brusca had *risk tolerance*. That's what Jeffrey called it. Investors are great, he told me, when everything is going up, but when it's going the other way, some of them get very, um, anxious. Human nature, I guess. I don't know about such things, I'm a poet."

Crawford cocked his head. "Are you really?" Poets were not commonly encountered in Palm Beach.

"Well, I started out as an adjunct English professor at Columbia married to a man named Harding Leitner. Anyway, Harding and I got divorced and that's where I met Jeffrey."

It seemed she was going to skip the chapter about having an affair with Fisk, then divorcing Leitner and marrying Fisk. That was all right with Crawford since it wasn't particularly relevant.

"Jeffrey was an Econ professor believe it or not. Maybe should have stuck with it, but he was always talking about Wall Street guys...men who were 'half as smart as me, making fifty times the money,' he'd say. So one day he got some investors, a few of them who he'd taught, and boom! He started a fund."

"Interesting. Just like that," Crawford said and snapped his fingers.

"Pretty much."

"Tell me more about Henry Brusca. I remember your husband's partner, Mr. Zoller, mentioning his name."

She laughed. "You've heard enough about my poetry and being a professor, huh?"

"No, I—"

"I'm kidding. So a man recommended Jeffrey's fund and introduced Brusca to Jeffrey. Jeffrey told me he should have listened to what his gut was telling him about Brusca."

"Because Jeffrey told you later the man had no tolerance for risk?" Crawford asked.

"Yes, exactly."

"Well, thank you Mrs. Fisk. Again, my condolences," he said, reaching for his wallet and a card. "If you have any more thoughts or anything at all, please don't hesitate to call."

She nodded. "I will, Detective, I certainly will."

*****

Ott called Crawford as he was headed back to the station.

Crawford had just received an urgent call from Norm Rutledge asking him to stop by his office ASAP. Rutledge was in there with Mal Chase, whom he described as being "anxious." That was not the mayor's usual state, which generally ran calmer than Rutledge's.

"How'd it go at the post office?" he asked Ott.

"Big strikeout. Our postman just went on an unscheduled one-week vacation. Told 'em it was 'stress-related.'"

"Where to?"

"He didn't say."

"Oh, swell," Crawford said with a groan, "did Rutledge call you too?"

"I got a text and I'm on my way to the station. Said he's there with the mayor, who is quote, unquote restless."

"Told me he was anxious."

"Just what we need, an anxious *and* restless mayor."

"I'll see you there in a little while."

"Can't wait."

*****

"So, bring me up to speed," Mal Chase said to Crawford and Ott. "I didn't really like the direction of our meeting this morning"—he turned to Rutledge—"though I've got to say, Norm, you deflected things well. Nice work."

"Thank you, Mal," Rutledge said.

Chase was normally very supportive, calm and easygoing. But by the look on his face, today might be an exception.

Ott looked to Crawford to lead it off.

"Okay, Mal, I'll tell you exactly where we are at this point and I'm going to be perfectly frank," Crawford said.

"You always are."

"Most of the time," Rutledge said.

Crawford ignored that.

"So give me some specifics, guys," Chase said,

"All right," said Crawford. "I think I can speak for Mort on this…so far several of the suspects we've looked at, along with their motives, are, what I'd call, something of a reach. Pretty weak, in fact. What I'm talking about, specifically, is a guy going into the Ocean Club and killing three people and injuring six others, one critically, because the club shot him down for membership. That's suspect profile number one and I think we can all agree…unlikely. Two, we have a man going into the Ocean Club and targeting a man—specifically, Jeffrey Fisk—because all his money went down the tubes with Fisk's fund. Let's call him an *enraged investor*. This guy's name is Henry Brusca. The others that got shot, in that scenario, were collateral damage."

Rutledge thrust his oversized head forward. "So, you don't think that Brusca coulda done it?"

"Coulda, yes," Ott said. "Did it? Also unlikely. Let's just say it would have been an extreme overreaction."

"Which, to me, is an understatement," Crawford said. "I mean, think about it. You lose all your money and you go to a club and start shooting everyone in sight. No, that doesn't happen in real life."

"Okay," Mal Chase said, "I know how you guys operate: you look over possible suspects and rule them out one by one, but who the hell are you ruling *in*?"

There was a little more heat than usual in Chase's tone.

"I'm getting to that," Crawford said, "but first let me ask you both, how would you describe a typical shooter—if there is such a thing—in a situation like a school shooting, or a work-related shooting, or a hate shooting?"

"Off his fuckin' rocker," Rutledge blurted.

Ott chuckled silently.

"Well, suicidal for one thing," Chase said. "Wants to take some innocent people along with him before he's killed or kills himself."

Crawford nodded. "Yup, that's certainly one profile."

"A racist," Rutledge said. "Like that guy in the Charleston church or the Pittsburgh synagogue. Or hates his boss for some reason or the people he works with."

"Absolutely, so that covers most of 'em," Crawford said.

"And some of the killings just have no rational explanation why they happen," Ott added.

"So, instead of those I mentioned, we're looking at two primary suspects who've been on our radar for a while."

"I thought you said there were three." Chase said.

Crawford held up a hand. "Hold on, I'll get to him."

Crawford described Marlon Celestine and Alain Fournier and their efforts to find them and bring them in for questioning.

"The bad news is, as far as Celestine goes, we haven't been able to locate him yet. We're pretty certain he's somewhere in West Palm, but since, as I explained, he recently broke out of a mental institution in Miami and is a fugitive, he not making himself easy to find. Same goes for Fournier. But I'm going to let Mort tell you about him because he's more up to speed on him."

Ott explained that Alain Fournier was being looked at as a suspect in the *disgruntled employee* profile. That he had been fired and struck back at his employer, or in this case random club members. He too was being sought but so far without success, Ott added. He noted that Crawford had spoken to him briefly about meeting with him and that Fournier had hung up on him. That evoked a 'hmm" from Mal Chase and a frown from Rutledge.

"Number three," Crawford said, "is a man named Jason Reardon, someone we just found out about, who apparently just went on a stress-related vacation."

Crawford went on to detail his phone call with Reardon's psychiatrist.

"In any case," Crawford added. "We'll find 'em and will requisition other guys if we need them."

"Okay, I've heard enough," Rutledge said, waving his arms frenetically, "why the hell don't we have everyone in our department and half of the West Palm cops out on the street looking for these guys? I mean it's fucking unacceptable to say you've got three possibles but, sorry, you just can't find any of 'em."

Crawford's immediate reaction was to reach across Rutledge's desk and throttle him. He slowly counted to ten instead. He found that actually worked.

"Okay, Norm, I figured you'd weigh in with your typical restraint—"

Chase put up his hand. "I actually tend to agree with Norm on this," he said.

Rutledge pointed at Crawford. "So don't gimme that shit."

"Just listen to me, for Chrissake, and I'll tell you exactly what we've done. Number one, we printed out two hundred flyers with photos of Marlon Celestine and Alain Fourier and took 'em to the West Palm Police station and asked a couple of detectives there—Keith Aaron and Sif Navarro, who we've worked with before—to hand 'em out, put them on the visors of squad cars and on bulletin boards all over. They owe us a favor and said they'd get 'em out and were happy to help out. Number two, we have two detectives going around, as we speak, to all the homeless shelters in West Palm. If we don't find Celestine we'll expand the search to surrounding cities and towns. And number three, Norm, number three—"

"Okay, okay, I got it," Rutledge said. "But doing is one thing, succeeding's another."

Crawford was grateful Rutledge had interrupted because he didn't have a number three.

"Is that something you picked up from Dale Carnegie?" Crawford said.

"What?"

"'Doing is one thing, succeeding's another,'" Crawford said. "Sounds like a quote."

Ott laughed; Chase stifled a chuckle.

Rutledge shook his head. "Ott's usually the wiseass; this is a new role for you, Crawford."

"Oh, so you want me to jump in?" Ott said.

Rutledge just kept shaking his head. "Funny fuckers, the both of ya."

"So that's where we are," Crawford said, glancing from Chase to Rutledge. "Obviously, we'd like to have solved it because we know you guys are feeling heavy pressure. I also don't need to tell you that Mort and I are putting in eighteen-to-twenty-hour days—"

"You just did," Rutledge said.

Crawford chuckled. "Yeah, guess you're right, I did," he said. "So…anything else? Or are we done here?"

Rutledge glanced over at Chase.

"Yes, we're done here," Chase said. "Good luck with this. It seems like you got your work cut out for you."

No shit, Mal, brilliant.

What Crawford didn't tell the chief and mayor was that they had abandoned their search for the murder weapon at the gun shops. It was simple: between them and the other three cops they had enlisted, they had now canvassed every single shop on the list. And they had struck out at all of them.

TWENTY

Crawford was leaning up against Ott's cubicle, getting the full download on Jason Reardon, the postal worker who had suddenly gone on vacation with little warning to his boss or co-workers.

"I got a few names of friends and a brother of Reardon they gave me at the post office where he works, but no wife, girlfriend, or other immediate family," Ott completed the wrap-up.

"I wonder if he really went on vacation or somehow got the sense we were looking for him and took off."

"Doesn't much matter which 'cause we got no clue how to find him," Ott said, then flipping his head in the general direction of Rutledge's office. "So what did you think?"

"Of our little meeting?"

Ott nodded.

"It's just part of the old script when we don't nail a perp right away," Crawford said. "They figure they gotta give us a kick in the ass even though they knew we're doing everything we can."

"I know, but sometimes I'm like, 'oh Christ, do we really have to go through this song and dance again?'"

"I know and the answer, I guess, is 'yeah, seems like we do.'" Crawford's cell phone rang. He slid it out of his pocket.

"Hello?"

"Hey, Charlie, it's Sif Navarro." It was one of the West Palm Beach detectives who owed him a favor. "We just had a sighting of your guy Celestine, but, sorry to say, guy got away."

"Where?" Crawford said, immediately jacked-up, as he hit the speakerphone button so Ott could hear.

"On South Dixie, two blocks south of Southern," Navarro said, also amped up. "Uniform IDed him from the guy's photo in his squad car, ordered him to stop. But he ran. Down a side street. Nottingham, between Dixie and Georgia."

"Thanks, man, we're on our way," Crawford said as Ott quickly got to his feet.

They both ran to the back door of the station.

"Stay with me, will ya, Sif?" Crawford said into his phone. "We're ten minutes out."

They got into their Crown Vic, Ott behind the wheel, and a minute later were going sixty down South County Road, siren blaring.

"We got probably thirty guys canvassing the area right now," Navarro said, "but no sign of him."

"What was he wearing?" Crawford asked as Ott took a skidding hard right onto Southern just past Mar-a-Lago.

"Dark pants, dark shirt, scruffy beard—which he didn't have in the photo—but our guy said he was sure it was him."

"Or else why would he run?" Crawford said.

"Exactly."

"Okay, we're almost there. Last seen running down Nottingham, between Dixie and Georgia you said, right?" Crawford asked.

"Yup, but that was fifteen minutes ago. Cop said he was a fast runner."

"My partner can chase him down," Crawford said, as Ott chuckled and turned hard left onto Dixie.

They could hear the sirens and the flashing lights quickly came into view.

Ott skidded right onto Nottingham and they saw cops everywhere.

"I think I see you. White Vic, right?" Navarro said.

"Yeah, that's us," Crawford said, seeing a white Dodge Charger flick his lights at them.

Ott pointed at a black armored vehicle up ahead.

"Holy shit, you got SWAT guys here, too," Crawford said. "That was quick."

"Hey, man, we don't fuck around," said Navarro.

"I'm going over to Georgia and maybe a little further west," Ott said. "You guys got this area covered."

"Cool," said Navarro. "If we get him, I'll let you know right away."

"And vice versa."

*****

A half an hour went by and no Marlon Celestine.

Sif Navarro called back, the animated tone gone from his voice. "Sorry, man, no go."

"Hey, we tried," Crawford said. "This guy's been pretty slippery. We're trying a bunch of homeless shelters."

"I got a suggestion for you," Navarro said.

"Let's hear it."

"We got this new woman on what's called our On-Street Homeless Engagement Team, I think they call it. Name's Allie Agostino, she's tight with all the people at the shelters, might be someone you should talk to."

"Good to know, got her contact info?"

"Hang on a second…yeah, here you go," Navarro gave him two numbers.

"Great, we're gonna give it another twenty minutes or so," Crawford said. "But I don't think driving around is gonna be enough to find the guy."

"He's probably hiding out in one of these warehouses," Ott said, pointing at a two-story warehouse. "Waiting for us to clear out."

"I'm gonna make sure a bunch of guys stick around," Navarro said.

"Okay, thanks for giving us a heads-up," Crawford said. "I'm gonna give Allie Agostino a call now."

Crawford dialed the number and a chirpy voice answered. "Hi, this is Allie, Outreach."

"Hi Allie," Crawford said. "My name's Charlie Crawford, I'm a Palm Beach homicide detective. Sif Navarro gave me your name and number."

"Hi, Charlie, what can I do for you?"

"I'm working a murder case and looking for a guy who's maybe looking for a bed at one of the homeless shelters in West Palm."

"Oh, yeah, I think I heard something about this. Can you give me his name and what he looks like?"

Crawford did.

"Okay, and does he have any mental health issues you're aware of?"

"I was just going to tell you. Were you in West Palm five years ago?"

"I sure was. Born and bred here."

"Do you remember a case where a guy slashed a bunch of people in The Square, back when it was called Cityplace? Nobody killed but some pretty serious injuries."

"I sure do. Didn't he end up in a mental institution somewhere?"

"Yeah, he did. Down in Miami. Anyway, he escaped from there and we know he ended up in this area."

"Wait a minute…those three people killed at that club in Palm Beach, that's your case, right?"

"Yes, it is."

"So you're thinking he went a lot further this time? From a knife to a semiauto rifle, from six wounded to three dead?"

"And five more seriously injured."

"I got it. Well, I'll get on this right away. Check around and see what I can come up with."

"Appreciate it," Crawford said and clicked off.

"Sounds like a good contact," Ott said of Allie Agostino.

"Yeah, I agree," Crawford said. "All right, let's get out of here."

"Back to the station?"

Crawford looked at his watch. "Yeah, I got that guy, Henry Brusca who threatened the hedge fund vic, coming in half an hour."

Ott nodded. "Just want you to know, Charlie, I was ready to hop out of the Vic, chase that guy down and tackle him."

"I know you were, Mort. Fastest guy in Palm Beach."

TWENTY-ONE

Henry Brusca, the man who had allegedly threatened to kill the hedge fund owner/Ponzi-schemer Jeff Fisk, arrived fifteen minutes late.

Bettina took him back to Crawford's office and introduced them.

"Sorry, I'm late," Brusca said, "I've got hell of a lot of issues I'm in the middle of at the moment."

Crawford nodded. "Have a seat, Mr. Brusca," he said. "I'm going to get my partner to join us."

He gave Ott a quick call. Ott came in a few moments later and Crawford introduced them. Ott sat down next to Brusca, a tall man who slouched and had a veiny, hooked nose.

"So, Mr. Brusca, we've been told by two sources that you threatened the life of Jeff Fisk. Allegedly for his fund's poor performance. And, well, now we know it's totally collapsed."

"That's bullshit," Brusca said. "I was like a lot of other guys in Fisk's fund, deceived and pissed off. But threaten to *kill* him? You gotta be kidding me."

"Well, why do you suppose we were told you did?" Ott said.

"Probably his partner and his wife, right?"

"Doesn't matter," Ott continued. "What matters is what you *did* say to Fisk."

"That he was a scammer and a crook. I mean, Christ, I may have said something like, 'I could kill you for losing all my money,' but it was just, you know, a figure of speech."

"So that was before the fund totally crashed?" Crawford asked.

"Yeah, a couple of weeks ago, when it was obvious the whole thing was toast," Brusca said. "Fisk was lucky he wasn't around to see it go to zero."

"Lucky," Ott said, "to get shot in the head?"

"I didn't mean it that way," Brusca said. "But in a way he's better off dead."

"What do you mean?" Crawford asked.

"Well, he doesn't have a wife who's leaving him," Brusca began, clearly describing himself. "Or a girlfriend who's cutting him loose because I can't pay her twenty grand a month rent anymore and she's gonna get evicted. Shit, I can't even pay her dues at the Carriage House."

"What's the Carriage House?" Ott asked.

"This new club for the nouveau rich and famous, which I'm sure as hell *not* anymore. Just down South County from here."

"I feel your pain, Mr. Brusca," Ott said. "You shoot guns, by any chance?"

"I hunt a little. Went hunting in Africa a while back. Bagged a lion, well, actually the guide did, but I got the credit."

"Credit?" Ott said.

Crawford could see his partner fuming under the surface.

"Credit for shooting a lion?" Ott said, shaking his head. "What a man, you must have been really proud of yourself"—then dropping his voice—"fucking pathetic."

"We had in mind something more like a semiautomatic assault rifle," Crawford said.

"No, never had one, never even seen one."

"You sure?"

"I'm sure."

Crawford had heard enough to know Brusca was not their man. Insufferable yes, a killer, no way in hell.

"Okay, Mr. Brusca, you can go," Crawford said, sneaking a glance at Ott, who was still shaking his head.

"That's all? I figured you'd have a lot more quest—"

"You heard the man, Mr. Great White Hunter," Ott said with a shooing motion, "the door's thataway."

TWENTY-TWO

Ott walked out of Crawford's office, still shaking his head over Brusca claiming false credit for killing a lion. His plan now was to meet with a brother of Jason Reardon—effectively his nearest kin, according to Reardon's supervisor. Ott also wanted to call a woman who had purportedly dated Reardon but lived in South Carolina now.

After Ott left, Dominica ducked into Crawford's office.

"You busy?" she asked.

"Oh, man, like a damn three-ring-circus around here," he said. "What's up?"

"I just wanted to give you a quick update on the continuing saga of Rose and her Brit friend, Alastair. Well, ex-Brit friend that would be."

"What happened?"

"The bastard beat her up."

"You're kidding! Is she all right?"

"She's okay. Nothing that a bunch of makeup can't hide," she said. "So the good news is, it's over. I never trusted the guy in the first place."

"I remember, but what was the fight about?"

"Not much of anything, as far as I can tell. She was paying for everything when they went out and one time she said something like, 'Hey, it's your turn.' That apparently got him seething, so when they went out to the parking lot, he just punched her. Like with his fist, not just a slap. Knocked her down, actually."

"You're kidding, she should press charges," he said, starting to seethe himself.

"I know, that's what I said."

"And?"

"She told me she didn't want it getting around. Might be bad for her business somehow."

"How?"

"I don't know. I guess she really just doesn't want to be the subject of the latest gossip."

"Well, I get that," he said. "So she dumped him."

Dominica nodded. "Like the proverbial ton of bricks," she said. "So how's the case coming along?"

"Well, we've gone from zero suspects to almost too many."

"But isn't that better than none?"

Crawford said. "Yeah, it is, but how 'bout just one guy dead to rights in handcuffs."

Dominica leaned across Crawford's desk and patted his hand. "Be patient."

Crawford laughed and pointed at himself. "Me? Charlie Crawford? Never."

TWENTY-THREE

Ott drove into the driveway of Jason Reardon's brother's house in Palm Beach Gardens. It was a two-story colonial with green shutters and surrounded by pygmy date palm trees.

A man in his thirties with a short ponytail and a gold earring opened the door.

"Mr. Reardon?" Ott said.

"Yeah, hi, Detective," Dave Reardon said. "Come on in."

Ott followed him into the living room and saw a woman in the adjacent kitchen. He gave her a wave and she smiled and nodded.

"Have a seat," Dave said.

Ott sat, and Dave sat down facing him.

"Well, as I said on the phone," Ott said, "I wanted to ask you a few questions about your brother. See, I tried the cell number I have for him but it just rings and rings."

"I'm a little unclear why you want to know about Jason? Did he do something wrong?"

"Tell you the truth, I'm not sure. But speaking to him might confirm that he didn't. So I'm going to just summarize what I heard: that Jason struggled with severe depression and had mentioned that he had considered suicide on a number of occasions. And one of the times he mentioned it he said he might want to—quote, unquote—'take a bunch of people along with me.'"

Dave shrugged and looked genuinely surprised. "Really? That's the first I've heard of it. Who told you that?"

"Sorry, I'm not at liberty to say. But someone who I'd deem reliable. He never talks to you about any of this?"

"Hey, look, I'm not going to sugarcoat it, Jason has struggled all his life."

"How so? Can you be specific?" Ott said.

Out of the corner of his eye Ott could see the woman leaning closer to listen in.

"Well," Dave went on, "just that he's always had a dark side and, as you said, struggled with depression. And yes, it was pretty severe. Plus, when he was eight or so, our father went to prison for manslaughter. Which really kind of crippled Jason. Emotionally, I mean. I was much younger and didn't even understand it, so it really didn't affect me."

"So, being as specific as you can be, have there been any incidents where he might have acted out? Or any attempts at suicide that you're aware of? Any violent acts of any kind?"

Dave glanced over at the woman in the kitchen, who tried to look busy mopping the counter with a sponge.

"Well, yeah, there actually was one really big one," Dave said, his eyes darting around nervously.

"Tell me."

"Well, we lived in this little town with kind of what you'd call a one-room schoolhouse…"

"Okay, and?"

Dave lowered his voice. "He burned it down."

"The schoolhouse?"

Dave nodded. "So, um, I guess you could call that a 'violent act,' even though lighting a match isn't exactly violent, but…"

"How old was he when this happened?"

"Twelve."

"And what happened after the fire?"

"He basically got off, because of his age and I guess they decided he had some pretty serious mental issues, but my mom moved us out of that town to down here. Jason went to a new school and nothing much happened after that."

"No other incidents?"

"No, but same old depression. He's just stay in his room a lot and read Harry Potter books."

"Last time he was here," said the woman in the kitchen, raising her voice, "I saw him reading *Miss Peregrine's Home for Peculiar Children*. I thought he was a little old for that."

"Oh yeah, I remember," said Dave.

"What's that, I'm not familiar with that book?" Ott asked.

"They made a movie of it," the woman said.

Ott nodded. "Okay, so do you know where Jason might have gone? He told his boss that he was stressed out and needed to take a vacation."

"Sorry, no clue. I haven't heard from him in at least a month."

"Will you do me a favor and call him? He might answer if he sees your number."

"Sure, I'll do that," Dave said, taking his iPhone out of his pocket and dialing. It rang and rang. He clicked off after ten or so rings.

"Sorry," Dave said, then he squinted. "I just hope he's all right."

Ott nodded. "Let's hope so," he said, getting up. "Okay, well, thank you for your time, I appreciate it."

Dave nodded.

"If you speak to Jason would you ask him to give me a call. I just need to ask him a few questions, then hopefully I can scratch him off my list," Ott said, even though Jason Reardon had just climbed to the top of his list alongside Marlon Celestine and Alain Fournier.

"Sure, no problem," said Dave, "I will."

"Again thanks," Ott said walking toward the door and glancing at the woman in the kitchen. "And thank you too, ma'am. What was the name of that book again?"

"*Miss Peregrine's Home for Peculiar Children*," she said.

"Sounds interesting," said Ott.

On his way back to his office he called the woman who had moved to South Carolina and according to a friend had briefly dated Jason Reardon. Her name was Alicia Sands.

She answered. "Hello."

"Hello, Ms. Sands?"

"Yes."

"My name is Detective Ott. I'm with the Palm Beach Police Department. I was told that you dated Jason Reardon back when you lived in this area."

"Yes, for a while, it didn't last long," her voice was thin and reedy, as if she was sick or in a weakened state.

"I'm actually trying to reach him. I have this number." Ott gave her the number. "Do you know any other way to reach him?"

"No, that's the only number I have, but we don't speak anymore anyway," she said.

"I understand. I hope you don't mind if I ask you some personal questions about Jason."

She took a while to answer. "Okay…I guess so."

"Thank you. When you dated—"

"It was only for about four or five months."

"Okay, well, when you did, did you see signs of him being depressed?"

"Yes, on and off."

"And what about, did he ever mention suicide?"

"Him doing it, you mean?"

"Yes."

"No, no, I don't remember him ever saying anything about that."

"Did he ever…did he ever say anything about harming other people?"

"Wait a minute," her voice suddenly got stronger, "I read about those murders in Palm Beach. That's not what you're calling about, is it?"

"Yes, actually it is, we've been interrogating a lot of people. Jason is just one person on a long list we'd like to talk to."

There was another long pause. "You might already know this, but Jason worked at that club, where it happened. A few years ago."

Ott got a sudden shiver. "No, I didn't know that. At the Ocean Club, you're saying?"

"Yes, he was a waiter. Before he got the job at the post office. It didn't last very long. The job at the Ocean Club, I mean."

"Why not? What happened?"

"The people he worked with there were mean to him. Picked on him."

"How so?"

"Well, Jason has this facial tic. Kind of a nervous thing around people. And he, well, tended to sweat a lot too. He's a nice man but, like I said, people picked on him. The other waiters and people in the kitchen too. I think even some of the members there. It was just not the right job for him and so he quit."

"I'm sorry to hear that," Ott said, animated now. "Did he ever…did he ever say anything about, um, about wanting to do something to those people who picked on him. To go back and harm them maybe?"

"No, never," she said. "I think he just wanted to forget about it. Get another job and move on with his life."

"I see. That was probably the right thing to do. And, last question. Did Jason own a gun, do you know?"

"I don't know. But I do know that he went hunting once with his brother. So maybe."

"So he never said anything about a gun? For protection maybe?"

"No, never."

"Okay, Ms. Sands, you've been very helpful, and I can't thank you enough," Ott said. "I might want to call you back if I have any other questions. I hope that's all right?"

"Sure, that's fine."

"Or my partner, his name is Detective Crawford, he might want to call you. Is that all right?"

"Sure."

"Oh, and do me a favor, please don't mention we had this conversation to anyone. Especially if you speak to Jason."

"I won't. We don't speak anymore," she said. "Things just got a little weird."

TWENTY-FOUR

Crawford got a call on his cell phone. He looked down at the display. *Delbert Roth,* it said. The club manager.

"Hey, Delbert."

"Hello, Detective," Roth said. "I wanted to tell you about something I just found out. It may be totally irrelevant to your investigation and you definitely didn't hear about it from me because it concerns a member here."

"Don't worry, Delbert, just about everything I hear, I never repeat."

"Okay, that's good to know…it's about the husband of the woman who got killed in the shootings."

"Warren Faircloth?"

"Yes, have you spoken to him?"

"Yes, a few days after the shootings."

"Well, supposedly he is a huge collector of old guns but has a lot of new ones too. I heard he has machine guns and lots of other guns like that. I don't know much about the things, never shot one in my entire life, but I heard he's got a whole room off of his living room with nothing but guns in it. Maybe that's helpful, maybe not."

"And, by any chance, did you hear whether he shoots them or just displays them?" Crawford asked, remembering what David Balfour had told him about Faircloth being a fanatical Civil War reenactor and wondering if that was the reason for the collection.

"The person who told me said he goes to a range in West Palm all the time," Roth said. "I guess that's his golf or tennis. He also told me that Mr. Faircloth goes to these paintball battles they have out at some place out near Lake Okeechobee. Belle Glade, I think he said."

"Really?" Crawford said. "But you have to be in shape to do those kinds of things. There's a lot of running around, I know. When I met with him he looked a little…well, out of shape."

"Don't kid yourself, Detective. He's a regular in the gym here. He may not look it but, trust me, he's in shape. Damn good shape, too."

Crawford flashed to Ott: short, 90 percent bald, and kind of dumpy, but the guy could bench press 250 pounds and outrun him on the beach. And Crawford himself: college jock, football and lacrosse star, erect posture and flat stomach, but Ott was the one you'd be wise to put your money on in a race or a fight.

"What else did you hear, Delbert?"

"Well, that's all. I just figured I'd tell you, particularly with what happened to his wife."

"Are you thinking that he might have had something to do with…what happened at the club?"

"No, no, not at all, I'm just…you know, putting it out there. Let you see whether there's something to it or not or, you know, something relevant."

"Okay, and I appreciate that. I'll tell my partner about it too, and maybe get back to you if I have any more questions."

"Be my guest," Roth said. "I hope you don't think I'm bringing up stuff I shouldn't bring up—"

"No I don't. I appreciate any help I can get."

"Part of it's just…well, I want to do what I can to remove the stigma from the club. I'm not even sure that's possible. We already had some members resign."

This was the first Crawford had heard about that, but he wasn't too surprised.

"What I've heard," Roth continued, "is that they don't want to go back to a place where people were killed. It's like when they closed down that school where all those kids were killed because parents didn't want their kids to have to go back there."

"I get it," Crawford said, "but hopefully in time the memory will fade."

"I hope so, but I don't know," Roth said. "One of the members who resigned said something like, 'I can never go back to the pool or the outdoor bar, I just think of all that blood everywhere.'"

"I never thought of that," Crawford admitted, grimly.

"So if you catch who did it, it might bring some relief. Though I'm not really sure. Well, I'll let you go, Detective. Go find the guy who did it…please."

As if Crawford needed urging.

TWENTY-FIVE

Crawford called up David Balfour right after he hung up with Delbert Roth.

"Hey, Charlie, you want to pick my besotted brain again?"

Crawford glanced at his watch. It was just past three. He guessed Balfour might have had a late boozy lunch at the Poinciana Club. After his usual golf game, which typically ended around one.

"Just a couple of quick questions about Warren Faircloth?"

"You mean, General Faircloth. Second in command to Robert E. Lee," said Balfour.

"You're kidding—that's the role he plays?"

"Yup. I mean, look at the guy. Can you ever see him as a lowly sergeant or corporal?"

"Now that you mention it, definitely not."

"So what's the first question, Charlie?"

"When I met with him, he just looked like just another old man. Probably headed for a wheelchair in a year or so. But I've been told that he's in really good shape, runs around playing paintball somewhere, goes to the gym five times a week. What do you know about that?"

"That looks can be deceiving? What I can tell you is this: I've seen him in a bathing suit before and…he's in really good shape. I definitely can believe he goes to the gym five times a week. As far as the paintball thing, who knew? But for these Civil War nuts, they can't get their fill of gun-shooting and pretend killing…wait a minute, Charlie, my besotted brain just caught up with you…you're thinking Warren Faircloth—"

"Where are you, David?"

"The bar at the Poinciana."

"Anybody around you?"

"Um, the bartender."

"I thought you couldn't use cell phones at the Poinciana."

"So shoot me."

"I don't want to have this conversation where someone could walk in and overhear it. Do me a favor and go out to your car."

"Okay, Charlie, this is getting interesting," Balfour said, and clicked off.

Crawford waited a few minutes then called Balfour back.

"Okay Charlie, I'm in my car, safe from eavesdropping ears."

"I know I don't need to say this because you don't have loose lips, but we never had this conversation."

"By now I know the drill. If I ever spill the beans, you'll never talk to me again. And I like our conversations."

"Good. So what else can you tell me about Warren Faircloth?"

"Funny you should ask because I did hear something else recently. You know what an organ recital is?"

Crawford had no idea where this was going. "Sure. A concert where an organ is played."

"Yes, but it also means the kind of coffee klatch where old people sit around and talk about their maladies. They get together and…well, what else are they going to talk about but what ails them? So I was out to dinner a few nights ago, and I was the youngest one there, when an organ recital broke out. My aching back this, falling down and almost breaking my hip that, and someone said, 'Did you hear about Warren Faircloth?' And someone else said, 'No, what's wrong with him?' And the woman who brought it up said, 'I heard he's got prostate cancer.' 'Poor guy,' said this other guy, 'it's not that uncommon.' Then the woman lowered her head, dropped her voice and said, 'But I heard it's terminal.'"

That was a pretty long story to get to the punchline, thought Crawford.

"Poor bastard," Balfour said, lowering his voice.

"Yeah, I know. But I think I see where you're going," Crawford said, "and thanks for the information."

"What else do you want to know, Charlie?"

"Um, that's all for now," Crawford said, "you can go back to the bar now."

"You know what…I think I'll take a nap right here."

Crawford didn't say what he was thinking: *It's called passing out, David.*

*****

Just before four o'clock Ott walked into Crawford's office and relayed his double bombshell about Jason Reardon burning down his schoolhouse when he was a kid and having worked at the Ocean Club.

Crawford shook his head. "Jesus Christ, man, I'd call that a possible warm-up for shooting all those people at the club."

"Yeah, no kiddin'. Particularly about him working there."

"But you got no clue where he went on his last-minute vacation?"

"Nobody does. He just seems to have…vanished."

"A common theme in this case."

"I know."

"So listen to this, here's an interesting update on Warren Faircloth, who is—"

"I know, the husband of the dead woman Lauren."

"Right. So the guy when I interviewed him struck me as old and rickety but he's actually a guy who goes to the gym regularly and participates in Civil War reenactments and paintball battles at someplace out near Lake Okeechobee."

"Yeah, but…so?" Ott asked raising his hands and shrugging.

"So…I don't know. He's also, supposedly, got prostate cancer. I know, your response is still *so?*"

"Well, I mean, I'm sorry about the cancer, but because the guy shoots pretend guns and paintballs, how does that make him our killer?"

"I'm not saying it does. Just that it was kind of a curveball. Unexpected, you know. That maybe since he's gonna die, and has nothing to lose, he might do something…really radical."

"Yeah, I hear you on that," Ott said.

"So now we got three guys to find. All of them with histories that suggest they could have done it. And one septuagenarian, who knows about him?" Crawford concluded.

"Oh hey, by the way, I thought of something that Celestine and Fournier have in common," said Ott.

"Oh, you mean knives."

"Yeah, guess you already thought of that."

"Oh, also," Crawford said, "something else you're not going to be too thrilled about."

"What's that?"

"Rutledge called me and said we got another meeting with him and Chase and the boys and girls who run the Worth Avenue shops tomorrow morning."

"Oh shit, really?"

Crawford nodded. "But he said if we caught our killer before then, he'd call it off."

"That's a hell of an incentive," Ott said. "Makes me want to work all night to duck that meeting."

"Which we're pretty much already doing."

TWENTY-SIX

It was 7:15 p.m. at the station. Most people had gone home. Not Crawford and Ott. Crawford had just Googled "Experts in Mass Shootings." The first thing that popped up was "Mass Shootings Experts Available." The second one was "The Violence Project: Mass Shooting Data & Research." A little further down was a *New York Times* article entitled "What Are the Real Warning Signs of a Mass Shooting?" He decided to read them all.

He noticed that most of the writers on the subject had PhDs after their name. He remembered that several of the PhDs he had run across in life tended to spout a fair amount of hot air but he certainly wasn't going to eliminate all of them because of the hollow words of a few. His plan was to try to contact some of them and ask them questions. Hopefully they wouldn't charge him for a short conversation, but he wasn't so sure about that.

He read the *Times* article next. The subhead of the article was "While some mass shootings are committed by people with diagnosed mental illnesses, a life crisis is a better predictor of violence, researchers say." That was interesting, but not surprising. That seemed to fit Marlon Celestine best. In his case. That, one, he had mental illness, but two, something had set him off, i.e., a *life crisis*.

He read on with keen interest:

The real problem, those experts say, is that mental illness is not a useful means to predict violence. About half of all Americans will experience mental health issues at some point in their lives, and the vast majority of people with mental illness do not kill. Instead, many experts have come to focus on warning signs that occur whether or not actual mental illness is present, including marked changes in behavior, demeanor or appearance, uncharacteristic fights or arguments, and telling others of plans for violence, a phenomenon known as "leakage."

He was staggered by the claim that "half of all Americans will experience mental health issues at some point." He couldn't believe that. It sounded like a gross exaggeration.

He also realized that while the article contained good, worthwhile information and he found it revealing, he knew it had very little to do with him. No, his job was not to identify potential killers, his job was to catch them and take them off the streets after the crime was committed, the damage done. It didn't much matter what the cause was, or what had precipitated the heinous action, he just had to find who did it, put them behind bars, and make sure they never did it again.

One thing he noticed was there seemed to be no incidents where one person had committed two mass shootings, mainly because the perpetrator was either caught or dead. The article went on to point to other things that had caused mass killers to become mass killers. The list was long: drugs and alcohol use, being bullied, being schizophrenic or severely delusional, a desire for fame, radicalization on the internet, childhood trauma, and on and on and on.

One paragraph dealt with the Columbine killers. The memory of the two raincoat-clad killers and their guns and bombs made Crawford shudder:

One journalist "deflated many of the myths surrounding the massacre when he revealed that the Columbine perpetrators were neither outcasts nor bullied. Rather, he reported, one of the two gunmen was a psychopath, lacking in conscience and empathy but abundant in grandiose ideas, and the other was a suicidal depressive who just went along with the plan."

Next, Crawford launched into the Violence Project article. It turned out to be a vast database of incidents and deaths from violent mass shootings. What was disturbing to Crawford was a huge bar graph entitled, "Mass Public Shooting Death by Incident, 1966 to Present." The worst year appeared to be 2017 and the best—that is, the fewest deaths—2020. He absorbed a lot of the data, but it soon became a depressing blur.

He rubbed his eyes and glanced down at his watch: 10:07. He spent the next half hour making plans for the next day, then went home, fearful of what he might dream of that night.

TWENTY-SEVEN

Crawford and Ott were meeting with Norm Rutledge and Mal Chase for their second gathering with the merchants of Worth Avenue. Crawford recognized Fred Burgess, the head of the Chamber of Commerce, and Jake Kaufman, owner of the oldest and most exclusive men's shop on Worth. There were a couple of new people who hadn't been there the last time, he noticed.

"Well, once again," Chase started out, "I welcome all of you owners and operators of Worth Avenue shops, galleries and restaurants. Also, Fred, our Chamber of Commerce head. I'll get right to the point. Obviously, though I'd like it to be otherwise, the shooter at the Ocean Club is still at large. I can assure you we have our best men on it"—he nodded at Crawford and Ott—"who have been working around the clock and have been making considerable progress—"

"What's considerable progress?" Fred Burgess blurted.

"Well," Chase glanced at Crawford, "Charlie, would you like to take it?"

"Yeah, okay," Crawford said, eyeing Fred Burgess. "At present we have three solid suspects—"

"In jail?" Burgess cried out again.

"No, but I expect one of them might be shortly, just as soon as—"

"You find 'em?" Burgess said, which got a few laughs. "Detective, that's not good enough for any of us in the room here. It's been close to a week and you've got nobody."

"Time to quit screwing around and bring in the FBI," said a man who hadn't been there for the first meeting.

"Sir," Ott said, "sorry, I didn't catch your name?"

"Copeland, I manage the Brown, Harris, Stevens real estate office, where our traffic has slowed down to a trickle and where people are putting their houses on the market 'cause they're scared to live in this town."

"So," Ott chimed in, "as Detective Crawford just told you, we've got three solid suspects and expect to be close to solving the case soon"—Crawford winced, hearing Ott being a little too optimistic—"and rather than bringing in the FBI and having to spend all our time bringing them up to speed and hand-holding them, we're proceeding with dispatch to catch this killer."

"Might just be that you're better at bringing the FBI up to speed than solving the case, Detective," said a short woman with thick black glasses and a scowl to match.

"Let's try to be constructive, Nancy," Jake Kaufman cautioned the woman.

"I thought I was," she retorted. "I think we've given the local guys here a shot and now it's time to bring in the cavalry."

"My men are pros," came the sharp protest from a surprising source: Norm Rutledge.

Ott smiled in disbelief.

"Look," Rutledge continued, "these guys are the best around. They've got a stellar record, better than anyone in the state. The FBI? Sometimes good, sometimes not so good."

"That's very touching, Chief," Nancy said. "Well then, how about we put a time limit on it? Give your guys another…say, three days, then the FBI?"

"I don't like that," Rutledge said. "This case is not like solving a routine break-in with fingerprints and clues all over the place."

Fred Burgess stood up. "I make a motion to give these guys three more days—"

"Make it a week," Rutledge said.

"Five days," said Nancy.

Rutledge glanced over at Crawford, who didn't move. "All right, five days," he said. "If we don't have the killer in custody in five days, much as I think it's the wrong move, we'll call in the FBI."

*****

Crawford and Ott stuck around after the merchants of Worth Avenue, along with Mal Chase and Fred Burgess, filed out. They took their usual places facing Rutledge.

"Wow, was that really you?" Ott said to Rutledge.

"I didn't mean a word of it," Rutledge said, shaking his head. "I just have a thing about the Federal Bureau of Incompetence."

"Deny, deny, Norm," Ott said with a smile, "but you sounded like you really meant it to me."

"Leave it alone, huh? What I did was buy you guys some time," Rutledge said. "But time flies, so get your asses in gear and go get the guy."

Crawford leaned back in his chair facing Rutledge. "I noticed you did something very crafty there, Norm."

Rutledge squinted. "What are you referring to?"

"You said, 'if we don't have the killer in custody in five days, we'll call in the FBI.' We could have *anyone* in custody, and how would those people know whether it's the actual killer or not."

Rutledge smiled. "You liked that, huh?"

"Crafty, Norm. Very crafty."

TWENTY-EIGHT

Short of driving around all day hoping to bump into Marlon Celestine, Alain Fournier, or Jason Reardon, Crawford decided to go back to Google again, and as he had done before he typed "Mass Shooting Experts." He clicked on one he had scanned the day before: "Mass Shooting Experts Available." He counted eleven out of the twenty-three listed were PhDs. He scanned the thumbnail photos next to their names looking for the ones who seemed to have the most compassionate and wise faces. Almost all were smiling, but he narrowed it down to five contenders. He clicked on one name and had to jump through a few hoops—an email and brief questions—but finally got phone numbers for three of them.

He dialed the first one and it was answered right away.

"This is Dr. Malachi, who's calling, please?"

"Hi, Doctor," Crawford said. "It's Detective Crawford, I just emailed you a little while ago."

"Oh yes, hello, Detective. I just want to tell you that my charge is five hundred dollars an hour, but only four hundred an hour if we speak for three hours or more."

"I just wanted to ask you a few quick questions," he said. "Shouldn't be any more than ten, fifteen minutes."

"Well in that case, it's twelve dollars a minute…starting right this second."

"Ah, thank you, doc, but I'm afraid I can't afford you." He was thinking that if it went an hour or so, Rutledge would hit the roof.

Click.

As he was about to dial the next number, he got a call. It was David Balfour.

"Hey Charlie, I gotta make this quick 'cause I got a tee time in ten minutes, but I got a scoop for you on our friend Warren Faircloth."

"Let's hear it."

"So this is from what I'd call a quasi-reliable source. She told me that Lauren Faircloth had a serious boyfriend on the side who wanted to marry her. Which would mean she'd lose her pre-nup, but she was seriously thinking about doing it anyway. Then she found out Faircloth had prostate cancer and decided to hang in there until he croaked. Then, in the meantime, the old man found out about the boyfriend."

"I get it, so Faircloth might have been thinking she was just waiting for him to die and get his money. He couldn't stomach that and—"

"The bullets start flying."

"Not very sensitive, David."

"I know, sorry. Hey, I gotta go."

"Thanks."

Crawford went back to the Mass Shooter Expert list and dialed the next number.

He got an answering machine and left a message.

He dialed the third number.

"Hello."

"Yes, hi, is this Mr. Ellis?"

"Yes, Professor Ellis. Who is this?"

"Detective Crawford, Professor. We just went back and forth via email."

"Oh, yes Detective, you mentioned you're investigating a mass shooter case."

"Yes, I am. It took place in Florida a little over a week ago."

"I read about it. In Palm Beach, right?"

"Yes, exactly," he said. So far Ellis wasn't putting the bite on him for money so he kept going. "Can I ask you some questions?"

"Sure, but I have a class in about an hour. I'm going to need to allow fifteen minutes to get there."

"Thank you very much, so I noticed it said on your website that your field of expertise is, ah, Law Enforcement Mental Health—I'm reading now—Psychology of School Shooters, Law Enforcement Mental Health, Crisis Counseling and Homicide Investigations."

"Yes, that's correct."

"Well, what I thought I'd do if it's okay with you is spend ten minutes giving you profiles of my suspects," Crawford said. "See, this is my first mass shooting and me and my partner need all the help we can get."

"Understood. Go right ahead," Ellis said.

"Okay, thanks, Professor."

"Just call me Don."

"Okay, the first suspect escaped from a mental institution in Miami recently. In fact, it was two days before the homicides. He was in there because five years ago he took a knife and slashed a bunch of people in a shopping center near here."

"Let me guess," Ellis said, "he was ruled mentally incompetent to stand trial?"

"Yup, halfway through it. He's at large at the moment and knows we're after him. Though he may think it's only for breaking out of the institution."

"So not in police custody?"

"I wish."

"Okay, who's the next one?"

Crawford told him about the former Ocean Club chef, Alain Fournier, then Jason Reardon, the postal worker, who had burned down his school when he was a kid. Crawford added that, they, too, had not been found yet.

"All these men seem like pretty good suspects," Ellis said. "Now all you need is to catch 'em."

"We're tryin'," Crawford said and proceeded to delve into the long-shot candidates. First, he talked about hypothetical suspects who wanted to take out two people on the Ocean Cub Membership Committee because of the role they played in rejecting them for membership.

"I'd say that's a little thin," Ellis reacted. "I can't really see that. Though I've never had any interest in getting into some fancy club and can't imagine what that rejection would feel like. Still, how bad could it be?"

Next Crawford walked Ellis through the irate-investor scenario, where Henry Brusca lost all his money, donned tennis whites, a floppy hat and shades and went up to the Ocean Club and mowed down hedge-funder Jeff Fisk along with the others who had the misfortune of being there. Even as he spelled it out to Ellis, he again realized how flimsy it was and wanted to toss it out for once and for all. Even before Ellis gave his feedback.

"No," Ellis said, "why wouldn't he just ambush this guy Fisk as he was going home or in his office. That's about a one in a thousand."

"Yeah, I know, I agree with you," Crawford said. "All right, how about this one?"

Next he described Warren Faircloth, Civil War re-enactor, gym rat, and widowed husband of the much younger victim, Lauren Faircloth. Then he added the latest wrinkle from David Balfour, the theory that Lauren was going to divorce him, marry a much younger man, but found out her husband had a probable death sentence and decided to wait it out.

"Now that's interesting…all except the mass shooting part. Again, why kill all those other people? Why not just concoct something…I don't know, that a burglar broke into their house, she surprised him and he shot her. Or fake some scenario where the boyfriend shot her because she said she was no longer going to marry him and live forever on the pre-nup money. But still, I don't think you should throw that one out. I'd put that in the *maybe could be* category."

Crawford looked at his watch. He had plenty of time before Ellis had to go to his class, and he could tell the professor was getting into it.

"But you're going with one of the first three as most probable?" Crawford said.

"Yes, or another one altogether."

Crawford groaned. "Oh, God, I hope not. I hope it's just a matter of catching the three and figuring out which it is."

"I hope so, for your sake," Ellis said.

"Well, so Don, your job seems pretty damn interesting to me—"

"—I was just going to say the same about yours."

"Some days. Most days it's just wearing out shoe leather and sitting in a car with my partner…who, trust me, can get pretty ripe," Crawford said. "So besides mental illness, what are the main reasons why people shoot up a school or a church, or in my case, a club?"

There was a pause. "Um, I'd say the feeling that they were wronged."

"Bullied, you mean?"

"Yes, that, or something that happened on the job, as with your chef and postal worker. But even just being singled out or picked on unfairly. It builds up and you think the world is against you, or a single group is. Like jocks or the popular kids, they make fun of you and mock you. And it builds some more, until it finally explodes."

"Scary."

"Sure is. It's a crisis, which I define as *when ones circumstances overwhelm ones coping mechanisms,* shortly before carrying out their crimes. I saw this TED talk once, I'll never forget what it was called, 'I Was Almost a School Shooter.' The guy who gave it talked about a time when he was really down and bummed out about life and drifting toward doing something suicidal, maybe taking people along with him, when, out of the blue, this guy asked him if he wanted to go a movie. That simple act of friendship, or whatever you want to call it, turned him around. I also remember the quote he ended it with, 'When someone treats you like a person when you don t even feel like a human, it ll change your entire world.' Kid got a lot of applause."

"I bet he did," Crawford said, looking at his watch again. "Well, I better let you go, Don. Don't want to make you late for class. Hey, I really appreciate your time. And thanks for weighing in on my case."

"Any time, Charlie, let me know when you got the guy locked up."

TWENTY-NINE

And that's exactly what happened next. They found Alain Fournier and though they didn't lock him up, they brought him in to the station for extensive questioning. One of the plainclothes cops whom Ott had requisitioned to keep an eye out for Fournier at a bar in West Palm Beach he was known to frequent had finally spotted him walk in with a woman and sit down at the bar.

He let Fournier order a drink, get halfway through it, and then sidled over to him. The cop, named Jim Werwaiss, was reluctant to make a scene in the bar. He sat down next to Fournier and said under his breath, just loud enough so only Fournier could hear:

"Mr. Fournier, I'm Officer Werwaiss, Palm Beach Police, I have a warrant for your arrest and have been instructed to take you in for questioning. I don't want to embarrass you or make a scene here, so finish your drink, then I'll follow you outside and you'll get in my car and go with me to the Palm Beach Police station."

Fournier shook his head and rolled his eyes. "For Chrissake, what is this all about?"

"I said I have a warrant. That's all you need to know. Of course, you can retain a lawyer, if you choose, while you're being questioned."

The woman glanced over at Werwaiss having not been able to make out the conversation, but having seen Fournier's perturbed reaction.

"What's wrong, Alain?" she asked.

"Nothing at all. But I'm afraid I've got to leave you for a little while," Fournier said, then to Werwaiss: "How long's this going to take?"

"I can't answer that. I don't know."

Fournier pulled out his wallet, took out a twenty-dollar bill. "Save my seat," he said to the woman, "this shouldn't be long."

Werwaiss didn't tell Fournier he was being a tad optimistic.

*****

Werwaiss called Crawford from his car. "I got your fugitive, Alain Fournier, in the car with me, Charlie." He pronounced it "For-knee-err."

"It's Fournier—" said the ex-chef derisively, pronouncing it, "Fourn-yeah."

Werwaiss shrugged.

"Good goin', man," Crawford said. "He give you any resistance?"

"Just at pronouncing his name. Nah, he was fine, probably not happy about breaking up his date at a bar."

"All right," Crawford said. "I'm going to get Ott. Meet us at the interrogation room. He want a lawyer?"

Werwaiss glanced over at Fournier. "You want a lawyer present?"

Fournier just shook his head.

"He says no."

"Okay, how far away are you?"

"Just going over the middle bridge. Be there in five."

*****

Werwaiss took Fournier into the interrogation room and asked him if he wanted something to drink.

"Yeah, another pinot noir," Fournier said.

"Sorry we got Coke and water."

"Water."

"Please," said Werwaiss.

Fournier just groaned.

Two minutes later, Crawford, with a bottle of water in hand, and Ott walked in.

"I'm Detective Crawford and this is my partner, Detective Ott," he said, handing Fournier the water.

"So is this about what happened up at the Ocean Club?" Fournier said.

"Yes, where you were head chef for…how long was it?" Crawford asked.

"Eight years," Fournier said.

"Let me just explain something to you, Mr. Fournier," Crawford said. "We wouldn't have needed to go to all the effort of getting a warrant and tracking you down if you just came in willingly. Instead of hanging up on me."

"See, that tends to make us a little suspicious, Mr. Fournier," Ott added, pronouncing it "For-neer."

"For Chrissake, it's Fournier."

"Whatever," Ott said. "So we have a lot of questions for you. First of all, where were you Friday the second between two and four in the afternoon?"

"Wait a minute," Fournier said, sneering, "you're not thinking I had something to do with what happened at the Ocean Club?"

"How come you know when it happened?" Ott asked.

"What else would you be referring to?" Fournier said, twisting off the top of the water bottle. "I read the newspapers."

"Where were you?" Crawford asked.

"I guess I was at my new apartment," he said.

"You guess? Doing what?" Ott asked.

"I don't know. Putting up a few pictures or something. I had just moved in."

"Okay. And was anyone there with you?" Ott asked.

"No. I was all alone. All afternoon long. Then I went out for dinner after that. With the same woman who was with me at the bar before your…*sidekick* rudely interrupted us."

Ott glanced at Crawford and chuckled.

"Are you seriously thinking that it was me who went up there and killed all those people?" Fournier asked.

"We're *seriously* asking you," Crawford clarified. "'Cause it seems like you might have a motive."

"Temperament too," Ott added.

"What the hell's that supposed to mean?"

"Well, a guy who throws a chef's knife at someone certainly has a temper, wouldn't you say, Alan?"

"It's Alain," he said contemptuously, "and that's bullshit. It never happened."

"Oh," said Ott, "so maybe it was just a butter knife?"

Fournier seethed silently.

"Did you know a waiter there by the name of Jason Reardon," Ott asked, taking a different tack.

Fournier laughed. "Jason the nebbish," he said, "yeah, I knew him. He didn't last long."

"What was your take on him?"

"He was an okay waiter, but he sweated all over the members' food. He got canned or quit after a few months. I don't know which."

"Did he ever threaten anyone or act hostile at all?" Crawford asked.

"I don't know. I never heard anything. I said maybe ten words to the guy the entire time he was there. He had this tic, too, as I remember."

Crawford nodded. "Let's go back to you and talk about your possible motive," he said. "But first, let me ask you a question: have you ever heard about a mass killing where an employee kills his boss, or maybe an owner, along with other coworkers?"

"No, I haven't. The last thing I do is spend my time reading about what homicidal maniacs do. I've got better things to do with my time."

"Okay," Crawford said. "But if you did, you'd know that there are dozens of cases where that's exactly what happened."

"What about the time where you shoved someone in the kitchen so hard that he fell down and needed medical attention. Is that bullshit too?" Ott asked. "Because we have eyewitnesses who saw it happen."

"Oh my God," Fournier said, "it was just a shove. He fell down and hurt his elbow, supposedly. It wasn't like they had to rush him off to Good Sam."

"Do you like to shoot guns, Mr. Fournier?" Ott asked.

"I've got a shotgun from my father that I've never shot," he answered directly.

"What about a gun that fires five bullets a second, or three hundred rounds a minute?" Ott asked.

Fournier shrugged. "I have absolutely no idea what you're talking about."

"I'm talking about an Steyr AUG semiautomatic."

"I wouldn't know an Steyr AUG semiautomatic if it bit me in the ass," Fournier said with another shrug.

"They don't bite, they kill," Ott said.

"So you have never possessed an a Steyr AUG?" Crawford asked.

"Hell no. And you suggesting that I'd go up to the Ocean Club disguised as a tennis player and kill all those people. That's just plain ridiculous," Fournier said. "I haven't even been back there since…I quit."

"Oh, is that what happened?" Ott said, sarcastically. "'Cause we heard it a little differently. From a man who heard you actually got fired by the head of the Board of Governors of of the Ocean Club."

"I don't give a damn what you heard. It was a shitty place to work. All those stuffed shirts and pompous phonies."

"Okay, so help us out here a little bit, *Alain*," Ott said, emphasizing the name, "if you were really at home hanging pictures, who do you think might have been at the Ocean Club shooting at all those stuffed shirts and phonies."

"*Pompous* phonies," Crawford said.

"Sorry, pompous phonies," Ott said.

"How the hell would I know," Fournier said. "What? Am I some private investigator now? Clearly, you guys don't have a clue and are desperate to bring me—or anybody—in here and waste my time. I should sue you for false arrest or something."

"We didn't arrest you," Crawford said. "Do you remember us reading you your Miranda rights?"

"Or handcuffing you or saying you're under arrest," Ott said.

"In that case, I want to leave."

Crawford put up his hands. "So leave, we're done here. But just be careful about throwing knives at people or, I guarantee you, we will arrest you."

Ott shot him a little wave, daintily wiggling his fingers. "Bye-bye, *Alain*."

THIRTY

Ott drove Alain Fournier back to the bar in West Palm, where, it turned out, the bartender gave Fournier the bad news that the woman he had been with left with another man twenty minutes before.

"Shit," Fournier said, "she probably bought him drinks with my money."

Ott shrugged and walked out.

Ott went back to the station and he and Crawford huddled to compare notes on Fournier and decide on their next moves.

"I'm not completely ruling him out," Crawford said, referring to Fournier, "but we obviously gotta get something solid on him."

"Got any ideas how we can do that?" Ott asked.

"Not really. I mean we looked into his past to see if he had a sheet or anything and he was completely clean. Maybe we get a warrant to search his new place for the Steyr AUG, but if he ever had it he's probably either dumped it or got it hidden so well we'll never find it. So that doesn't get us anywhere. Plus, I don't know, I just don't feel it."

"I still have a few more people, friends of his supposedly, who I want to talk to. Maybe something will come up there," said Ott.

"Maybe. In the meantime, why don't you focus on Jason Reardon. Take another close look at those security cams at the Ocean Club. See if you can find a close shot of the guy, see if he's sweating profusely."

"Yeah, not a bad idea. Talk about being in a situation where he'd be sweating his ass off."

"I know," Crawford said, "in the meantime, I'm doing round two with Warren Faircloth."

"Oh, you set up another interview with him?"

Crawford looked at this watch. "Yeah, in a little over an hour. I suggested we meet at the Ocean Club, it's open again, to see how he'd react to going there. You know, the scene of the crime. But he said no, come to his place again."

Crawford's cell phone rang. He looked at the display.

"Oh, hey it's Allie Agostino, from that West Palm homeless outreach team."

He clicked his iPhone. "Yeah, hi Allie."

"Hi, Detective. I'll make this quick. Someone from a place down on Datura just called me and said your guy Celestine spent the night there last night."

"Okay, thanks." Crawford said, snapping his fingers excitedly. "Got a name for me and the Datura street number?"

"Sure do," and she gave him both.

"Okay, my partner and I are headed there right now."

"Good luck."

"Thanks."

He and Ott got to their feet and ran to the back of the station and hopped into their Crown Vic.

"You know where Datura is, Charlie?" Ott asked.

"Sure. Between Clematis and Evernia. See, the east-west streets there are alphabetical. It goes Banyan, Clematis, Datura, Evernia, Fern."

"No shit. Who knew?"

"Me."

"You know everything, Charlie."

"Fuck off," Crawford said. "Let's go get the sonovabitch."

*****

They didn't.

Marlon Celestine had left the shelter an hour before and the woman in charge said her sense was that he wasn't coming back. She commented that he seemed to keep looking behind, and all around him, as if he was scared someone might be sneaking up on him. Well, in fact, that was the case. They spent the next half hour driving around the immediate area, then fanning out a little further. But nothing. Then Crawford dropped Ott off back at the station and went to meet with Warren Faircloth for a second time.

This time Faircloth was wearing shorts and a collared Polo shirt and Crawford could clearly see the man had biceps. Nothing huge, but hard with none of the droop to them which was common with men his age. Same with his legs. Particularly his quads. Solid.

They sat down out on his porch, which overlooked a long narrow lap pool and a high, thick hedge behind.

"You swim a lot, Mr. Faircloth?" Crawford asked.

"Yes, every day," Faircloth said. "Best exercise there is. Works every muscle in your body."

Crawford nodded. "I should do it."

"You look like you're in pretty good shape, Detective."

"I may look it…." Crawford's voice trailed off as he wondered how he was going to start off his Q & A, since both his talking points were extremely delicate.

"By the way," Faircloth said, "do you want something to drink? Coke or water or something?"

Crawford got a silent chuckle: The same stuff they served in the interrogation room at the station a little while ago.

He put up his hand. "No thanks, I'm fine," he said, mentally rehashing his conversation with Ott where they speculated that maybe Faircloth just couldn't live with the idea that his much younger wife was going to marry a much younger man and live on his money happily ever after. It would be a pretty hard pill to swallow was their conclusion.

"So, Mr. Faircloth, you know how Palm Beach is a small town and how it's known for, among other things, its gossip?"

Faircloth eyed him warily. "Just where are you going with that thought, Detective? I have a feeling you're referring to some gossip about me. If you are, go on, out with it."

Well, that made his job easier. He didn't have to beat around the bush anymore.

"All right, I'm just going to come right out and say it…I've been told that your wife might have been having an extramarital affair."

His words seemed to clunk loudly to the floor.

"Oh, have you now?" Faircloth said, but surprisingly his tone had not changed. "I guess you're throwing that concept of not speaking ill of the dead right out the window."

"Mr. Faircloth, please understand I'm trying to solve a multiple homicide—"

"And are you suggesting I might have had something to do with it?"

Crawford beelined to a favorite default. "What I do is go around and talk to a lot of people. Gather up as much information as possible which then, with any luck, leads to making an arrest and catching my killer."

"So should I feel honored that this is your second go-around with me?"

"Feel however you feel, Mr. Faircloth. So is that true about your wife?"

"I'm going to answer your question this way: *it's none of your goddamn business.* And, two, it's absolutely irrelevant to finding whoever killed Lauren and those others." Faircloth took a deep breath and continued: "See, I've had a lot of time to think why you called me up and asked to meet with me again, and here's what I came up with: You caught wind of some local gossip, since Palm Beach is without a doubt the gossip capital of the world, and also heard that I like to participate in reenactments of Civil War battles. Your keen mind then surmised that, 'Aha, he must love guns' or maybe you heard I have a world-class collection of them, then you thought, 'Faircloth must be the killer because his wife was'—you'll excuse the crude way I'm putting it—'screwing around on him and so the old bastard killed her.' Is that pretty close, Detective?"

Pretty close? It was right on the money. "Yes, Mr. Faircloth, something like that did cross my mind." And this "old bastard" was a hell of a lot sharper than he appeared the first time.

"Well then, Detective, one of two things: either you have a wildly vivid imagination or you're desperate to find this guy who killed my wife and the others. And on that note, I am concluding our meeting because I need to do my laps for today, so I'll be in good shape on the battlefield at Appomattox."

THIRTY-ONE

Crawford left Warren Faircloth's house in kind of a daze. The old guy had run circles around him and, he decided, maybe it was time to let him off the hook. But he had to clear his head first before he decided for sure. Whatever the case was, Marlon Celestine and Jason Reardon remained the leading candidates. Alain Fournier? Insufficient evidence. TBD. Warren Faircloth? He put the man in a distant fourth place.

Crawford decided to give a call to a man who had started out low on his list of suspects. And still was. It was John Zoller, Jeff Fisk's partner, mentioning Olive Fisk's affair with Fisk when she was married to Harding Leitner. And Zoller adding, "I can't imagine Harding was too happy about it." His unhappiness, Zoller posited, might have led to Leitner possibly going to the Ocean Club and killing Fisk along with the two others. This struck Crawford as a giant leap—similar to how he now viewed Warren Faircloth—but in the absence of having Celestine and Reardon in custody, he figured he'd better take a look anyway.

So, he called Harding Leitner, who answered immediately.

"Yes, hello Mr. Leitner, my name is Detective Crawford, Palm Beach Police—"

"Well, hello, Detective," Leitner said almost jubilantly. "'Bout time you got around to me. I was beginning to feel left out."

"I'm sorry, sir, I'm not sure what you mean by that," Crawford said, truly perplexed.

"I'm referring to the fact that you've spoken to just about every man in Palm Beach as a possible suspect in those murders up at the Ocean Club."

"Ah, sir, that's a bit of an exaggeration. Would you be available to meet with me, either at your house or the police station in Palm Beach."

"Any time you say, Detective, I'll happily clear my calendar to get in on this."

Ugh, thought Crawford, now feeling like this might well be a colossal waste of time. But he couldn't very well back out at this point.

"Okay, Mr. Leitner, can you stop by the police station at 370 South County Road at two o'clock this afternoon? Ask for me."

"It's a date," Leitner said, and Crawford wondered what kind of life the man had, as this seemed to be the high point of his day, maybe his week.

*****

Crawford was down at Ott's cubicle discussing things when Bettina announced that Harding Leitner had arrived. Crawford asked her to take him into his office while he finished up with Ott.

A few minutes later, Crawford went to his office where Leitner was sitting and introduced himself. Ott had asked if he should sit in, but Crawford told him he was a long-shot suspect and not to bother.

In an effort not to waste any more time, Crawford skipped the warm-up.

"Mr. Leitner, it's come to my attention that Jeff Fisk, one of the casualties of the Ocean Club murders, had an affair with your then-wife. I guess, a few years ago."

"Oh my God, talk about old news. When was it? Four years ago," he answered his own question. "So what are you suggesting…I went out and bought a semiautomatic rifle, dressed up in tennis whites, went up to the Ocean Club and shot Fisk and those others?"

"You framed the question: What is your answer, please?"

"No is the answer, that's absurd," Leitner said waving his hand dismissively. "I barely remember what my wife looks like anymore, but I might have a scoop or two for you."

"Okay, let's hear it," Crawford said, somewhat warily.

"Well, I heard the killer may have come ashore by boat," Leitner said.

What, like a marauding pirate...in tennis whites? Crawford thought. But instead he said, "Okay, go on. Who was he?"

Leitner scratched his cheek. "Um, the guy who told me wasn't really sure."

It was time to give the guy the boot.

Leitner continued: "Someone else told me it might have been Hank Koehler."

Crawford was familiar with the name because his brother Cam knew him from New York. "You mean, the head of Goldman Sachs?"

"Yes, exactly," Leitner said. "'Cause the Ocean Club dinged him for membership. Two of the guys on the Membership Committee got shot. Right?"

"Ah, thank you, Mr. Leitner, but we've already gone down the road with that scenario and didn't feel it panned out."

"Okay, well there were a couple others, but I can't remember 'em off the top of my head," Leitner said.

"Well, listen, thank you for coming in and I really appreciate your feedback," Crawford said.

"Is that all, Detective?" Leitner asked, seemingly disappointed with the brevity of the interview.

"Sorry, I've got to get to another appointment," Crawford said. He didn't.

Reluctantly, Leitner stood up, revealing his full height: He was all of five feet, six inches, max.

Mentally, Crawford kicked himself. Why hadn't he asked the man his height like he had everyone else?

He was really slipping.

THIRTY-TWO

Crawford had had his fill of comic relief and harebrained theories.

Meanwhile, down the corridor, Ott was just beginning to interview a friend of Alain Fournier, a big bear of a man named Mel Craig who barely squeezed into Ott's cubicle.

"So, Mr. Craig, tell me about Alain Fournier," he asked. "What's your impression of him?"

"Well, like a lot of French people, Alain can be arrogant. Opinionated as hell about everything, and never wrong about anything," Craig said, "but beneath all that was a pretty decent man."

"You knew him socially, right?"

"Yeah, socially. Well, athletically, I guess you could say. We met playing pickleball and hit it off. We'd go out together at night, chase women…he was much better at it than I was."

"Did you ever see a side of him where he maybe lost his temper and was out of control, violent even?"

"Oh, my God, no," Craig said, "nothing even close to that."

Ott nodded. "Or did he ever talk about a hatred he had for the people at the Ocean Club after he lost his job?"

Craig nodded. "Oh, I see where you're going now," he said. "Alain Fournier would no more lose his mind and go shoot all those people at that club than you or I would. Yeah, I'd see him get pissed off every once in a while, but then it would pass. I'm sorry, Detective, but you're barking up the wrong tree if you're looking at Alain to have done something like that. No way in hell."

"Okay, well, I appreciate your coming in and meeting with me. Fournier is lucky to have you as such a good character witness."

Craig stood up. "I'm just telling it like it is, Detective."

"Well, thanks again."

*****

Ott got a call on his cell phone as Mel Craig departed. It read UNKNOWN on the display. He answered it anyway.

"Hello?"

"Detective Ott?"

"Yes, who's this?"

"Dave Reardon, Jason Reardon's brother."

"Oh yeah, hi Dave, what's up?"

"I got a call from Jason a little while ago and thought I better tell you."

Ott pressed his phone closer to his ear. "What did he say?"

"He was rambling a bit, almost like he had been drinking, but he doesn't drink. He went on and on about how he hated everyone he worked with—"

"At the post office on Military?"

"Yes."

"Go on."

"He said how they persecuted him and made fun of his sweating. Did I tell you about that?"

"No, but I heard about it from someone else. Keep going?"

"So he was going on and on about people there and then he said something like, *I wish someone would just torch the whole damn place*. It really scared me."

"I don't blame you. But did he say that about 'torching the place' meaning when everyone was there…actually in the post office?"

"He didn't say that, but it sounded like that's what he meant. And, like I said, what he said was, I wish *someone* would torch the place, he didn't say, *I'd* like to torch it. There's a difference. Know what I mean?"

"Yeah, I hear you, it's still pretty scary that he's even thinking like that," Ott said. "So did you ask him where he was?"

"Yeah, I did, and he said he didn't want to tell me, he just said it was a place—a motel, he said—he had gone to with a woman once."

"And who was she?"

"I asked him that and he wouldn't tell me that either."

Ott wondered if it was the woman who he had talked to, who had moved to South Carolina. Alicia Sands.

"Did he say anything else, Dave?" Ott asked.

"No, it was like he was obsessed with his coworkers and how they always made fun of him and harassed him. I've heard him mention it before, but never like this."

"Okay, well, can you call him back and try to find out exactly where he is. My partner and I need to talk to him, or better yet, see him in person."

"Sure, I'll try, but there's no guarantee he'll tell me or even answer his phone."

"I understand. Just do your best, please."

"Oh, trust me I will. He definitely needs professional help."

Ott recalled Crawford's discussion with Reardon's psychiatrist and wasted no time in going straight to Crawford's office and telling him about the call from Dave Reardon.

Crawford listened, then said. "Okay, first thing we gotta do is get some guys over to that post office and make sure Jason doesn't show up with a couple gallons of gas."

"Yeah, I know, I was just about to do that, but I wanted to tell you first."

"And secondly, we gotta find where he is and go there fast," Crawford said. "I mean, this guy sounds like a real loose cannon."

"Sure does," Ott said. "So right now I'm gonna call the woman who I spoke to who went out with him. I'm hoping she was the one who went with him to this motel wherever the hell it is. Will you take care of getting guys over to the post office?"

"Yeah, I'll do that right now. If that woman tells you where the motel is, we gotta go there immediately."

"I agree," Ott said, pulling out his cell phone and dialing as he walked back to his cubicle.

He got Alicia Sands's answering machine. "Shit," he mumbled to himself, then he left a message. "Ms. Sands, it's Detective Ott in Palm Beach, Florida, we spoke a little while ago and it's important that I speak to you again. Please call just as soon as you get this. Thanks."

He clicked off as Crawford was on the phone lining up cops to go to the post office on Military Trail.

Ten minutes later, Ott got a call back from Alicia Sands.

"Hi, Alicia, thanks for getting back to me so fast," he said, hoping she was the woman who had accompanied Jason Reardon to the motel. "Did you, by any chance, ever take a trip with Jason Reardon and stay in a motel somewhere?"

"Yes, yes I did, it was to a place called Mount Dora, north of Orlando, about two and half hours north of where you are. But I'm sorry, I don't remember the name of the motel. Just that it had a pool and this…what's it called, when you roll those balls on the ground?"

"Bocce?"

"Yes, exactly. It had this bocce…court, I guess you call it, and we played a few times."

"Is there any way you can remember the name of the motel. Maybe you had a receipt from there or something?"

"No, Jason paid for it, sorry."

"Well, that's helpful, Ms. Sands, I really appreciate it. If the name comes back to you, please let me know."

"I will, definitely."

Ott called Bettina. "I have a puzzle for ya. Are you busy?"

"For you or Charlie, I drop everything."

"Thank you. Could you look up motels in a place called Mount Dora, Florida. I'm looking for one that has a pool and a bocce court. Then if you find it, I want to see if they have a man registered there by the name of Jason Reardon. Just make sure that whoever you talk to doesn't mention to Reardon that you called and asked if he was there."

"Got it. I'll get on it right now."

She called Ott back ten minutes later.

"Well, that was a piece of cake," she said. "Why don't you give me something more challenging? The name of the motel is the Wagon Wheel. And your guy Jason Reardon checked in three days ago. It's 114 miles from here and about a two-and-a-half-hour drive. Two-fifteen with you at the wheel."

"Thanks, kid," Ott said. "I'll try to give you something a little tougher next time."

He was already halfway to Crawford's office. His partner ended his call as Ott strode in.

"All right," Ott said. "I know where the motel is."

"Already?" Crawford said, standing up.

"Well, Bettina…"

"Say no more. Meanwhile, I got Wiley, Jimenez, and Del Bianco headed over to the post office."

"You think Reardon's our guy?" Ott asked, as they went out the back door of the station to the Crown Vic.

"I don't know. Good possibility, I'd say. In any case, we're narrowing down our list."

THIRTY-THREE

They put a cassette of The Band's greatest hits on their way up to Mount Dora. Both of them had compatible tastes in music and were old-school in that neither subscribed to Sirius or Amazon Music or anything else on their car stereo.

"They're all dead now, I think," Crawford said of the members of The Band.

"Yeah, Garth Hudson was the last to go. Died earlier this year in Woodstock."

"Where it all began, right?" Crawford said.

"Well, actually it all began for most of 'em in Canada. But they got famous in Woodstock with Dylan. I know these guys inside out. Right up there with the Stones, Tom Petty, and Waylon Jennings."

"I thought you were a big Dire Straits fan."

"I am. Mark Knopfler's the man, one of the greatest guitar players ever," Ott said. "Speaking of motels, Rich Manuel was the first member of The Band to go."

Crawford turned to him. "What do you mean 'speaking of motels'?"

"Dude hung himself in a motel room after a concert. In Winter Park, actually, not that far from Mount Dora."

"Wow, you know your stuff."

"You know who was next?"

"To die you mean?"

"Yup."

"Who?"

"Rick Danko. Throat cancer, I think it was," Ott said. "He was only in his mid-fifties."

"Your age, huh?"

"No, Charlie, I'm only in my early fifties. And as fit as the proverbial fiddle."

"So I see," Crawford said. "So who was next?"

"Levon Helm, cancer, too," Ott said. "Then a couple years back, Robbie Robertson."

"You know what's amazing…Keith Richards survives 'em all," Crawford said.

"Not just alive, but still strumming and touring, and Jagger's up there onstage dancing like a teenager."

"Incredible," Crawford said. "Both in their eighties and going strong. You know that place Big Pink?"

"Sure. Where The Band lived for a while. West Saugerties, New York," Ott said. "Not far from Dylan's place in Woodstock. Their first album was called, *Music from Big Pink*—what about it?"

Crawford shook his head. "Now you're just showin' off."

Ott laughed. "Yeah, well, I saw that movie about 'em probably a dozen times."

"Well, anyway, I was up in that neck of the woods like twenty years ago and went by the house. You know, a visit to a rock 'n' roll shrine. It was still standing and it was still pink, but, Christ, was it ever ugly. And, just for the record, damn thing's not big at all."

*****

Mount Dora was a little city on a picturesque lake that seemed to have a funky vibe to it and judging from its downtown, a fair amount of culture and history. It was a far cry from the beach towns and cities that Crawford and Ott were used to down south. Crawford had Googled the town on the way up and read that at its highest point it had an elevation of 184 feet above sea level, which struck him as unheard of in Florida, but he read on and saw that a place called Britton Hill in a town called Lakewood Park was 345 feet above sea level.

"Feels kind of high up here," Ott said, as they drove into the city, playing into Crawford's hands.

"How high would you say?" Crawford asked.

"Um, maybe 125, 130 feet above sea level?"

"Nope, 184 to be exact. Only place higher is in Lakewood Park at 345 feet."

"So suddenly you're an expert on all the elevations in the Sunshine State," Ott said and chuckled. "Someone stuck his nose in Google."

"No, I just know stuff like that," Crawford said with a straight face.

"Bullshit."

"You got this motel on your GPS?" Crawford asked, turning business.

"Sure do. The Wagon Wheel is just a mile, mile and a quarter from here," Ott said. "You getting woozy from all this altitude?"

Crawford laughed. "Yeah, they probably got a ski area around here somewhere."

The pulled up to the Wagon Wheel two minutes later and first thing they saw was the bocce court. Unoccupied at the moment. They got out of the Crown Vic and went in the door marked *Office*. It was cluttered with little rectangular signs all over like, "Don't molest the alligators." Another said, "Four seasons in Florida: summer, hurricane season, lovebug season and football season,." A third said, "Don't touch your seatbelt during summer, you'll get second-degree burns!" And finally, "Say what you will about Florida but no one retires here then moves up North."

"Someone's got a real funny bone," Ott murmured as they walked up to the desk.

"Hi," Crawford said to the young woman with glasses and a nice tan sitting at the front desk. "We're detectives from Palm

Beach"—he flashed her ID—"and we called earlier about a guest of yours here by the name of Jason Reardon."

"Oh, yes, but I think he just went out a little while ago."

Ott groaned. "But he hasn't checked out, has he?"

"No, I think he said he planned to stay here three days and it's only been two."

"Would you mind calling his room just to make sure he's not there?" Crawford asked.

"If he answers, just hang up," said Ott.

"Sure, no problem," she said, and she reached for a phone and dialed.

It rang and rang and after about ten rings she hung up.

"Okay, thanks," Crawford said. "We'll just wait around for him."

Ott looked up at Crawford. "How's your bocce?"

Crawford chuckled. "I don't know, I've never played. We're not exactly dressed for bocce."

"How do you know? Is there a dress code?"

"All right, come on," Crawford said, then to the woman at the desk. "But first…what kind of car is he driving?"

"It's a white SUV. Maybe a Honda or a Toyota?" she said. "You're going to need bocce balls if you're going to play."

She reached under her desk and pulled out a transparent rectangular plastic bag that had eight large balls in it and one smaller white one. The large balls were red, green, blue and yellow—two of each. "Normally I'd charge you two bucks and a ten-dollar security deposit, but for officers of the law, it's on the house."

"Thank you," Crawford said, taking the bag. "We'll bring 'em back."

They walked out of the office. "Another sport I'm gonna kick your ass at," Ott said.

"Oh yeah, what were the others?"

"'Member when we played miniature golf that time with Dominica?"

"The way I remember it, she kicked both our asses. What else?"

"Pool, that time."

"You were just lucky. What else?"

"Ah, let's see…Baldur's Gate 3."

"For Chrissake, that's a computer game," Crawford said, shaking his head.

"So, it's a game, isn't it?" Ott said as they approached the bocce court.

Crawford looked around to where they had driven into the Wagon Wheel, noting to himself to keep an eye on it.

He looked down at the bocce court, which was little more than a long, skinny lane of packed dirt.

"We should be facing that way," Crawford said. "So we'll see the guy drive in."

"Yeah, definitely," said Ott.

Crawford took off his jacket and put it on a bench. "How the hell do you play this anyway?"

"One of us rolls this little white ball, I think they call it a jack, and then we both roll four of these"—he pointed at the eight larger balls—"and whoever gets closer wins."

"Well, that's pretty basic," Crawford said. "That's all there is to it?"

"Yup, course if one of your balls gets really close, I try to hit your ball and knock it away."

Crawford laughed. "That would be a nasty thing to do."

"Yeah, well, whatever it takes to win. You ready?"

"Yup, so why don't I roll the jack."

"Hey, go for it," Ott said, handing him the little white ball.

Crawford gave it a toss and it rolled about twenty feet away from them.

"Good toss," Ott said.

"You mean, there's such a thing as a bad toss?"

"Well yeah," Ott said, "if you throw it too close…"

Crawford laughed. "You say that so authoritatively, was bocce a big sport up in Cleveland?"

"Yeah, I got an athletic scholarship to Cuyahoga Community College for it," Ott said with a straight face.

"Oh, did you now? A free ride, huh?"

"Yeah, guys like you go to fancy Ivy League colleges 'cause you're good at stuff like football and lacrosse, guys like me…bocce and bowling."

"Okay, quit your bullshitting and toss the ball," Crawford said.

Ott took a red ball in his right hand and rocked it back and forth a few times, getting the feel.

"Okay," he said, "watch out—" and he flung it onto the packed dirt.

It rolled up to within an inch of the white jack. Ott turned to Crawford with a wide grin.

"You gotta be shittin' me," Crawford said. "How'd you do that?"

"You thought I was kidding about the scholarship," Ott said. "Well, maybe I was…but, see, I'm just a natural athlete."

"Okay, so that means I have four balls to knock you outta there," Crawford said.

"Good luck with that—" And then, just as Crawford was about to throw a ball, they both saw a white Toyota Corolla SUV drive into the Wagon Wheel, a white male at the wheel.

They just watched the SUV drive up and park midway down the row of two-story motel rooms. They started walking as the man got out. There was no question about it. He fit the description of Jason Reardon. He walked toward a stairway going up to the second story. They walked faster, both looking for a telltale bulge in his pockets, but they could clearly see he wasn't packing.

They followed Reardon up the stairs, taking them two at a time, and saw him take his key out, ready to open the room door.

"Jason Reardon!" Crawford said with authority. "Palm Beach Police, we need to speak to you."

Reardon's eyes darted around, like he was thinking of running, but there was nowhere to go unless he felt like jumping from the second floor.

"We just want to talk to you," Ott said in as soothing a tone as he could muster. "We're not arresting you or anything."

Reardon pulled the key out of the lock. "What? What do you want to talk to me about?" he stammered as they approached him.

Crawford held up a hand. "There's a coffee shop next to the office. Let's go talk there."

"I said, about what? What do you want to talk about?" He was full-on jumpy now.

"We'll tell you when we get there. Now come along with us," Crawford said.

Ott smiled at Reardon in an attempt to ease the tension. "Just want to talk, Jason."

"Do I need to get a lawyer or anything?" Reardon asked.

"If you want one. Do you know one around here?" Crawford asked, knowing the answer.

"I don't know one anywhere," Reardon said. "I never needed one."

"Well, that's good," Crawford said. "Come on, let's go."

Ott took the lead, walking back to the stairway, then down the steps. Crawford motioned for Reardon to go down the steps in front of him.

The three walked, with Reardon in between them, up to the office and through the door. The woman on duty looked up and smiled.

"Is it okay if we bring the bocce balls back to you in a little while?" Ott asked.

"Yeah, sure," she said.

The walked into the small coffee shop and the woman at the front desk followed them.

"I'm the waitress too," she said with a smile. "We're kind of a low-budget operation."

"Gotcha," said Ott as the three sat down at a table.

"What do you want, Jason," Crawford said. "We're buying."

"Um, just maybe a Coke is all," he said.

"Come on, we're buying. Get yourself a burger or something," Ott said.

"Sorry, no burgers," said the woman, with her pad out now. "We got hot dogs, though."

"Last chance, Jason?" Crawford said.

"Just a Coke, please?"

"I'll have one too," Crawford said.

"Coffee for me, please," Ott said.

"That's all?" said the woman.

Crawford nodded. "So, Jason," he started out, "we know you went on vacation from the post office on Military a few days ago. Kind of sudden, wasn't it?"

"Well yeah, I guess. I just felt I needed it," Reardon said.

"People at work bugging you, huh?" Ott said. "Getting in your face?"

Reardon looked surprised and frowned. "How do you know that?"

"Your brother Dave. He was concerned about you," Crawford said.

"You got a good brother there," Ott said. "He just wants to make sure you're okay."

"He told us about something you said that got him really concerned," Crawford said.

"What was that?" Reardon said.

Crawford leaned closer to Reardon as the woman brought them their two Cokes and a coffee.

"Thanks," Crawford said, and waited for her to walk away. "Dave said you said, *I wish someone would just torch the whole damn place*. Meaning the post office."

"Did you say that, Jason?" Ott said.

"I don't know, I was mad. There're a bunch of assholes who work there, always giving me shit about something. I couldn't handle it anymore."

"But would you ever do something like that?" Crawford asked. "'Torch the whole place.'"

"Nah, 'course not, I was just talking."

"But you did that once," Ott said.

Reardon's frown got deeper. "Did what?"

"You burned down your school, back when you were a kid," Ott said.

"How—? That was a long, long time ago."

"We know," Ott said, "and sometimes people repeat past actions."

"Not me, I would never do that, I was just talking. Getting it off my chest."

"How do we know that for sure, Jason?" Crawford said.

"'Cause I'm telling you."

Crawford glanced over at Ott. "Let's talk about something else. Did you hear about those murders in Palm Beach that happened a while back? Three people got killed and a bunch of injuries."

Reardon picked up his Coke and took a long sip. Crawford noticed his tic for the first time.

"Yeah, I heard. What about it?"

"You don't know anything about that, do you?" Ott asked, pouring the contents of a sugar packet into his coffee.

"Well, just what you said. Three people got killed and a bunch of injuries."

"No, what I meant was you didn't have anything to do with that, did you?"

"Are you crazy? Why in God's name would I have anything to do with that? You think I went out and shot all those people?"

"Do you have a semiautomatic weapon, Jason?" Crawford asked.

"No, of course not, I don't go around shooting guns, for God's sake."

"But I heard you went hunting with your brother a while back," Ott said.

"That was for deer, not people."

"Yeah, I know," Ott said. "You used to work there, didn't you?"

"Work where?

"At the Ocean Club in Palm Beach. Where the shooting took place."

Reardon let out a long sigh and glanced away.

"Jason, my partner asked you a question," Crawford said. "You used to work at the Ocean Club in Palm Beach where those people were killed, didn't you?"

Reardon's eyes slowly circled back to Crawford. "Yeah, I did, so what? I wasn't there long at all. Only a couple months."

"Yes, but people there made fun of you, bullied you, didn't they?" Ott said. "Which was why you quit, right?"

Reardon sighed again. "Yes," was all he said, the tic getting worse.

"Did you go there and shoot those people?" Crawford asked. "Dressed up in white tennis clothes and wearing a white floppy hat and wraparound sunglasses? Did you, Jason?"

"No, of course, I didn't. You think I'm a murderer?"

"I don't know, you talked about torching the post office. If you did that, you'd certainly be a murderer. Wouldn't you?"

"Yes, but it was just all talk. That's all I ever do. Just talk."

"But that one time you acted. That was not just talk." This time it was Crawford.

Jason buried his head in his hands.

"We need to know the truth," Ott said. "Your supervisor said you were going door-to-door in a mail truck on the afternoon the murders took place in West Palm. What was your route?"

"Mainly the Northwood section of West Palm," Reardon said.

"The Northwood section?" Crawford said. "So that means that you could have taken the north bridge over to Palm Beach, then it's just a short drive up to the Ocean Club?"

"I guess so, but I didn't. I just did my route in the Northwood section like I always do."

"Then what?"

"Then I went home. Like I always do."

"So you never drove over the bridge to Palm Beach?"

"Nope, never did."

"'Cause if you had, it would have been easy to change into tennis clothes in the truck, park a block or two away from the Ocean Club, then go and shoot those people. Then go back to the truck, change back, and go on delivering mail."

Ott nodded. "Like nothing ever happened," he said. "Mail truck would have blended in nicely. Nobody's gonna go, 'hey, what's a West Palm mail truck doing in Palm Beach?'"

"Well, as I told you, that never happened," Reardon protested, his voice approaching a wail. "I just did my route in West Palm, like I said."

"You've got to convince us," Ott said.

Reardon rubbed his chin with his hand. "Even I know it's the other way around," he said. "*You've* got to prove I did anything. And there's no way that's going to happen, because I didn't do it. I just delivered mail that afternoon the way I always did."

"And you had no automatic weapon in the mail truck with you?" Crawford asked.

Reardon shook his head. "Just mail."

Crawford glanced over at Ott. Ott shot him a barely perceptible shrug.

"When do you plan to go back to your job?" Crawford asked.

"*If* I go back to my job," he whispered.

"So you're thinking about quitting?" Crawford asked.

Reardon nodded. "Thinking about it."

"So what would you do instead?" asked Ott.

"Get another job…not working with assholes who are always on my case," Reardon said. "This guy I know is a toll both collector. He doesn't work with anybody. Just makes change. I might like that."

Crawford wanted to be careful not to divulge his source on what he was about to say. "Jason, you once told someone that you were so depressed that you might want to commit suicide. Is that true?"

"It's true that I've had depression for a long time and sometimes it gets really bad."

"So bad that you've thought about killing yourself?"

Reardon smiled an uneasy smile. "Well yes, but, as you can see, I'm still here."

"I can see that," Crawford said. "And you also said that if you did it—killed yourself, that is—that you might want to take some people along with you."

Reardon held up his hands. "No, I don't think I ever said that. No never."

"We're pretty sure that's exactly what you said, Jason," Ott said.

"Well, I don't remember that," Reardon said, picking up his Coke and draining it. "And if I said it, I didn't mean it."

"But it's possible you might have forgotten saying it?" Ott asked.

"I don't think so."

Crawford pointed at Reardon's Coke. "You want a refill?"

"No I'm fine," Reardon said. "Are we almost done?"

Crawford and Ott both knew they had no smoking gun going in, and they still didn't have one now. But they still had to keep trying. Jason Reardon and Marlon Celestine were their best leads.

Only problem was, they didn't have anywhere left to go.

"So when do you plan to go back home?" Crawford asked. "Even if it's not back to your post office job?"

"A couple days, I've kind of mellowed out up here," Reardon said. "It's a nice place here, Mount Dora."

"Yeah, seems to be. What do you do for fun up here?" Crawford asked.

"Um, go to a karaoke place at night, just hang out at the pool during the day."

"You ever play any bocce, Jason?" Crawford asked.

"Nah, I don't even know how to play."

"Well, Detective Ott here could show you how. He's a pro."

"You are?" Reardon said.

Ott laughed. "Don't listen to him."

"All right," Crawford said. "So we're gonna let you go now. We might want to talk to you again back home. In the meantime, if you leave the post office, good luck with your next job."

"Thanks."

"Okay, Jason," Ott said, standing up and grabbing the check. "You take it easy."

"I will."

They went back to the bocce court, gathered up the balls and went back inside and paid their bill.

As they walked to their car, Crawford turned to Ott. "I'm gonna call the guys at the post office and let 'em know we don't need 'em there anymore."

THIRTY-FOUR

"So what did you think?" Ott asked as he drove out of the Wagon Wheel on their way back down to Palm Beach.

"I think...I don't know."

"That's an answer I've never heard from you."

"Yeah, well, on paper he's the perfect profile of our killer. A violent action in his past, granted it was thirty years ago, but still. Plus, his occupation itself and its history of mass shooting incidents. Not to mention, his easy access to the crime scene area at the Ocean Club that afternoon. Just drive his mail truck over the bridge from Northwood, and bang! bang! bang! then back to Northwood a few minutes later."

"Definitely could have. But?"

"Observing him in the coffee shop. Asking him a bunch of questions, I just didn't think I was looking at or talking to the guy who did it. Did you?"

"I don't know. Put it this way, I definitely didn't rule him out, but I definitely didn't rule him in either. But even if he did it, we don't have anything on him anyway."

Crawford just nodded.

"So it's back to Palm Beach," Ott said and took a deep breath, "empty-handed."

*****

They were driving past Melbourne on I-95 when Crawford's cell phone rang. He glanced down at the display.

"Oh Christ, Rutledge," he said.

"Hello, Norm," he said, doing his best to sound *up* and happy to hear from him.

He put the call on speakerphone so Ott could hear.

"Where the hell are you? I've been looking all over for you and Ott."

"Outside of Melbourne on—"

"Well, get your ass back here. We've got a dead body up on Peanut Island. It's a suicide and his name is Marlon Celestine."

Ott accelerated so hard Crawford's head snapped back into the headrest. "You're kidding, what did he do?"

"Shot himself. Left a note too."

"You gonna read it to me?"

"No, the first-on-scene cop left it in place," Rutledge said. "Said he didn't want to touch it. Taint the evidence."

"All right, we'll be there in a little less than two hours," Crawford said, looking down at the speedometer, up to 120 mph now: "Make it an hour forty-five."

*****

An hour and twenty minutes later they were staring down at the bloody head and body of Marlon Celestine, lying on a beach at the north end of Palm Beach. Also at the crime scene was Medical Examiner Bob Hawes, two crime scene techs, Candy Tamposi and Dominica McCarthy, and two cops, posted to keep gawkers away from the scene. They had strung up yellow tape but already two teenage boys and an older man were craning their necks to get a better look at the dead body. There was also a helicopter from one of the local TV news stations chopping the air a hundred feet above, no doubt describing the morbid scene below to viewers.

Crawford and Ott had just joined the group.

They walked up to Bob Hawes. "What do you know, Bob?"

"Old guy walking on the beach found the body two hours ago and phoned it in," Hawes said, then he glanced over at the cops. "Those two cops were the first ones here."

"One shot?" Ott asked.

"Yeah, that's all you need when the barrel's pressed right up to the head," Hawes said, known to not be the most sensitive guy around. He pointed. "Had that Ruger 9 in his right hand."

Crawford saw the dark tan pistol in Celestine's hand.

Crawford turned and walked toward the two cops, Ott right behind him. "Hey," he said to them. They were Mars and Whittaker, uniform cops. "How long do you figure he'd been here?"

"Shit, Charlie, hard to tell," Johnny Mars said, "maybe better to ask the techs."

"My guess is not too long," Whittaker said. "There're a lot of walkers who come up this far. Or go to Peanut Island."

Peanut Island, in its former life, had been the location of a fallout shelter that had been built around the time of the Cuban Missile Crisis in the 1960s for President John F. Kennedy, who came to Palm Beach during his presidency and stayed at the family compound at the north end of North Ocean Boulevard. The small, spartan building was built to shelter the president in case enemy missiles were launched.

"So definitely a suicide?" Crawford asked.

"Yeah well, what else could it be?" Whittaker said. "I mean that Ruger in his hand."

"Thanks," Crawford said, and he and Ott walked over to the body and the two techs who were crouched down around it.

Dominica McCarthy looked up at Crawford. "This is one of your suspects for the Ocean Club, right?"

"Yup," Crawford said, "top of our list, matter of fact."

"We did a GSR and neutron activation on his right hand," said Tamposi.

Crawford nodded and noticed a folded piece of paper in the breast pocket of Celestine's shirt.

"That's the note, I take it?" Crawford said, taking out latex gloves from his jacket pocket.

Dominica nodded. "Have a look," she said.

Crawford, in a crouch, reached in and slid the piece of yellow lined paper out of the pocket and opened it up. Ott, his knees popping, got down in a crouch beside Crawford. They read it together:

I don't need the cops catching me and killing me, I can do a cleaner job myself. Just for the record, so you can wrap this whole thing up with a neat little red bow, I killed those people at that club. You see, I have a thing about rich people and how high and mighty their behaviour always is. I was planning to go to the Poinciana club next. Lay waste to some more fat cats. But I had to get rid of the semiautomatic fast. Those Palm Beach cops were all over the place in a hurry. Almost caught me. So good-bye cruel world, I'm off to a better place. Sincerely yours, Marlon Celestine, now deceased.

"Wow," Ott said. "They're not usually that long."

"Yeah, I know, kind of strange," Crawford said, glancing contemplatively off in the distance, then taking a picture of the note, folding it up like it had been before and handing it to Dominica, so she could bag it.

"What do you think about that?" Ott asked his partner.

"I've got a couple of reactions," Crawford said.

"Well, care to share 'em with me?" Ott said.

"I want to think it through a little," Crawford said.

Ott stood back up and his knees popped again.

"Snap, crackle and pop," Dominica said.

Ott chuckled. "One day you'll get as old as me," he warned her.

She smiled back at him. "Not for a while."

Crawford's gaze returned to the two techs. "And the slug, you found it yet?"

"No, not yet," Dominica answered, "we've been sifting through the sand but no luck so far."

"Gotta be there somewhere," Ott said, glancing down at the pistol in Celestine's right hand again, then glancing over at Crawford eyeing the footprints around them in the sand.

"I know what you're looking at," Dominica said to Crawford.

He looked up at her. "Okay, what do you think I see?"

"Two sets of footprints. Even though they're not exactly footprints, since you can't have footprints in the sand. But one set are Celestine's, and another right behind him," Dominica said, as Ott came over to take a look. "But I think what it might be is the prints right behind Celestine's are from the guy who discovered him."

"Could be," Crawford said with a nod. "Or could be someone walking behind Celestine with a gun on him."

"Jesus, Charlie, that's a hell of a leap," Ott said. "So you're saying maybe Celestine was shot as opposed to offing himself?"

"You really think so?" Dominica asked, looking up at Crawford.

"I don't know, it's a possibility is all," Crawford said.

"Okay, maybe it is a possibility," Ott said. "But, the question is, who would want to kill Celestine and why. Unless maybe one of the people he injured in that knife attack five years back. But, that makes no sense. That was a long time ago. And how would they find him anyway?"

"I'm just throwing stuff out there. Probably did kill himself. Figured he was eventually gonna get reeled in by us or the West Palm guys," Crawford said. "Obviously hated being incarcerated. Even in a mental institution. Plus, nobody was willing to take him in. His sister, that friend of his."

"Jimmy Wray," Ott said.

Crawford nodded. "But you know me, I don't always buy the simple, logical explanation."

Ott nodded. "Yeah well, for good reason."

"Sometimes," Crawford said. "And fact is that Celestine also seemed to have suicidal tendencies, just like Jason Reardon."

"How do you know that?" Dominica asked.

"Because it came out before he was judged mentally incompetent to stand trial five years ago—that he was expecting the whole slashing thing to end in 'suicide by cop.' Remember?"

Dominica nodded. "Oh, gotcha."

Crawford glanced around at the two cops, Mars and Whittaker, and took a few steps toward them. "Do we have any clue how the guy got here? 'Cause we know he had no means of transportation."

Ott shrugged "Maybe Uber until his money ran out?" he posited, one step behind Crawford.

"There's one of those motorized bikes back there in the direction of his footprints," Whittaker said. "Maybe he stole it or something?"

Crawford nodded. "Did you see any security cams anywhere? Maybe at the end of the street?"

"We weren't really looking for them," Mars said. "But we can do a thorough search of the area. See what we come up with."

"Yeah, do it. There's gotta be some in the area," Crawford said.

"The damn things are everywhere," Ott said.

Crawford nodded.

"So when you guys canvassed the immediate area," Crawford turned to Mars and Whittaker, "you didn't see anything else, huh?"

"No, not really, we can do another search if you want," Whittaker said.

"Nah, that's okay, Mort and I can check around some more," Crawford said. "I'm guessing there's probably not a hell of a lot more to find."

Then Crawford turned to Ott: "I think we gotta go talk to Norm. I don't know about you, but I've gotten four texts in the last hour alone to meet him in his office right away."

"Only three for me," Ott said. "Guess he likes you more."

Crawford rolled his eyes. "Lucky me."

*****

A half hour later they were sitting in Norm Rutledge's office. As Crawford guessed would be the case, Mayor Mal Chase was there too.

Chase led off the meeting. "So the big question is, how do we play this with the media?"

"And the next question is," Rutledge said, "do we know for absolute fact Celestine was the Ocean Club shooter."

Crawford glanced at Ott, then Rutledge. "No, we don't know for absolute fact that Celestine was the shooter. But he's always been at the top of our list. It would, obviously, have been better if we caught him and he confessed. Instead of the suicide note."

"What the hell's wrong with a suicide note?" Rutledge demanded.

"I don't know," Crawford said. "It's just not the same as a confession from a living perp. Plus, there a couple things about it that bother me."

"Like what?" Chase asked.

"Well, like that whole diatribe about rich people in the notes," Crawford said. "A while back I looked at the transcript from his trial five years ago after he went on the knife rampage. Every single vic was a woman. So it seemed like maybe he had a thing about women."

"As opposed to a thing about rich people?" Chase said.

"Yeah, exactly," Crawford said. "Plus there's another thing I want to think through some more."

"What's that?" Chase asked.

"I need to give it more thought," Crawford said.

"Okay, so that *neat little bow* Celestine talked about in the note isn't so neat to you?" Chase said. "Is that what you're saying?

"Yeah, we're not there yet," Crawford said.

"So the question remains, how do we play this with the media?" Chase said, turning to Rutledge. "What do you think?"

"I think we gotta do something fast. Before there's a leak and everyone knows about Celestine's suicide…if that's what it was. Hold a press conference and say something like, 'we found the body of a man named Marlon Celestine who was our leading suspect in the horrible tragedy that occurred at the Ocean Club.' Ah, let's see, 'and he committed suicide and left a note confessing to having done the shootings. Five years before, some of you may recall, there was an incident where a man went on a rampage with a knife at The Square in West Palm Beach and severely injured five innocent victims there'"—Rutledge paused for a moment—"'and that was this same man…Marlon Celestine. We feel that the modus operandi were similar, though of course, the attack at the Ocean Club was far more deadly.'"

"That's pretty good, Norm," Chase said, turning to Crawford and Ott. "What do you guys think?"

"I think that's okay," Crawford said, "but it doesn't go far enough. By that I mean, we should say, something like, 'nevertheless, Palm Beach homicide detectives are still looking into the Ocean Club murders and won't curtail their investigation until they're one hundred percent certain that Celestine was the killer.' That way—"

"Yeah, yeah, I agree with that," Rutledge said.

"Me too," Ott said. "'Cause what if we find out the real killer turns out to be someone else altogether. We'd be looking pretty stupid if we had put all our eggs in the Marlon Celestine basket."

Chase chuckled. "Funny way to put it, but I totally agree."

"Yeah, who knows," Crawford said, "someone not even on our radar screen might suddenly come out of nowhere."

"You really think so?" Chase said.

"You never know," Crawford said. "We're still digging."

"Okay, what I want to do before a press conference is have a quick meeting with the Worth Avenue merchants, to make them feel that keeping them informed is a top priority," Chase said.

Crawford got the sense Chase's motivation might have everything to do with votes and keeping his constituents happy.

"I'm not quite sure why we need to do that, Mal. They'll find out at the same time we give the press conference," Crawford said.

"Yeah, why's that necessary?" Ott asked, cocking his head.

"Let's just do it," Rutledge said. "We can make it brief. Just basically make it be an announcement."

Crawford shrugged. "Okay, can't really hurt, I guess."

"All right, I'll alert them and schedule it for two o'clock. Because it's such short notice, I'm sure a lot of them won't be able to make it anyway," Chase said. "Okay, so we're agreed on how we're going to play it. Norm, why don't you lead off a press conference and you guys flank him and field any questions because I have a feeling there're going to be plenty. Are you guys good with that?"

Crawford and Ott nodded.

"You don't want to be part of it, Mal?" Rutledge asked.

"No, it's strictly a police matter, let's just keep it to you three," Chase said. "I hate those press conferences I've seen on TV where everyone on the whole police force, including goddamn meter maids, show up all stoned-face and solemn."

THIRTY-FIVE

They met with the merchants of Worth Avenue at a little after two o'clock.

Crawford's read on the group—which numbered only about half as many as the time before—was they didn't seem as hostile this time. Not loaded for bear anymore. He figured that was probably because the meeting had been called by Mal Chase, which likely signaled to them that he and his law enforcement guys had some positive news to report on the case. And, of course, they were right.

"Thank you all for coming on short notice," Chase said. "I'm going to follow this up with an email and send it out to all of you, plus those who couldn't make it here this afternoon, summing up what we're about to tell you. A man was found dead of an apparent self-inflicted gunshot wound on the beach just south of Peanut Island late yesterday afternoon. His name is Marlon Celestine. We believe that he was the shooter at the Ocean Club less than two weeks ago. He, in fact, left a note saying he was responsible for that. The reason I'm saying, *we believe,* is that the homicide detectives here in charge of the case, Detective Crawford and Detective Ott, have not fully concluded the investigation yet. Nevertheless, Celestine was the detectives' prime suspect, and as I'm sure you all know, the general pattern of shooters in mass murders is that many of them kill themselves after committing the crime."

"Though usually not this long after, right?" asked Jake Kaufman, the owner of the exclusive men's shop on Worth Avenue.

"That is true," Rutledge said, "but it is not unheard of."

"Well, that is good news," said Fred Burgess, the head of the Chamber of Commerce, turning to Crawford and Ott. "But when are you going to be able to say, 'we have no doubt whatsoever that this man Celestine committed the murders at the Ocean Club'?"

"Yes," said the woman who owned an art gallery, "otherwise people will think, well, it looks like he did it but the cops aren't a hundred percent certain?"

"Soon," said Rutledge.

"As soon as possible," Crawford added.

"Those are not the same thing," said the woman.

"Allow me to jump in here," said Chase the conciliator. "Charlie and Mort have one other suspect who they need to know, beyond a doubt, had nothing to do with it"—he glanced at Crawford—"then, is it safe to say, Charlie, there'll be no question Celestine was the perpetrator?"

"I think that's safe to say," Crawford said, "but I can't say that with absolute certainty."

"But what about the note," said Kaufman, "isn't that enough for you guys?"

"I've seen suicide notes that weren't actually written by the person who seemingly took his own life," Ott volunteered.

"Okay, everyone," Chase said, clearly eager for the meeting to end. "The detectives and Chief Rutledge have a press conference to prepare for, but we felt it was our duty to first give you people a heads-up to where things stand."

Chase stood up, thereby ending the meeting even though some of the merchants didn't look entirely satisfied.

*****

Earlier Chase had put the word out to the media that they were going to conduct a press conference that afternoon at three o'clock. Rutledge added a little teaser announcing, "the purpose being to report a significant development in the Ocean Club shootings," knowing that was sure to pack the room.

And sure enough, it was packed. And latecomers were even turned away after it was observed that there were already too many people in the room, which was a violation of the fire code allowing a maximum of two hundred people in the reception area of the police station. In front of the police station on North County Road a throng of cars and news vans double parked and took handicap spaces, which kept the squad of meter maids busy issuing tickets and calling a towing company to haul away the offending vehicles.

The press conference began with Rutledge making an announcement that the body of an escapee from a Miami mental institution had been discovered and was a presumed suicide. There was a triumphant tone in his voice as he said the man's name was Marlon Celestine, and then added that Celestine confessed to the Ocean Club murders in a suicide note. But Rutledge then emphasized, as he had discussed with Chase, Crawford, and Ott, the case was not officially closed as the homicide detectives on it felt that there were still some "loose ends" that needed to be tied up.

"These 'loose ends' you mentioned," the question came from a reporter of the local CBS affiliate, "care to elaborate what they might be?"

"Yes, and why would there be any loose ends when you have a suicide note confessing to the murders?" a woman crime reporter from the *Palm Beach Post* asked.

Rutledge glanced at Crawford who took a step forward. "For the simple reason that we have at least one other possible suspect who we haven't completely eliminated."

"But what more than a confession do you need?" the woman crime reporter followed up.

There were a flurry of nods.

"Put it this way, I've heard of, and even personally come across, written confessions that were bogus or doctored before," Crawford said.

"Are you saying that's the case here, Detective?" another reporter asked.

Crawford remembered seeing the man on CNN.

"No, I'm not," Crawford said. "My partner and I are just trying to cover all our bases."

"Any other questions?" Rutledge asked.

"So, Marlon Celestine, I remember that name," another woman asked who Crawford remembered seeing on the local news. "Wasn't he the man who assaulted and injured all those people at The Square in West Palm five years ago?"

Ott fielded this one. "Yes, ma'am, he is."

"Because I covered that and, as I recall, he targeted just women. Isn't that the case, or don't you know?"

"I believe you're right. Yes ma'am, that's my recollection, too," Ott said, as Crawford nodded. "And I think I can see where you're going: the Ocean Club shooter killed two men and a woman and injured one woman and four men. So, obviously, he didn't target women exclusively this time. So, the honest answer is that we don't have an explanation for that."

"Because, as I recall," the woman continued, "after those knife attacks it was concluded, or at least hinted at, that this man, Celestine, was a misogynist, since all his targets were women."

"I think you might say that was theorized, not necessarily decided for certain, because my reading of the case was that he never came right out and said he was a misogynist and targeted women. Celestine, that is," Ott said.

Crawford nodded, impressed at his partner being so fast on his feet.

"So bottom line it for us, Detectives," said a reporter from the *Glossy*, who Crawford knew to be somewhat of a wiseass and know-it-all, "are you saying the case is, what? Ninety percent solved? Ninety-five percent solved? What?"

Dick, thought Crawford, letting Ott take that one since he was on a roll. "I'd say, give us just a little bit more time to be at hundred percent."

Crawford read Norm Rutledge's face, which virtually broadcast the fact that he was starting to feel uneasy. Sweating a little too. His detectives were walking a fine line between being certain they had their killer and having niggling doubts about it, despite the dead man and the suicide note.

"Okay, everyone," Rutledge said. "Thanks for coming today and, of course, we'll keep you informed of all developments."

And with that, he strode purposefully away from the Klieg lights and microphones.

Crawford had to hand it to him: when Rutledge wanted to end something, he ended it.

THIRTY-SIX

After the press conference ended and everyone left, a lot of the attendees came charging back into the police station, irate and demanding to know what had happened to their cars or news vans. Bettina, at the reception desk, calmly gave them the phone number and address of the towing company. They stormed out swearing under their breath or, in some cases, at the top of their lungs.

Crawford got a call on his cell phone ten minutes after getting back to his office.

"Hello," he answered.

"Is this the detective?" a voice croaked.

"Yes, Detective Crawford, who's this?"

"It's Marvin...Marvin the homeless dude you met."

"Sorry, Marvin, where'd we meet?"

"You know, up on Dixie, where we sleep under the stars...or sometimes the frickin' rain."

"Oh, yeah, I remember now," Crawford said, recalling when he went up to where homeless people were sprawled out on the sidewalk under a building overhang. He had tasked them to call him if Marlon Celestine returned there again. "So what's up, Marvin?"

"Well, so you said you'd pay a hunnert bucks if we told you that guy came back, 'member?"

Crawford felt a tug in his gut. "Yeah, sure, I remember. Did he?"

"You gonna give me a hunnert?"

"Yes, I will. Did he come back?"

"Sure did."

"When?"

"Yesterday."

"What time?"

"Inna afternoon. Around two or three."

"Well, why didn't you call me right away?"

"Well…I…"

"Listen, Marvin, I'm coming up there right now. So don't move."

"I, I'm not there, I'm at a pay phone."

"Okay, go back to your place right away."

"Okay, okay, I will."

"I'll see you in a few minutes." Crawford said and clicked off.

He practically ran down to Ott's cubicle. Ott was on the phone. "Come on," Crawford said.

Ott, surprised, looked up. "Gotta go," he said and clicked off.

"We're goin' to West Palm," Crawford said. "I'll explain in the car. Take the north bridge."

They ran to the Vic. As usual, Ott was faster. They jumped in, Ott started the engine and, tires squealing, pulled out onto South County Road.

"Celestine showed up at that homeless place on Dixie yesterday afternoon," Crawford said as Ott headed to the north bridge over to West Palm.

"Holy shit, musta been right before he offed himself," Ott said.

"If he did."

"I hear ya," Ott said, crossing the bridge at what could have been deemed a dangerously high rate of speed.

Three minutes later he skidded up to the homeless place, and they both rushed out.

Three men and a woman were all leaning up against the outside wall of an abandoned building, half on the sidewalk. One white guy, two Black guys and a Black woman. There was a ratty-looking sleeping bag, circa twenty years ago, a tattered army blanket, a bottle of half-drunk Night Train Express wine, two empty plastic water bottles, and a beat-up red bike, for decor. Looking closer, Crawford spotted a tiny mutt—maybe a poodle, or Havanese or Schnauzer mix—being petted lovingly by the woman.

"Hey, where's Marvin?" Crawford asked.

"He went out," said the woman.

"To make a call," said the white guy.

"What can we do you for, Detective?" one of the Black guys asked.

"Okay," Crawford said. "Marvin called me ten minutes ago and said that guy Marlon who we've been looking for showed up here yesterday."

"Gets confusing…Marvin and Marlon, huh," the Black woman said with a smile that highlighted a gold front tooth.

"Here he comes now," the white guy said, pointing to Marvin walking toward them. Seeing them, he broke into a trot.

"Wow, you boys got here fast," Marvin said. "Got my hunnert?"

Crawford pulled out his wallet and opened it. "All I got is sixty," he said to Ott as he handed Marvin three twenties.

Ott pulled out his wallet and dug in. He handed Marvin a twenty and two tens.

"All right, Marvin, talk to us," Crawford said.

"Okay, well like I said the guy you were looking for showed up yesterday"—he glanced at the four others—"when was it, like two or three o'clock?"

The Black woman shrugged. "How the hell would we know, none us got a watch."

"Okay," Marvin said, "well, I could tell by the sun, it was about two or three—"

"Anyway?" Ott said impatiently.

"Anyway," said Marvin, "so Jo-Jo called this other guy to tell him this Marlon cat was here—"

"Whoa, whoa, wait a minute!" Ott said, looking at the other man. "Who's Jo-Jo?"

"And who's this 'other guy'?" Crawford asked, getting in Marvin's face.

"Jo-Jo ain't here," Marvin said. "He's down at the recycle place, getting money for his soda cans."

"Okay, so who did he call?" Crawford asked again.

"Like I told ya, this other guy," Marvin said.

"Marvin," Crawford said, raising his voice, "who is 'this other guy'? We need to know."

Marvin held up his hands. "See, what happened was right after you came here and offered a hunnert to call if Marlon came here, this other guy came along right after you left, parked over there, and asked us why you were here, what you wanted."

"And blabbermouth Jo-Jo says you were looking for a guy named Marlon," the white guy said.

"So this other dude says, 'I'll give you fifty bucks if you call me instead of the cops if Marlon shows up.'"

"I go, 'c'mon, man, make it worth our while,'" Marvin said. "The cops offered us a hunnert if we called and told 'em he was here."

"So the guy goes, 'okay, I'll give you two hunnert if you call me first if Marlon shows up.'"

Crawford let out a long sigh. "So you called him first? Before me?"

Marvin nodded.

"And he came?" asked Ott.

Marvin nodded. "Right away."

"And, I'm guessing, he took Marlon with him?" Crawford said. "Probably told him he had a nice place for him to stay? Something like that?"

"Yup. How'd you know?" Marvin said.

"Lucky guess," Crawford said. "So for our hundred bucks, I want a *very* accurate description of what this guy looked like."

"And what kind of car he drove," Ott added.

"Okay," Marvin said, "well, he had kind of blond hair, kind of on the long side. A little like you. Um, and as I remember blue eyes—"

"No, green," said the Black woman.

"Okay, green then, probably about your height," Marvin said to Crawford.

"Any tats or scars, or a facial growth, a mustache, a beard, what?" Ott asked.

"Nope, nope and nope," Marvin said. "Clean-shaven dude."

"Kind of a pretty boy," added the Black woman. "Kind of a Fancy Dan, too, if you know what I mean? Expensive clothes, shoes with buckles on 'em or some shit."

Ott was taking notes on his ancient leather pad. "What else? His car?"

"It was white."

"SUV, sedan or what?" Ott asked.

"A white Mercedes sedan, I think."

"No, it was a Lexus," the Black woman said.

"Girl knows her cars," said Marvin with a shrug.

"Well, hell, we look at 'em drive past all day," the Black woman said.

"What else?" Crawford said.

"That's about it," Marvin said.

"You're forgetting the most important thing," said the Black woman, stroking the dog's head.

"Whazzat?" said Marvin.

"Dude's English accent."

THIRTY-SEVEN

Crawford and Ott were on their way back to the station.

"So, question is, who's the limey?" Ott asked.

Crawford was scrolling back on the photos on his iPhone. "You know how I said there was something else in the suicide note that bothered me, beside the fact that the guy seemed to have it out for rich people, instead of women, who Celestine seemed more likely to single out?"

"Yeah, you never said what it was," Ott said.

"Because I wasn't sure it meant anything…here it is," Crawford said pointing at a photo of the suicide note, "he spelled behavior, with a *u*. English people spell it b-e-h-a-v-i-o-u-r."

"Yeah, you're right. They do that with a lot of words. Like favorite…f-a-v-o-u-r-i-t-e and color, c-o-l-o-u-r."

"Exactly."

"So that confirms it, the writer's a Brit. Killed Celestine to take the heat off himself, even though we were never looking at a limey. Thing is we got more than a few of 'em in town, or at least ones that affect English accents."

"True," Crawford said, "but I've got a pretty good idea who it might be."

"Who?"

"I gotta check out a few things first. No point in spinning our wheels if I'm off base."

*****

The first thing Crawford did when he got back to the office was call Dominica. He asked her if she could come to his office and she said she had to wrap something up, give her twenty minutes.

He waited for her with anticipation, going through the conversation he had had about two weeks ago with her. Actually, it was the day of the Ocean Club massacre.

After what seemed more like an hour, Dominica appeared. He was tapping a pen on his desk as she walked in. She was wearing a short beige skirt and a blue silk top, her thick, dark hair encircling her jutting cheekbones and stunningly beautiful face.

She walked in and pointed at his face. "Oh, I know this Charlie…nervously tapping his pen. You have something you either want to get off your chest or are dying to hear some insights I might have," she said with a knowing smile. "Which is it?"

He laughed. "Who's the detective here?" he said. "It's the latter."

"Insights. Okay, what do you want to know?"

"So the day of the murders at the Ocean Club, you stopped by and asked me to look into an English guy named Alastair…"

"Christopher."

"Right and I said I would, but then the murders put everything else on the back burner."

"Yes, including the dinner that night that got cancelled, I was going to make you one of my specialties."

"Which you'll recall we had later on."

"Oh, you mean, the night you bailed on me."

Crawford laughed. "So tell me more about Alastair?"

"Can I ask a question first?"

"Yeah, sure."

"Why do you want to know about him?"

"It's kind of a long story, but—"

"Okay, you don't need to tell me now," Dominica said. "So about Alastair...he comes across as very slick and charming, but something bothered me about him. I told you how when me and Rose were at LoLa and his eyes kept scanning the room, like maybe he wanted to upgrade, spot something better than me and Rose."

"Impossible."

"Thank you, Charlie," she said. "Talk about slick and charming. Anyway, I just—well, after that creep that Rose went out with—"

"The married creep."

"Exactly, after him, I wanted Rose to find the right guy, and I guess my gut told me Alastair wasn't him. And, turned out, my intuition was right."

"You mean, 'cause he beat her up that time?"

Dominica laughed. "Yeah, exactly. Plus, I got the sense he was kind of shaky financially, looking for a woman with money. And since then, I've heard more things about the guy."

"Like what?"

"Well, for starters, he was having an affair with one of your victims before Rose."

Crawford's eyes got big. "Wait, Lauren Faircloth, you mean?"

"Yes, exactly. The very married Lauren Faircloth."

"Oh, man, I know the whole story," Crawford said, excitedly. "Heard it from David Balfour, except he didn't know who the guy was. She was actually going to dump her husband and marry the dude. Which meant she'd lose a pretty sizable pre-nup, which, David said, she was thinking of doing anyway. But then she found out Warren had prostate cancer, so she figured she'd hang in there until he died. Then, after that, marry this guy, whose identity, like I said, David didn't know."

Dominica nodded. "It was loverboy Alastair with the nice dimple."

"So you're saying Lauren Faircloth dumped him?"

"Yup."

"Wonder why?"

"David didn't know?"

"I'll ask him again. Maybe it's leaked out by now."

Dominica smiled at Crawford. "So even though Marlon Celestine left that suicide note, you're looking at Alastair as the possible Ocean Club killer?"

Crawford nodded. "Yeah, could be. But at this point I don't have nearly enough proof," he said. "I do think, though, that he and I should have a little chat."

"Find out why Lauren Faircloth dumped him, maybe?"

"Among other things. But I'm thinking I better know the answer before I talk to him," he said, then smiling at Dominica. "As always you've been a fountain of information. Thanks. Oh, one last thing, can you ask Rose for the guy's number?"

"Sure will. I'm sure she still has it."

"Thanks."

She got to her feet. "You're very welcome. Just remember that dusk-to-dawn promise of yours as soon as you wrap this thing up."

THIRTY-EIGHT

Then they got lucky. And the timing couldn't have been better.

Crawford got a call on his cell.

"Detective Crawford?"

"Yes."

"Hi, it's Tim Cutter, head of Membership at the Ocean Club, remember me?"

"Yeah, sure Tim, how's it going?"

"Well, remember we had that conversation—that off-the-record conversation, I should remind you—about people who we turned down for membership at the Club?"

"Yeah, sure, I remember."

"And how I couldn't remember who the other guy was?"

"Yup."

"Well, I remember now because I saw him across the room at BrickTop's"—a Palm Beach restaurant—"and it jogged my memory. It was a British man named Alastair Christopher."

It hit Crawford like cold water splashed in his face.

"Really?" Crawford said. "Do you remember why you turned him down?"

"I sure do. One of our members found out in the due diligence, which we always do, that he embezzled money from his grandmother in England, by forging something in her will, and his British employer found out about it and fired him. I just thought you'd like to know, and I hope it goes without saying, we never had this conversation."

"Don't worry, I won't tell a soul…well, except my partner," and with that, Crawford hung up and put in a quick call to Ott to come to his office.

*****

"That's incredible timing," Ott said, high-fiving his partner after Crawford delivered his bombshell. "It's about time we got a break on this damn thing."

Crawford nodded.

"So how do you want to proceed?" Ott asked, putting his leg up on Crawford's desk.

"Well, we talk to him, for starters."

"Yeah, but how do we play it?"

"We keep it casual, 'cause at this point we got nothing to convict him," Crawford said. "By now, everyone and their mother knows what happened to Celestine and probably assumes that's it, case closed. So we lead in by saying to Christopher, we're just trying to wrap up a few loose ends, speaking to everyone we can who either knew one of the vics pretty well, worked at the Ocean Club, or might have known our suspect, Marlon Celestine."

"So do we let the cat out of the bag, say we know he was banging Lauren Faircloth and got dinged by the Ocean Club?"

Crawford laughed. "I love it," he said. "If there's a way to describe something in the cheesiest way possible, you'll find it."

"Why, thank you, Charlie."

"And yes, I think we tell him that we know about that. I'd say we don't lead with it but in the course of the conversation spring it a little later."

"I agree, just kinda…slip it in there"—Ott laughed at what he had stumbled onto—"just like ol' Alastair did."

Crawford ignored that. "I've already got Bettina on the case, tracking down Alastair, finding out where he lives, trying to piece together his backstory," he said. "Also Dominica is having Rose call me with Alastair's number. She also told me about one time when she was with Rose and Alastair at that bar LoLa and how Rose kept going on about us, how we're the greatest homicide guys in the world. Never had a case we couldn't solve, and blah, blah, blah."

"Good to hear," Ott said, with a thumbs-up, "but what's your point?"

"That maybe…who knows, maybe Alastair followed us around, looking to see who we were after, what suspects, I mean, so maybe he could try to frame one of them—in this case, Celestine."

"Oh yeah, I see what you mean. That's a damn good theory. So maybe he was following you when you went to that homeless place on Dixie."

Crawford nodded. "That's exactly what I'm thinking," he said. "Now, as far as motive, I'm going to take a guess that when Alastair got *dinged* by the Ocean Club, that might have had something to do with Lauren Faircloth cutting him loose."

"Another good theory, and maybe why the two other vics who got killed were on the Membership Committee with her," Ott said.

Crawford pointed at Ott and nodded. "I was just going to say that…but they're all just theories, we got a long way to go from theories to definitive proof," he said, tapping his pen on the desk again. "I didn't tell you about this guy I spoke to who was…speaking of definitive, a definitive expert on mass murders along with a bunch of other related things. Anyway, I got the sense the guy really knew his stuff, not like some long-winded bullshitter, and he said one of the most common things that sets off a mass murderer is called a *life crisis*. Which is just like what it sounds like. So it looks like our boy Alastair had a couple of 'em at the same time."

Ott was nodding now. "Ocean Club committee blackballs him. That hurts bad. But when his girlfriend dumps him over it, it's bad to worse. That on top of it all, further back, him getting fired from his job in England for trying to rip off his grandmother."

"In a lot of cases, just one can be enough to drive a guy over the edge. This expert also said something that I thought nailed it…something about how some people go on sudden killer rampages when 'their circumstances overwhelm their coping mechanisms.'"

"Huh, sounds about right," Ott said. "And some people are just born evil."

"Yeah, well, there's that too."Crawford nodded. "And every single dead victim had something to do with the failures in Alastair Christopher's life."

"But one question I have," Ott said, "is how he knew all the vics were going to be at the Ocean Club at the same time."

"That's a damn good question," Crawford said. "I'll give Delbert Roth a call. Maybe he'll have some idea."

Ott let out a long sign. "He's the guy, Charlie. He's *definitely* the guy."

"Yeah, I think so too, but how are we ever gonna prove it?"

THIRTY-NINE

Rose got back to Crawford while Ott was still in his office. She gave him the information he requested. One was Alastair's phone number and the second was his address.

"What do you want this for?" she asked.

"Just trying to wrap up a few loose ends on the Ocean Club investigation," Crawford said.

Rose was silent for a moment. "Charlie, Charlie, Charlie...I know you're bullshitting me, and there's nothing worse than try to bullshit old Rose."

He laughed. What else could he do?

"Okay, Rose, so if you ever had to keep something completely quiet, strictly between us, this is it. I'm not gonna give you any of the *hows* or *whys* but we're looking at him as a suspect in the Ocean Club murders."

"Get out of here, seriously?" she said. But then: "Well, he certainly has a violent side."

"That's all I'm going to tell you, but once we've wrapped up the case, I'll give you all the sordid details. But you absolutely have to keep this—"

"Charlie, relax. I walk around every day with a huge headful of secrets. You don't think in the real estate business I hear everything there is that's floating around out there? Your secret is safe with me."

"I know that," Crawford said. "So I'm sure you heard about the connection between Lauren Faircloth and Alastair?"

"Now I do. I found out about it a little while ago. Apparently I caught him on the rebound."

"After what he did to you, you're so better off," Crawford said. "What can you tell me about him?"

"Oh, Christ, do I need to dredge it all up?"

"Just some, you know...general impressions."

She sighed. "Okay, my first impression was he was a real dreamboat: a great-looking guy with nice manners and dreamy eyes, and, of course, that English accent that all women fall for. Second impression after we went out: a little...moody, sometimes a little demanding, and completely self-absorbed; third impression: strictly out for himself, sometimes rude, sometimes arrogant...at that point I was thinking seriously about bailing. What am I up to?"

"Fourth impression."

"Oh yeah, fourth impression: mean, with a cruel streak, and, God forbid, violent."

"Really? How so? Besides when he hit you that time?"

"Well, he played rugby with these guys—mostly English guys and, I guess, some Irishmen—at this park in West Palm some weekends. Anyway, I was there watching this one time—talk about a dumb sport—and Alastair at one point just hauled off and slugged this guy on the other team in the mouth. Then they really went at it, I mean a full-scale brawl until the others broke it up. The other guy was bleeding and had to go to Good Sam."

"Jesus, you're kidding."

"No, coincidentally that was the night he beat me up, not to mention my last date with him," Rose said.

"Not soon enough, huh?" Crawford said. "So that address you gave me for him on South Ocean Boulevard. I noticed that's just a little north of the Ocean Club. Whose house is it, where he's staying?"

"This South African friend who works up in New York. I don't think he's been down here for a while. Alastair's just kind of house-sitting. I don't think he pays the guy anything."

"Pretty good deal, huh?"

"That's for sure. Another impression: he's very cheap…or maybe just broke," Rose said. "Thank God he's way back in my rearview mirror. So now, of course, Dominica is on the case, trying to find another guy for me. But, at the moment, I'm kind of off guys. I'm thinking of going to the dog pound and finding a nice mutt just starving for affection."

*****

Crawford dialed Alastair Christopher's number, having given a lot of thought to what he was about to say.

A man with an unmistakable British "hullo" answered.

"Hi, is this Alastair?" Crawford asked.

"Yes, it is," he said, "but I don't recognize your voice."

Crawford suddenly got the British accent thing. How it gave the man a head start with women. He could hear the charm too.

"My name is Detective Crawford, I'm with the Palm Beach—"

""Yeah, hi, Charlie. I know all about you. You go out with that luscious Dominica."

"Yes," he said, eager to move past his personal life, "I'm one of the detectives on the Ocean Club murders and we're trying to wrap up the investigation with the last of our interviews. Could I schedule a quick Q & A with you? It won't take long at all."

"Why me?" The charm remained but it had faded.

"Well, because we know about you being friends with Lauren Faircloth and we're talking to everyone we can who either were relatives of the victims or friends of theirs. It's just normal protocol."

"But I don't understand what's left to do. The man who did those horrible things killed himself and left a note."

"This is just standard procedure for all our cases," Crawford repeated. "It won't take much of your time at all."

Alastair sighed. "All right," he said. "I don't see what harm it can do. When would you like to have this…interview?"

"As soon as possible," Crawford said. "Either you can come to the police station on South County or I'm happy to come to you."

"All right, why don't we do it this afternoon at, say, one or two. I'll come to you. What's the address there?"

"It's 345 South County."

"All right, see you at two."

*****

Crawford and Ott went to lunch at their favorite spot in Palm Beach. Well, one of the few spots they could afford—Green's Pharmacy and Luncheonette. Crawford had his usual: sardine platter with egg wedges and tater tots. The sight of the smelly little fish always made Ott gag, which was part of the reason Crawford ordered it. Ott went with the Philly Cheese steak bomb and Crawford shot him a variation on his usual comment: *Can never get enough cholesterol, can ya, Mort?* Nowadays, Ott ignored him altogether, or pointed at his puny garden salad, which, he argued, transformed the whole meal into something healthy.

"So did he sound the least bit nervous?" Ott asked.

"He sounded totally cool," Crawford said, "which Rose told me is the first impression he creates."

Ott nodded after he sipped his milkshake. "Then it goes downhill from there?"

"Yup, exactly," Crawford said. "So I don't think we good cop, bad cop him, just act friendly and like all we're doing is checking one of the last people off our list."

"Okay, then what? How we gonna reel him in?"

"Well, at some point I think we're gonna want to get a warrant to search that place where he's housesitting. But we're not there yet."

"To find the Steyr AUG?" Ott asked.

"To find anything. The tennis whites, the floppy hat, the shades. We got pretty good shots of all those things on the Ocean Club cameras and if we find them we're halfway home."

"What if we don't find anything?"

"Then…I don't know," Crawford said. "I also want to see if he's driving a white Lexus. I'll get Bettina to check DMV."

"Why didn't you just ask him?"

"Because that might tip him that we're looking at him. I want it just to seem like this is SOP in wrapping up murders. Knowing everything there is about the vics, in this case."

Ott nodded. "Got it. Make it seem he can be useful and maybe provide information about Lauren Faircloth?"

"That's it," Crawford said. "Did you hear back from Mars or Whittaker whether they found anything on any security cams up at the north end?"

"No, nothing."

"I guess that means they didn't. Which means we've got to get our people to look at every camera along the route from where Alastair picked up Celestine at the homeless place to where we found him. That's probably about five miles…we should find something on at least one of 'em."

"All we need is him driving the white Lexus and Celestine in the passenger seat," Ott noted.

"That would go a long way," Crawford said as his sardines arrived.

*****

Crawford and Ott were back at the station after their lunch when Crawford's in-house phone rang.

It was Bettina, at the front desk, whispering. "Wow, who is this dreamboat?" she murmured, using the exact same word Rose had used.

"Alastair Christopher, you mean?"

"Yes, I just sent him back to you."

"Thanks, Bettina."

Crawford called Ott and told him Christopher was on his way.

As, he clicked off, he heard a "Knock, knock," then the handsome face of Alastair Christopher appeared. "Detective?"

Crawford stood up behind his desk as Alastair walked in and put out his hand. "Yes, hi, Mr. Christopher, thanks for coming." He pointed to a chair facing him.

"Please, call me Alastair," he said, sitting.

Crawford nodded. "My partner's going to be joining us," he said, and just then Ott walked in.

"Hi, Mort Ott," he said shaking Alastair's hand and sitting next to him facing Crawford.

"Doesn't look much like Sam Spade's office," Alastair said. "Bet you don't have a bottle of whiskey in one of your drawers?"

Crawford laughed. "No, and nobody's ever confused me with Humphrey Bogart."

"Or Clive Owen," Alastair said.

"Who?"

"He plays a retired Sam Spade, living in France, past his prime," Alastair said.

"Oh, yeah, I heard about that one," Crawford said. "So, Alastair, we're looking into whether the man presumed to have killed the three people at the Ocean Club and left the suicide note specifically targeted his victims. Since you were a friend of Lauren Faircloth, do you know of any connection she might have had with Marlon Celestine?"

"Good God, no," Alastair said. "What possible connection could there have been?" What I've read they certainly traveled in…rather different circles, shall we say."

"So she never mentioned his name to you?" Ott asked.

"Certainly not," Alastair said. "I thought those killings were a random act. Of that psychopath?"

"Well, probably," said Crawford. "What about Jeff Fisk and Roland Embry?"

Alastair's head jerked back almost imperceptibly.

"Did Mrs. Faircloth know them or were they friends of hers?"

Alastair shrugged. "I don't know those names. Are they the other victims?"

"Yes," said Ott, "their names were in all the papers."

Alastair didn't respond at first. Then: "Sorry, just didn't ring a bell."

Crawford shot a quick glance at Ott, then back to Alastair. "Just curious, how did you meet Lauren Faircloth?"

"I'm not sure how this is relevant to anything, but it was at Club Colette," Alastair said, "or wait, maybe it was the Carriage House, I'm not sure."

They were two exclusive clubs in Palm Beach that were extremely particular about who they let in.

"Do you live here in Palm Beach?" Ott asked, casually.

"Yes, I'm staying at a friend's house on North Ocean."

"What's the address?" Ott asked.

"Number 745. North Ocean and Fairview."

Ott nodded. "Oh, so near the Ocean Club?"

"Yes, just a little south."

Ott kept nodding. "So, just curious, did you, by any chance, hear the shots? At the Ocean Club?"

Alastair hesitated, then shook his head. "No, I was down at Publix, doing some shopping when it happened."

"Gotcha," Ott said.

"Well, thank you, that's really all we wanted to ask," Crawford said. "We appreciate you coming in. Your help gets us a little closer to completing our investigation."

"Yes, thank you," Ott said.

"You're very welcome," Alastair said with a matinee idol smile. Then to Crawford, "I've heard so much about you and all your exploits."

"Oh, have you?" Crawford said. "From whom?

Alastair's eyes got squinty. "I think you know who…well, good day, gentlemen," he said, getting up and walking out.

Crawford dialed a number on his landline. "Bettina, I need you to see what kind of a car the 'dreamboat' is driving. But don't make it obvious you're checking."

"Got it," she said, lowering her voice, "here he comes."

Crawford glanced at Ott. "Saves having to check DMV."

Ott nodded. "Well, we caught him in at least one lie."

"About not knowing Fisk and Embry from the Membership Committee, you mean?"

Crawford nodded as his landline rang. He picked it up.

"That was easy," Bettina said. "He parked right in front. A white Lexus ES350. Want the plate number?"

"Yes."

"25A65N."

"Thanks," Crawford said, clicking off and turning to Ott. "We're getting closer."

"Yeah, one inch at a time," said Ott.

Crawford dialed back Bettina.

"What'd you forget?" she asked.

"I want you to put a full-court press on the 'dreamboat.' Dig up everything you possibly can on the guy, please. Including when he lived in England. Leave no stone unturned."

"Oh also, Bettina," Ott said to the speakerphone. "If there's any way you can do it, check if Alastair used a credit card at Publix while the murders were taking place."

"Will do."

Crawford added, "He could have used cash if he actually went there," he said to Ott, "but it's worth a shot."

"Okay," Bettina confirmed, "one dreamboat dossier, coming up."

FORTY

"Don't you think we need to talk to Rutledge about all this?" Ott asked.

Crawford stood to leave. "I was just going to say that. Come on, let's go."

They passed Dominica on the way. "Where you boys headed?"

"Numb Nuts's place of business," Ott answered.

Dominica grinned and walked away in the opposite direction.

Rutledge was sitting in his office, staring into space. Some might deduce he was deep in thought about one of the cases under his jurisdiction, but Crawford guessed he was fantasizing about Ida, the motorcycle cop he was not so discreetly seeing on the side.

"Got a minute, Chief?" Crawford asked.

"Sure. What's up?" Rutledge said, putting his feet up on his desk.

Crawford and Ott sat down facing him.

"We want to talk to you about the Ocean Club killer," Crawford began.

"He's dead."

"Well, we're not so sure about that. He may well be very much alive," Crawford said and Ott nodded.

Rutledge's frown was immediate. "What the hell are you talking about?"

"This is gonna take a while," Crawford said, leaning back in his chair.

And it did. About Alastair's relationships with Lauren Faircloth and also with Membership Committee members Jeff Fisk and Roland Embry.

About their near certainty that Alastair had picked up Marlon Celestine at the place on Dixie where the homeless people lived, who themselves had identified Alastair's car as a match to the one he picked up Celestine in. About the suicide note and the British spelling of the word *behaviour*. About the simultaneous life crises—losing Lauren Faircloth and his membership bid—that, they suspected, might have driven Alastair over the edge. And finally, how Alastair had in person falsely denied knowing who Jeff Fisk and Roland Embry were, while confirming some degree of relationship with Lauren Faircloth.

There was more, Crawford assured Rutledge, they just hadn't uncovered it all yet.

In response, Rutledge asked one of his favorite questions: "So where's the smoking gun?"

"We feel that we've got almost enough circumstantial evidence to charge him with it," Crawford said.

Rutledge shook his head and sniffed. "The words that jumped out at me there were, 'almost enough.' As in, 'we almost got the guy by the balls, but not quite.' How do you think this is gonna look if we charge him? Everyone gonna go, 'wait, hold on, what about the guy who killed himself and left the note? That big press conference of yours and everything? You mean you guys screwed up, got it all wrong?'"

"As you'll recall, Norm," Ott said, "we said we believed he was the killer, not that he definitely, beyond a shadow of a doubt, was the killer."

"Yeah," Ott said, "remember that wiseass from the *Glossy* who said, 'So you're ninety to ninety-five percent sure you got him?' Well, turns out it was a lot less."

"You really think people are going to remember anything other than us making a strong case that Celestine did it?" Rutledge asked.

"'Cause if you think that, you're dead wrong. Everyone there, I guarantee you, came away with the sense he definitely did it. No two ways about it."

"Okay, we could debate this all day long," Crawford said. "Instead, can we get a few guys from you to check every security cam between Dixie and Twenty-fifth in West Palm and all the way up to where the body was found?"

"Hell, yeah, take ten guys, I'm not gonna slow you down. If there's something to this Alastair guy, I guess we gotta find it out."

"It would be nice if we got a shot of Celestine and Alastair coming over the bridge together in his car," Ott said.

"Yeah, that might be enough circumstantial evidence to take the guy in, even if it makes us look bad," Rutledge said.

"Okay," Crawford said, standing, "in the meantime we need to fill in a few holes."

"Like what?" Rutledge asked.

"Well, like how Alastair knew all three of his vics were going to be at the Ocean Club at the same time."

"Another thing we gotta do is broaden our search for the Steyr AUG and where it was bought," Ott said.

"Yeah, and include the Ruger 9 that we think Alastair killed Celestine with," Crawford said. "Go to gun shops maybe fifty miles out from here. Not just twenty-five like we did before."

"Those guns are the key," Ott said. "He damn sure didn't get 'em in Britain."

"Yeah," said Crawford. "And we need to look at it the other way around, now, too."

"What do you mean?" Rutledge asked.

"Well, originally we were looking for a sale of a Steyr with a custom stock to our killer."

Norm nodded.

"But one thing about Alastair—he's hard up for cash. He's also not dumb enough to keep those guns around. So *now* we're looking for the place where he sold or pawned off that Steyr AUG and the Ruger pistol."

"Okay," Rutledge nodded firmly. "Pawnshops and gun shops, bigger radius. I'll get the manpower for that too."

"Mort and I will hit some of 'em too, when we can."

"How many more shops is that, you figure?" Rutledge asked.

"I don't know," Crawford said. "Maybe another three, four hundred."

Rutledge shook his head. "Jesus Christ, why the hell do we need so many damn gun shops?"

Crawford glanced at Ott, then back to Rutledge. "That, Norm, is a whole different discussion."

FORTY-ONE

Crawford called Delbert Roth, the manager of the Ocean Club.
"Hi, Delbert, it's Detective Crawford. Got a minute?"
"Yeah, sure, Detective."
"So going along with your bartender's gut that the shooter was possibly targeting his victim," Crawford said, "my question is how would the shooter know that the three victims—Lauren Faircloth, Jeff Fisk and Roland Emery—were going to be there at that moment?"
"But didn't I just read that the official version was that this man Celestine was randomly shooting at people here? Which would, of course, contradict my bartender's observation."
"Yes, it would. But let's just play out what your bartender thought he saw, my question is how would the shooter know his targets were all going to be there?"
"Um, well, this is just pure speculation, but Fisk and Embry played backgammon with each other a lot. And maybe because it was Friday, I don't know, Fisk ducked out of work early to play. As far as Ms. Faircloth goes, I found out she had regular scheduled tennis lessons on Tuesday and Friday and always took a dip in the pool afterwards. Which the shooter would have to know."
"Understand," Crawford said. "Let me ask you this: is it possible that the shooter could have called there and asked if those three were there? Let's say, just before he went there himself?"

"Yes, that is possible. But I don't know if that happened or not. Put it this way, the two women on the switchboard never mentioned that. But I'll ask them."

"Yes, would you, ask them if there was a call to see if those three were there and did the caller have an English accent?"

"I'll speak to them right away," Roth said. "One's on duty now who worked that day, the other's off."

"Okay, I appreciate it, that's helpful," Crawford said. "How's it going at the club anyway?"

"Well, the good news is no other members have resigned and people are beginning to trickle back in. Our dinner reservations are almost back up to where they were before, and the tennis pro said that most players have come back to the courts. But things are still a little bit, um, subdued."

"Understandable. Well, thanks again, Delbert," Crawford said. "If you have any other thoughts, just give me a call."

"I will."

Right after he got into his car he got a call from Bettina. "Well, this is getting interesting," she said. "Alastair Christopher isn't such a dreamboat after all."

"Talk to me."

"So I spoke to Rose first, who told me he worked for Barclays Bank in London. So then I called the main office there and got tossed around to various people, but finally ended up with his old boss. A very nice guy, by the way. He told me to talk to a guy who he called a *constable*—which is British for street cop, I guess—and gave me his number. He wasn't there and I got bounced around a little more and was able to work my way up to an *inspector*—which must be British for detective. Anyway, he put me on with a guy who knew all about Alastair. Get this...Alastair apparently married his childhood sweetheart, who, after five years of marriage disappeared without a trace—like that Robert Durst creep in that documentary who killed all those people. How 'bout that?"

"Doesn't sound like such a dreamboat."

"Yeah, no shit," Bettina said. "Oops, sorry, I should watch my mouth."

Crawford laughed. "Good intel. Keep digging, girl."

"I will," she said. "The cop I spoke to gave me the number of another guy who was even more familiar with the missing wife case, but I haven't been able to track him down yet."

A few minutes after he hung up with Bettina, Crawford got a call from a highly amped-up Ott, who was also driving around to gun shops.

"Jackpot," he said. "I just got a call from Shaw who said a camera caught an image of a white Lexus ES350, plate number 25A65N, going up the Lake Trail with two guys in the car. He couldn't make out the faces, but was pretty sure they could be enhanced and be recognizable."

"He sure about that?"

"Not a hundred percent, but pretty sure."

"All right, I'll see you back here at the station when you get back."

*****

Bettina called Crawford a short time later. "Mort just came in, said to meet him at the crime scene lab. Plus, you're not going to believe what I just found out."

"Okay, you're next after I check out what Shaw came up with," Crawford said, clicking off.

He walked into the crime scene lab and saw Ott, Rob Shaw and Dominica McCarthy hunched over a TV screen.

Ott turned around when he heard Crawford's footsteps. A frown had replaced his amped-up tone from earlier.

"'Fraid we struck out on this," Ott said as Crawford bent over to see the screen. It was frozen on one frame of surveillance footage. "Just two blurry images."

"Is that the best you can do?" Crawford asked Dominica.

"Um yeah, I'm afraid it is," she said. "Sorry, we been working on the resolution and can't make it any better."

"Where's this from?" Crawford asked Shaw.

"A camera at North Lake Way and Miraflores," Shaw answered. "We found a couple of others, but this was the only one that showed a passenger. The other ones just showed a driver and then it got all blurry."

"Did you go all the way up to the end of the island?"

"No, not yet," Shaw said. "We still got a ways to go."

"You need more guys?" Ott asked.

"Yeah, we could use a few more."

Dominica smiled at Ott. "Guess you gotta talk to Numb Nuts?"

Ott laughed, but not with the usual gusto.

"All right," Crawford said. "Well, nice try. We'll get some more guys on the rest of the cams."

*****

Crawford beelined back to Bettina.

"As you were saying?" he said.

"Okay, well, get a load of this: so the other English detective called me back and said that Alastair's missing childhood sweetheart wife had been rushed to some hospital six months before she disappeared and was diagnosed as having poison in her system."

"You're kidding?"

"Nope, then he told me that what came out was that Alastair had a hot and heavy affair with this older woman at Barclays. So I called back Barclays and got a guy who worked with Alastair so I asked him about that. And this guy, not a big fan of Alastair's by the way, confirmed the affair with this older woman and said, get this, she came from a really wealthy family."

"Who's surprised?" Crawford said recognizing the same MO that had led Alastair to try to reel in Lauren Faircloth and Rose Clarke.

"Pretty incredible, huh?" said Bettina.

"Yeah, but hardly a shocker," he said and patted Bettina on the arm. "Great job as always."

Then ten minutes later, another shoe dropped when Delbert Roth called Crawford back.

"Guess what, Detective?" he said, "One of the women who answers our phone said that someone did call the afternoon of the murders and ask if his friends Roland Embry, Jeff Fisk and Lauren Faircloth were at the club that afternoon. But, sorry, he didn't have an English accent."

"Okay thanks, Delbert," Crawford said, assuming that one of the many things Alastair Christopher had mastered was speaking at least a few sentences in an American accent.

He went back to Ott's cubicle and told him what Bettina had found out, along with what Roth had just told him.

Ott nodded wearily. "No question now…now all we gotta do is prove it."

And that, of course, was the hard part.

FORTY-TWO

Later that night, Rose Clarke called.

"Hey, Rose," Crawford said.

"Hi, Charlie," she said. "So since you were inquiring about Alastair Christopher the other day. I thought I'd tell you what just happened."

"About him?"

"Yes, he showed up at my house last night. He had been drinking and was kind of a mess. Anyway, he asked to borrow some money from me."

"Wait, you let the guy in your house?"

"Yeah, I know, I know. I just felt sorry for him, he seemed so pathetic."

"And?"

"You'll be proud of me, Charlie," she said. "Despite the fact that I knew, firsthand, he could be violent, I turned him down cold. Told him to leave."

"Atta girl, well done. What did he say?"

"Well, he cussed me out like you wouldn't believe. Call me a bitch, called me the *C* word, you name it, but finally, I just slammed the door in his face."

"Nice work, I'm proud of you."

"Thanks, Charlie. No more Rose the Soft Touch. Hopefully I've now seen the last of the man."

"I'm guessing you have."

FORTY-THREE

Ott's phone rang at ten thirty that night.

It was Crawford.

"You're not usually a night caller. What's up?"

"Come on, let's go get him," Crawford said. "We got enough on the guy now."

"Whoa, whoa, where are you anyway?"

"The station. I've had a busy last couple of hours."

"What have you been up to?"

"Well, I called up our favorite judge around five this afternoon and asked him to play the par three with me. So an hour later we were out there 'cause if there's one thing he likes it's taking money from me on the golf course. So I played a little worse than usual, then we had a few drinks, then I popped the question."

"Which was?"

"Actually two. Would he give us a warrant to search the place where Alastair stays and would he sign an arrest warrant?"

"So you told him all the circumstantial stuff we have?"

"In vivid detail. Maybe a little exaggeration here and there," Crawford said. "Anyway, he did."

"Gave you both?"

"Yup," Crawford said. "Plus, I got call from Rose who said Alastair who showed up on her doorstep and practically begged for money."

"What did she say?"

"Slammed the door on him and told him to fuck off."

"Good for her. So the guy's desperate?" Ott said.

Crawford nodded. "And what do you do when you're financially desperate?"

"Um, hold up a bank?" Ott said.

Crawford laughed. "Not sure that's a British thing," he said. "You sell assets. And I'm guessing all he's got of value are the Steyr and the Ruger."

"What about the Lexus?"

"Then how's he gonna get around? Plus, Bettina checked DMV and just got back to me, it's a lease."

"So clearly his only play now is to sell the guns?"

"Yeah, definitely. What else has he got?"

"Okay, so what?" Ott said. "We head up there first thing tomorrow morning."

"No, let's make it last thing tonight. Right now," Crawford said. "Never know when the guys gonna get skittish and bolt for England."

"If they'd even let him back."

"Good point, so get ready and I'll come pick you up."

"But, wait a minute. I'm gonna play devil's advocate and put my Numbs Nuts hat on. Where's the—"

"Smoking gun?"

"Yeah."

Crawford said, "Hey look, there are plenty of convictions made with less than what we got. And if we find the Steyr or the Ruger or any of the tennis stuff we got they guy?"

"You sure, Charlie? I—"

"I'll be there in ten minutes."

*****

Crawford picked up Ott at just before eleven. Whatever hair Ott still had left on his head looked more matted-down than usual.

On the ten-minute ride up to the place where Alastair was staying, they rehearsed their lines. They decided Crawford would play the bad cop, even though Ott was dying for the role and he was the one who usually played it. They pulled into the driveway of 745 North Ocean, a smallish, two-story colonial on the ocean at just past eleven fifteen.

Crawford parked his car sideways in front of the two-car garage, just in case Alastair decided to make a run for it at some point. They got out of the car and walked up to the front porch.

Ott laid on the doorbell and, after a few minutes, Alastair came to the door looking disheveled, clad only in white boxers and a T-shirt that said *Giorgio Armani*, his blond locks going in six different directions.

"Jesus, I wake up from a nice dream to you blokes," he said, but the funny thing was, he was smiling.

"Alastair," Crawford held up a warrant, "this is a warrant to search your house. We have another one too, but this will do for now."

"What in God's name—"

"Step aside," Ott said.

"But before we do our search, we want to have another chat with you because we left out a lot of stuff when we met earlier," Crawford said.

"You can't be serious? It's eleven—"

Crawford and Ott walked past him and into the living room, sitting down without asking.

"Come on, sit, let's talk," Crawford said.

"This is so beyond incredible," Alastair said, shaking his head as dramatically as he probably could.

"It gets worse," Crawford said.

Alastair walked into the room, shaking his head and mumbling, "Utterly preposterous. And we got on so well last time. Okay, let's get this ridiculous charade"—which he pronounced *shah-rahd*—"over with so I can go back to my sweet dream."

"Okay," Ott said. "First, a confession, we weren't being entirely straight with you when we met with you earlier—"

"So, for example," Crawford said, "when you told us you didn't know Jeff Fisk and Roland Embry, we knew you were lying. You definitely knew them, since they shot you down when you applied for membership at the Ocean Club. Which we know was a nasty blow since it was at least one of the reasons why Lauren Faircloth cut you loose."

Alastair considered that for a moment. "Oh, so that's the way you're going to spin it."

"And then you jumped to Rose Clarke," Ott said, "a great woman who doesn't always have the greatest taste in men."

Crawford fixed a hardened gaze on Alastair. "And as you know, she's a personal friend of mine, this woman you beat up one night. Like the worthless piece of shit you are," he added. "But wait, there's more: Your childhood sweetheart who you married when you were twenty-five and got bored with a few years later. Or maybe she wasn't rich enough."

"Who went to the British hospital because they found poison in her system," Ott added.

"Gee, wonder how that got there," Crawford said. "Then she later disappeared and was never heard from again. Did you beat her, too, Alastair? Maybe went a little too far and killed her. Took her out in the country and buried in some…bog somewhere?"

Alastair tried to speak but Crawford charged ahead like a runaway freight train.

"Then there was your coworker at Barclays Bank, your very rich coworker. She shot you down too, just like Lauren Faircloth. Not suitable husband material, too many skeletons in your closet, was that it?"

"Okay, maybe we're not being fair," Ott said, doing his good cop thing. "We posed all those questions but never gave you a chance to answer, did we? Answered 'em all ourselves."

"So now it's your turn, Alastair," Crawford said. "We're gonna ask you a few questions and let you answer...take all the time you need. So, first, is a spelling quiz."

"What? Are you completely mad? This harebrained farce of yours is absolutely insane."

Crawford acted like he didn't hear a word Alastair said. "How you do spell *favorite*? As in, what's your favorite...rugby team?"

Alastair was back to shaking his head. "Now I understand. You two just came from a night at some wretched cop bar or something? Looking for a little sport, huh?"

"Come on, Alastair, play along with us," Ott said, "spell *favorite*, please."

He threw up his hands. "Oh, for fuck's sake, f-a-v-o-u-r-i-t-e."

"Very good," Ott said. "And last question, how do you spell behavior?"

"You really are mad, aren't you? B-e-h-a-v-i-o-u-r. Now are we done, and will you please leave?"

Crawford glanced at Ott and smiled. "Yes, we will, sooner or later, but now we're going to move on to the big event of the evening. It's called *find the evidence*."

"Sorry, you don't get to play. You're a spectator now," Ott added.

"Let me see that blasted thing," Alastair said pointing to the folded warrant Crawford was holding up in his hand.

Crawford handed it to him and Alastair gave it a cursory look for a few seconds, then thrust it back at Crawford.

"You got the gist, right?" Crawford said.

"Go on, then, get this damn farce over with!"

They'd talked about cuffing him but decided, *Where could he go?* And besides, the garage was blocked.

They spent forty-five minutes on the downstairs of the house, figuring that the upstairs bedrooms probably had the most promise. Ott also got the key to the Lexus and checked out the trunk and under the seats but found nothing. Then they went upstairs and realized that of the five bedrooms only two were in use. The master bedroom was as neat as could be with a walk-in closet that was half the size of Crawford's entire condo. Pants in one section were hanging side by side, perfectly creased and two inches apart, then in another section, jackets and suits as if right out of a London Jermyn Street clothing store. It didn't look lived in and they guessed it was the bedroom of the absentee owner, not Alastair. Ott decided to look it over anyway.

It was not hard to find the bedroom Alastair was staying in. The bed, which, obviously, Alastair had just crawled out of, was unmade, a drawer was half open, and there were some hangers on the floor of the walk-in closet and a button-down shirt on the floor. Crawford, wearing vinyl gloves, opened the open drawer all the way and saw two stacks of T-shirts. On top was one similar to the black one Alastair was wearing that read *Versace*. This was clearly his bedroom. Crawford inspected the bedroom thoroughly, going through all the drawers as well as the walk-in closet. Alastair was clearly not the neat freak that the owner of the house was, nor did he have the expensive suits, jackets, shirts and pants that the owner possessed. Yet his clothes were a long way from bargain basement either. Crawford noticed several Polo jackets, similar to Crawford's own and he wondered if Alastair also bought them at TJ Maxx.

He hoped to find tennis whites. But if Alastair was a tennis player, he didn't wear whites. There were zero white shirts, white shorts, or floppy white hats of the kind the killer wore. Crawford kept searching but found nothing of interest, no tennis clothes or tennis shoes matching those worn by the killer on the Ocean Club security cameras. Most importantly, no surprise, there was no Steyr AUG or Ruger 9. He was about to leave the room and see if Ott had found anything when he ducked his head into the bedroom's adjacent bath. There he saw a pair of sunglasses with phosphorescent blue lenses on a marble counter next to the sink. They had the exact same shape as those worn by the shooter at the Ocean Club.

He walked quickly to the master bedroom where Ott was finishing up.

Ott looked up.

"I got something," said Crawford.

"Something good?"

"Yup. Come take a look."

Ott followed him into Alastair's bathroom.

Then, seeing the sunglasses, he slapped his partner five.

"All right." Ott said, "so now we got plenty. Let's go cuff the bastard."

But now Crawford was the doubtful one. "Wait a sec," he said. "I don't know if that's enough."

"Christ, man, we got motive, and now we got proof," Ott said. "What more do you want?"

"Okay, hang on, let's walk through it," Crawford said. "We get the homeless guys to testify they saw Celestine get in a white Lexus with Alastair at the wheel, but that's where it ends. No clear shot of Alastair and Celestine driving toward the North End together in the Lexus. And, I think a sharp defense attorney might pick apart those homeless people as being unreliable. Or say something like, 'Okay, Celestine asked him for a ride, and Alastair, nice guy he is, gave him a ride. Is that against the law?' Then, about these"— Crawford held up the sunglasses—"he's gonna say something like, 'There have been—pick a number—half a million pairs of these sold in the last couple years, so just because the shooter in the Ocean Club security cam was wearing a pair, doesn't mean it's my client's sunglasses.'"

Ott slowly shook his head. "Yeah, I see what you mean."

"I mean, it's something, don't get me wrong," Crawford said, again raising the sunglasses, "but not enough."

Ott nodded glumly. "Sounds like what you're saying is only a smoking gun is gonna be *our* smoking gun."

Crawford patted his arm. "Well yeah, pretty much, then the rest is easy. If we find it we got the grooves inside the barrel and the striations on the bullets to match up and we got him," he said.

"Yeah, *if* we find it. A big if."

"Okay, let's take a few shots of these sunglasses where I found 'em on the counter next to the sink here."

Ott took out his iPhone and took pics of the sunglasses where Crawford had put them down.

"That marble top and the faucets are very distinctive," Ott said, as he snapped away. "At least no defense attorney's gonna be able to say they were a plant and were taken somewhere else."

"Oh, I don't know," Crawford said, "he could say we brought 'em with us."

"Well, yeah, I guess he could," Ott said. "So what do we do."

Crawford exhaled long and loud and put his arm on Ott's shoulder. "I fucked up, Mort," he said, lowering his voice. "Too damn eager. A goddamn rookie move. Played our cards too early." Crawford winced. "Nothing else to do but apologize to the guy. We just don't have enough. Say we're sorry, we got the wrong guy."

Now Ott winced. "Even though we're ninety percent sure that scumbag did it?"

"Yup. The good thing is he'll think he's in the clear. That because we didn't find anything, we ruled him out."

"He still might run, though."

"He might, but I doubt it. He's cash poor, for one thing…Still we're gonna need our best guys to keep an eye on him in case he does. Or, if he hasn't sold the guns yet, they tail him to a shop. I'm thinking we get Shaw and Rodrigo again. And you and me, we step it up. That's all we can do."

Ott nodded. "Okay, well, let's go. Put on our best acting job. You know, Sorry Mort and even sorrier Charlie."

They went down the stairs to the living room where, judging from the sounds coming from the TV, it sounded like Alastair was watching porn.

Going down the stairs, Crawford rolled his eyes at Ott. "Typical," he said under his breath.

Alastair saw them coming and hit the clicker. "Are you coppers finally done with this nonsense? Can I go to bed now?"

"Yes, we are," Crawford said, hanging his head, "and we—I—owe you a big apology. We realize we were barking up the wrong tree and are sorry to have bothered you like this. You won't be seeing us again, sir."

"I'm very sorry too," Ott said. "We just…well, what can I say? We messed up."

Alastair's face had brightened to the color of a Red Delicious apple. "So you didn't find anything that'll send me to the gallows?" he said in a tone laden with sarcasm.

"No, sir, not a thing," Crawford said.

Ott couldn't resist adding, "only thing you're guilty of, sir, is being a little messy."

FORTY-FOUR

"Wow, talk about laying it on thick," Ott said as they walked to their car. "You had me believing you were genuinely sorry, throwing in a few 'sirs,' even."

"Yeah, it wasn't easy, though," Crawford said. "I noticed you threw one in, too."

"Just following your example," Ott said, "but you pulled it off better than Brad Pitt."

"Please, Leonardo DiCaprio," Crawford said, "I'm gonna call Shaw first thing in the morning. Get him and Rodrigo to alternate covering the house here just to be safe, in case Alastair didn't buy our act."

"Oh, trust me, he bought it."

"Yeah, I think so, but meantime, we gotta find those damn guns."

*****

Crawford got to the station at eight o'clock the next morning and took a look at the blown-up map he had created with little red dots which indicated where gun shops were located between a twenty-five- and fifty-mile radius from the station.

Ott walked in and saw the map in front of Crawford.

Together they agreed the best use of their time at this point was to join in the search along with the gun expert Nick Boone and the others.

"We gotta just look at it like this: As boring as it is, it's just old-fashioned cop work," Crawford said. "Pounding the pavement, wearing out shoe leather, putting a bunch of mileage on our cars."

"I agree. Do you think there's any chance, if he hasn't sold 'em yet, he'll go to one of the shops where one of the guys has already been?"

"Maybe, but then the gun guys will call us. 'Cause I stressed to our guys to tell 'em how important it was to call us if he did."

"Okay," Ott said, "well, I'm gonna head out now."

"All right, I'm right behind you. I'll start in Lauderdale and work my way north."

*****

They were back in Crawford's office at the end of the day with nothing to show for their efforts, though they had whittled down the gun shop list to ninety-six to go.

"So who's watching Alastair's house now?" Ott asked.

"Rodrigo. He drew the straw for the eight to eight shift, Shaw's got the night shift. They're both pretty good at not getting made."

"You think Alastair's thinking about making a run for it?"

"I don't know, I think he's arrogant enough to think he committed the perfect crime. Us Yanks are too stupid to ever catch him. Besides where would he go?"

"Yeah, even jolly old England doesn't want him," Ott said. "But if he did make a run, what do you think, just jump in his Lexus and go? Or hop a plane. Or a bus, maybe? Though he doesn't strike me as a bus guy."

Crawford chuckled. "What exactly is a *bus guy*?"

Ott pointed at himself. "Me. I'm a bus guy…not a train guy. Although the Brightline's pretty good," Ott said, referring to the newer train line that ran from Miami to Orlando that was a definite step up from older trains. "You, you're a private plane guy. Ridin' around in your rich brother Cam's jet."

Crawford shook his head and rolled his eyes. "I've been on it exactly once. I'm hardly a private plane guy."

"Don't get all defensive. It was meant as a compliment. I mean, wouldn't you rather be a private jet guy than a bus guy?"

*****

Crawford and Ott, along with the other cops they recruited to search for the guns, got an early start the next morning. They planned to be on the doorsteps of the gun clubs when they opened.

By two in the afternoon, Crawford had gone to another eleven places and figured between the five of them trying to track down the guns, they might be done by the end of the day.

At the twelfth gun shop, something caught his attention. It was a flyer attached to a cash register with a piece of Scotch tape announcing the *Palm Beach Gun and Knife Show*. He read on with interest:

Admission Information: $12 Admission Free Parking

Children 12 and under free

Uniformed Law Enforcement Officers—Free

LEO and First Responders not in Uniform $1 off when showing ID

Over 500 tables of Guns, Knives, Safes, Optics, Tactical Gear and accessories for sale or trade. Customers may bring their own (unloaded) guns and gear to sell or trade as well.

Then he saw the event dates: yesterday and today.

He ran out to his Crown Vic, started it up, and jammed his foot down on the accelerator.

FORTY-FIVE

He got to the South Florida Fairgrounds where the gun and knife show took place twenty minutes later. It was just off of Southern Boulevard and the parking lot looked close to full.

He walked up to the gate and took out his wallet to pay. He handed a grizzled man at the ticket window a ten and two singles. The man glanced up at him and said, "Wait, ain't you that detective I read about?"

"I am a detective," Crawford said.

"Keep your money," the man said, waving it away, "it's free for LEOs."

That stood for Law Enforcement Officers.

"Thanks, man, appreciate it."

He walked into the enormous space, which held booths and tables displaying rifles, pistols, and knives as far as he could see. He went up to a man behind a table holding a SIG Sauer, showing it to a customer.

"'Scuse me," he said. "You know where I might find a black and white Steyr AUG A3M1 semiauto?"

"Um, well, I seen a guy walking out of here with one yesterday, 'cept it wasn't black and white," the gun dealer said. "Try that guy over there with the red hat, see him"—he pointed at a man in a red cap and a flannel shirt—"he might have one, or know where to find one. Damn fine piece, that Steyr AUG. Best bullpup you can find."

Crawford remembered Nick Boone's explanation of what a bullpup was the day after the Ocean Club massacre.

Crawford nodded. "Thanks."

He walked over to the man in the red cap and looked down at the display of semiautomatics on the table. He had a CZ Bren, a Ruger Mini-14, something called an FN SCAR 16S, but no Steyr AUG. The dealer looked up. "Help ya?"

Crawford showed him ID. "This is a long shot but I wondered if maybe you bought a black and white Steyr AUG A3M1 from an English guy recently."

"Sorry, man, only Steyr AUG I traded was a tan one to a Black dude 'bout a year ago."

"Anyone else that you know who I should ask?" Crawford asked.

The man pointed. "See that guy over there, bald guy with the beard?"

"Yup."

"Try him."

"Thanks, appreciate it."

Crawford walked over to the man behind the display table and looked down at his table. He had a SIG Sauer MCX, another one called a KelTec SU-16C, but no Steyr AUG. Or Ruger 9, for that matter. "'Scuse me," he showed ID again, "Any chance you bought a Steyr AUG from an English guy recently?"

"Nope. I never bought a gun from any English dude ever." He lowered his voice. "They're all a bunch of pacifists…but try Billy over there. He might be able to help ya."

"The guy in the green shirt and glasses?" Crawford asked.

"Yeah, that's him."

"Thanks," Crawford said, by now getting thoroughly sick of looking at guns both in all the countless shops he'd been to and the vast sea of guns here.

Ten feet away, he brightened because he saw what he thought was a black and white semiautomatic on the table in front of the dealer named Billy. As he got closer he realized it was a dead ringer for the one caught on the Ocean Club security footage.

"You Billy?" he asked.

"Yeah, sure am," Billy said with a smile.

Crawford showed him his badge, low-key. "I noticed that Steyr AUG…did you buy it from an English guy named Alastair—"

"Alastair Christopher. Sure did. Dude's like one of my best customers. I sold it to him about a month ago at my shop, and bought it back a little while ago. He paid twenty-five hundred for it and I bought it back for fifteen hundred."

Crawford was scanning the guns on display. "And that Ruger?"

Billy nodded. "Same guy. Good old Alastair."

"Nice little profit. So, just to be sure, guy's about my height, around forty or so."

"That's him. Not a lot of limeys buying guns like that."

Crawford's cell phone rang. He looked down at the display. It said, *Rodrigo*.

He held up a hand to Billy. "Hey, man, what's up?"

"I got eyes on Alastair Christopher coming out of his house with a big suitcase getting into his white Lexus."

It was uncanny. Almost as if Alastair expected he'd track down the guns by now. They had enough to take him in, but his fleeing would seal the deal.

"Okay, follow him, but stay back so he doesn't see you," Crawford said. "Stay on with me."

"Roger that," said Rodrigo.

Crawford put his hand over his cell and turned to Billy. "Thanks, man," he said. "I'm gonna need you to put these aside and not sell them. And I'll need the paperwork on the buy and sell. And then will you take 'em to the Palm Beach Police station? Don't worry I'll make it worth your while."

He wasn't quite sure how but he would. The man and his guns had just busted the case wide open.

"You got it," Billy said, "I got a buddy there and know exactly where it is."

"Thanks," Crawford said and started running, heading to the parking lot, his cell phone up to his ear. "Still there, Rod?"

"Yeah, he's headed down North Ocean."

"Okay," Crawford said. "I'm heading toward you, ten, twelve minutes away. Sounds like he might be going to the airport."

"We'll soon find out," Rodrigo said.

Crawford called Bettina at the station and asked her to see if Alastair had made a plane reservation. He told her to keep the line open.

A few minutes went by.

"Still on Ocean?" Crawford asked Rodrigo.

"Yup…hang on, he's got his blinker on for Southern."

"Gotta be the airport."

"Wait, he's going around the rotary, I'm on him…oh, shit, he made a full circle…I think he made me, Charlie."

"'Cause you followed him all the way around it?"

"Yup. Now he's headed back up north on Ocean."

"Yeah, must've made you…drop back a little."

"Okay…now he's pulling over."

"Okay, go past him. Turn left on Bellaria or…what's the next one? Clarendon. U-turn and wait for him."

A minute later: "I'm sure he made me," Rodrigo said. "Oh shit, he just went past. He looked over and saw me, he definitely made me now."

"Okay, man, take him!" Crawford yelled, feeling a sudden thumping in his chest and wishing he was in Rodrigo's place.

"You got it."

Crawford heard the roar of the cruiser and Rodrigo's sirens over the line.

"Oh, man, he's not pulling over. He's running."

"Stay on him!" Crawford said. "What's he doing?"

"Just took a left onto Worth, going like a bat out of hell. Fifty or so."

"Just stay with him," Crawford said, amped like he was the one chasing Alastair.

Bettina came back with a succinct message: "Eight thirty flight tonight to Portugal, then on to Morocco."

The speed limit was 25 mph on Worth Avenue, but a lot of drivers poked along at even less. "I'm crossing the Southern Bridge now," Crawford said, "so I'm not far behind you."

"Okay, we're going past the Poinciana Club turnoff on my left now," Rodrigo said.

"Looks like he's…hang on, he's pulling into a parking spot at the end…he's getting out…ran into the real estate office here."

It clicked. That was where Rose worked. The thumping in Charlie's chest became more insistent. "All right, go get the bastard, detain him 'til I get there."

"Will do," Rodrigo said, getting out of his car.

"Oh, my God, here he comes…with a woman. Shit, he's got a knife up to her throat."

"A tall blonde?" Crawford said.

"Yeah, exactly…and he's coming toward me."

*****

Alastair walked straight up to Rodrigo. "Tell Charlie Crawford to call off the dogs or his friend Rose here is going to be bleeding all over my nice white upholstery."

Rodrigo put his hands up. "Okay, okay, I'll let you go, won't follow you," he said.

"Good boy, give me your keys and gun," said Alastair. "Put them on your bonnet."

Rodrigo stared at him, bewildered.

Alastair sighed. "On your hood, dumb fuck. The hood of your car…also, you have handcuffs?"

Rodrigo nodded.

"Those too," said Alastair.

Rodrigo quickly complied while a small group of bystanders looked at the spectacle in horror and disbelief from the street. There were a few gasps and wide, incredulous stares. Real estate agents from Rose's real estate office had come out and were clustered at the door looking terrified at the plight of their coworker.

Alastair maneuvered Rose over to snatch Rodrigo's gun and keys, then pushed Rose into the passenger seat of his car, then ran around the car, and slipped into the driver's seat. In seconds, he was gone.

*****

Crawford heard the whole exchange because Rodrigo had his cell phone on speaker.

"Is he gone?" Crawford asked.

"Yup, just disappeared around the corner at the end of Worth."

"All right," Crawford said. "I'll position Shaw on the other side of the middle bridge, if they come across there. I'm gonna wait here on Southern and see if they come this way."

"So you think they're headed to the airport?"

"I know so. I had Bettina check flights. He's heading to Morocco, which has no extradition treaty with the U.S."

"Oh, shit. No kidding."

"Wish I was."

"What do you want me to do?" Rodrigo asked.

"Nothing. We don't want him making you again. Good job."

"Yeah, but he made me, and once he had the woman I couldn't—"

"Good job," Crawford repeated.

Crawford was parked in a parking lot across from the Bath & Tennis club. He was behind a hedge and was sure that a car turning right after Mar-a-Lago and going across the Southern Bridge had little chance of spotting him. Five minutes later he saw the white Lexus skid around the bend. He pulled out after it went by and let a car get between him and Christopher. He strained to see the license plate, but couldn't. But he was comfortable enough in knowing that the white Lexus was rare in a town full of black Bentleys, Maybachs and Aston Martins.

As the Lexus crossed the bridge, Crawford punched a number on speed dial.

"Hey, what's up?" Detective Rob Shaw said.

"Got our guy two cars ahead of me on Southern. He's got a flight on TAP to Lisbon, Portugal, then on Royal Air Maroc to Casablanca."

"Morocco, huh?" Shaw said, starting up his car.

"You know your geography."

"Seen *Casablanca* a million times. Okay, I'm on my way."

*****

The car in between Crawford and Alastair took a right onto Dixie, so Crawford could see the plate number. It was Alastair all right. Crawford didn't close the distance but waited and let another car cut in between them.

Crawford thought about Rose and was worried. Really worried. Her safety was the top priority. This was a desperate man after all who had killed three times. Quite possibly more. He had nothing to lose if he killed again. He better be prepared to kill Alastair to save Rose, though that was not his preferred scenario.

He hit Rob Shaw on auto dial. "Yeah, Charlie?"

"Where are you?"

"Parked at the entrance to the airport. Where are you?"

"Five minutes away. Here's what I want you to do: When you see him drive in, get behind him. He's only got two options, going into short term parking or dumping his car at Departures. I'm really concerned about the safety of his hostage. If it comes down to it, her safety's more important than apprehending him."

"Roger that."

"Meanwhile, I'm gonna make myself as invisible as possible and try to get him at the TAP counter."

"Gotcha. No way this guy's getting away."

"He has before."

"Ain't gonna happen this time."

*****

Rob Shaw saw the Lexus coming, then Crawford a hundred yards behind it. He slipped in behind the Lexus and followed it down the straight approach to the airport.

Alastair hit his blinker signaling a left turn into short term parking.

Crawford proceeded straight to Departures and parked at the curb. He waved to a nearby traffic cop and pulled out his ID. The cop came over.

"Hey, Detective Crawford, Palm Beach PD. I'm after a fugitive."

"No problem," the traffic cop said. "Hope you catch him."

"Thanks, shouldn't be long."

The cop shrugged. "It takes whatever it takes."

Crawford popped his trunk, went around and grabbed a blue baseball cap he used when he played golf and slipped on his Ray-Bans.

"Disguise?" the cop said.

"Yeah, guy knows what I look like," Crawford said as he ducked inside.

Crawford's mind reeled ahead and thought through the likely scenarios at the airport.

Alastair would walk in, suitcase in hand, Rose by his side, having made it very clear to her that the knife was just a short reach away, and he damn well wouldn't hesitate to use it.

Shaw called him on his cell.

"Yeah, Rob?"

"It's just him walking in," Shaw said.

"Where's she?"

"I don't know. I followed him into short term parking and only he got out," Shaw said.

Crawford was worried what Alastair might have done to her. His mind flashed to half a dozen dark places as he scanned the area for Alastair.

"Go check the car. Right away!" Crawford said.

"On it," Said Shaw. "He'll be there any minute."

"I got him," Crawford said, spotting Alastair. "Make sure she's okay."

Alastair stepped off an escalator, then walked toward the TAP counter. Crawford turned away from him, even though he could see that Alastair was singularly focused on getting checked in then getting the hell out of Palm Beach.

Crawford got twenty feet behind him, pulling his cap down, though he knew Alastair would probably recognize him if he turned. He put his hand on his holstered SIG Sauer inside his jacket, then got closer…ten feet…five feet…then slid the SIG out of the holster and pressed it against the back of Alastair's head.

"Your flight's been cancelled," he said. "Hands up."

Alastair did as he was told, as gasps of surprise and shock arose from the people near them. Others simply stopped in their tracks and watched the drama, which was over in seconds.

"Okay, go out the way you came," Crawford said, shoving him toward the escalator. "If you hurt Rose you're a dead man."

Alastair didn't say a word, just turned toward the escalator and started walking.

Crawford prodded him with his SIG. "Is she all right?"

"She's okay. And from now on I'm gonna let my lawyers do the talking," he said. "They'll sue the hell out of you, the Palm Beach Police Department, and the City of Palm Beach."

Crawford laughed and shook his head. "I've got some bad news for you, my friend, we found your Steyr AUG and Ruger, which your gun dealer buddy Billy sold you, then bought back."

Alastair's only reaction was his face turning a ghostly white.

Crawford chuckled. "That shut you up, huh?"

They got off the escalator and Crawford saw Rob Shaw running toward him.

"She's okay, Charlie," Shaw shouted. "He just cuffed her to the steering wheel of his car."

"If you had touched her," Crawford said from inches behind Alastair's ear, "I'd be dropping you off at Good Sam Hospital."

FORTY-SIX

Rose and Dominica were having dinner with Crawford and Ott at a restaurant in West Palm Beach called the Blue Door. It had a reputation for having great food and bartenders who didn't scrimp on their pours, which made Ott particularly happy. When he wasn't knocking back a Yuengling beer, he much preferred tasting the booze in his cocktails instead of it being drowned in tonic, soda, or some sweet fruit extract.

"Place is jammin'," Ott said, looking around at the people at the surrounding tables, a lot of whom were half his age. At fifty-two, he was also the senior citizen at his table, Crawford being forty, Rose thirty-six, and Dominica, the kid, thirty-one.

"So this was a fix-up, huh?" Ott asked Dominica. "Me and Rose?"

The other three laughed.

"What's so funny?" Ott said, with a straight face. "You don't think I'm worthy?"

"Well, I certainly do," Rose said. "You're not a murderer, like my last BF, or married, like the one before him. Are you, Mort?"

Ott laughed. "None of the above. Just suave, debonaire and, as you can see, incredibly good-looking."

The other three laughed at that.

He added, "And obviously...amusing as hell."

"Obviously," Dominica said with a nod.

Crawford mock-whispered to Ott, "This is your audition, so don't go overdoing it."

"I'll try not to, but as you know I can't always help myself."

"So what do you guys think is going to happen to Alastair?" Rose asked.

"Well, Florida has the death penalty," Crawford said.

"And having committed four brutal murders," Ott said, "he'd be a prime candidate."

Rose shuddered. "I wish I hadn't asked."

"Can we talk about something else, please?" Dominica suggested.

"Sure," Ott said, "how 'bout those Marlins?"

"Is that the football team?" Rose asked.

Ott laughed. "Close. They use a ball."

"Baseball," Dominica whispered to her friend.

Rose nodded.

They had another round and talked about a lot of things: the erratic stock market, the commander-in-chief who lived just down the road, the surging real estate market, and their favorite Netflix shows. They did not return to the subject of Alastair Christopher.

They left at 9:50 in three cars, just as they had come. Ott in his old, but beloved, beater, Rose in her shiny new Audi, and Crawford and Dominica in his four-year-old Lexus that had a ding on the front fender.

Crawford and Dominica took the elevator up to his eighth floor condo in the Trianon building on South Flagler Drive in West Palm Beach. He glanced down at his watch. "You ready?" he asked. "Remember?"

She nodded and gave him a kiss on the lips. "Of course, dusk to dawn. But we're getting a late start."

"That's all right, we'll just extend it a few hours past dawn."

Crawford unlocked the door. "After you, madame," he said, gesturing with his hand.

And those were the last words spoken for a while. Actions speak louder…well, you know.

Dominica unbuttoned her lime-green blouse, pulled it off, and flung it on the floor. Then in one swift flourish she did the same with her bra, tossing it in the air and sashaying across the living room.

Crawford followed suit with his jacket and shirt while Dominica wordlessly undid her short skirt and let it fall down her legs and onto the floor. A moment later, he did the same with his pants. Now they were both down to their underwear as they approached the bedroom.

At the doorway, she turned to him, put one arm around his neck to prop herself up, and, with the other, slid her skimpy black panties down her long, lean legs. He did the same with his boxers, then put both arms around her and they kissed like they'd both been in prison for a hundred years.

They never made it to the bed.

THE END

THE CHARLESTON-SAVANNAH ENIGMA

Exclusive sample

ONE

Billy Wofford was strolling around Colonial Lake in downtown Charleston, South Carolina. He kept looking at his watch because his love.springs.eternal.com date was late. In fact, a half hour late. It was dark now and he was hoping he'd recognize her from the photos, having never laid eyes on the woman in person. He didn't expect it to be difficult, though, as she was a five-foot-ten shapely blond and she said she'd be wearing a short beige skirt and a bright red collared blouse.

She had suggested they meet on the Rutledge Street side of the lake, which looked to be a three-block stretch, so he kept going up and down from Broad to Beaufain and back. He was strolling close to the lake by Trumbo Street when he heard a noise to his left from the water. Then he felt something tight around his ankle. He glanced down and saw it was a hand, a strong hand, then saw a man in the water pulling him toward the lake—now with his other hand around Wofford's other ankle.

"Help!" Wofford cried out, "Help! Jesus Christ help!"

But the man was too strong and there was no one around to help, and the last thing Billy Wofford saw was the flash of a knife, silhouetted by a street lamp, before it entered his chest and he sank to the shallow lake bottom.

TWO

Detective Nick Janzek of the Charleston Police Department was having his morning joe, espresso actually, from Bad Bunnies coffee shop on Spring Street. Every other time he went there he also ordered a bacon and cheddar croissant, which his girlfriend Ryder Farrell, a private investigator from Savannah, said was "to die for." Or maybe she used to say that, because Janzek thought that phrase had already run its course and was now passe. On his non-bacon-and-cheddar-croissant days, he ordered a lemon scone instead, which was almost as good.

As he finished the last bite of his croissant, his desk phone rang.

"Hey, Nick, it's Tommy Haase. I got a pretty grisly scene down here at Colonial Lake. A body just came up to the surface with a knife stuck in his chest."

"Whereabouts on Colonial Lake?" Janzek asked, getting up.

"Can't miss it, the Rutledge side. We got three squad cars here, light bars flashing."

"Be there in five," he said, fast-stepping out of his office.

Five minutes would be pushing it, even though his destination was straight down Lockwood from the Charleston police station. He wheeled up seven minutes later and his partner Delvin Rhett was already there. Rhett was a trim, wiry black man, on the short side, who had recently traded in his thick black Coke bottle glasses for a pair of rimless silver spectacles, giving him something of a scholarly, professorial look, though he probably would not be flattered to hear that. He was in his early thirties and had been pegged 'Urkel' by a traffic cop who liked to dole out nicknames, the reference being to a nerdy kid from a TV series back in the '80's. To his chagrin, the nickname had stuck. He had attempted to counter it by growing a long goatee, which he hoped might add a macho mien, and sprinkling his conversation with street talk, but neither seemed to help much. The nickname was there to stay. Today he wore tan chinos, a blue, long-sleeved, button-down shirt, and a rumpled brown corduroy jacket. Superfly he was not.

"Hey, Del, what we got here?" Janzek asked Rhett, who had been talking to the cop who called it in.

"It ain't pretty," Rhett said, flicking his head in the direction of the corpse under a sheet ten feet away. "Knife between the ribs or he drowned, hard to tell which killed hin."

They walked over to the victim, Janzek peeled back the sheet, and took a close look.

"So what's your guess?" he asked. "Stabbed, then tossed in the water?"

"Yeah, I guess," Rhett said. "It wasn't a robbery 'cause he's got his wallet and a Rolex on him. Name's William Wofford, address is down in Savannah."

"Wonder what he was doing up here?" Janzek said.

"No clue," Rhett said. "And don't know yet where he was staying or anything. I looked for a hotel receipt but nothing."

"He got credit cards?"

"Yup, a Chase debit card and a Bank of America credit card."

"We can check recent purchases with them and maybe get some answers."

Rhett nodded. "I figure there's a pretty good chance he parked somewhere around here."

"Yeah unless he's staying somewhere close and walked or took an Uber."

"True," said Rhett. "I got a couple uniforms looking for cars with Georgia plates in the area."

"Can't hurt. Maybe someone will miss him, call and report it."

Janzek got down in a crouch to get an even closer look at the vic. As he did, his right knee popped from an old football injury when he played wide receiver for Boston College. He looked the bloated body over from head to toe as Rhett watched from above.

"See anything else?" Rhett asked.

Janzek pointed at the victim's right ankle. "Check out those cuts," he said, "really narrow but jagged, like fingernail cuts or something—"then he glanced at the left ankle—"got 'em on both ankles."

"What do you s'pose from?" Rhett asked.

"Who knows? Bloating can deform the wounds, but I'm willing to say they didn't come from that knife."

"Wonder what they were doing here?" Rhett asked. "Wofford and the killer?"

"Beats the hell out of me. Maybe it happened somewhere else and his body got dumped here? Hard to tell. We'll see if the crime scene techs or Brayton have any theories." Neil Brayton had recently come aboard as the new medical examiner for Charleston County. "Anyone call him yet?" Janzek asked. "Brayton."

"Not that I know of. I just got here a few minutes before you," Rhett said.

"I'll call him. He's up in North Charleston, so it'll take him a while to get here."

"I don't mind waiting," Janzek said, "but it's pretty clear there're a hell of a lot of questions nobody can answer."

THREE

After calling the M.E., Janzek glanced over at the corpse again and had a thought. He speed-dialed Ryder Farrell, who lived in Savannah, two hours to the south. He had decided to leave Rhett in charge of the local investigation and all its follow-ups, which they were heading, and go dig around in Savannah, where his victim hailed from.

"Hey, honey," Ryder answered.

"Hey," Janzek said, "I'm looking down at a dead man from Savannah. I know it's a big town, but have you ever heard of a man named William Wofford?"

"No, sorry," Ryder said, "Got an address for him?"

"Yeah, hang on…1111 Priest's Landing Drive."

"Wait a second, that's out on Skidaway Island. At the Landings…where Jackie lives." Jackie was Ryder's older sister and investigative partner. "That's gotta be pretty close to her place. What happened to him?"

"Got stabbed in the chest and was dumped in Colonial Lake."

"Oh my God, that's off of Broad somewhere, right?"

"Yeah, exactly. Looks like he spent the night there, floated up this morning. I think I'm gonna head down to Savannah, nose around, see what I can find out about the guy. Got dinner plans tonight?"

"If I did, I'd cancel them," she said.

"Good answer. Where do you want to go?"

"Well. knowing you're a red-meat kind of guy, we could go to Ruth's Chris or, I don't know, Boar's Head Grill?"

"Yeah, but where do *you* want to go?"

"Oh, Nick, you perfect gentleman you, I'm fine with either steak place or maybe…Alligator Soul or Olde Pink?"

"Let's do Alligator Soul," Janzek said. "Can you book it? Figure I'll get in around six-thirty, quarter of seven."

"Perfect. I'll make a seven o'clock reservation. See you then."

"Oh, and can you give me Jackie's number? I want to see if she knows this guy."

*****

They both arrived at Alligator Soul on Barnard Street at nearly the same time and were seated at a table in a corner. It had more than a two-hour drive because Janzek hit rush hour traffic. He was ready for a cocktail. He ordered a Dewars and water and Ryder a glass of rosé.

When the drinks came, he raised his glass. "To the belle of Savannah. It's been too long."

"It only been a week, Nick."

"That's too long. Two weeks would be *way* too long."

"Well, if you'd just get a private jet…."

He laughed. "I'm workin' on it but it's tough on a detective's salary," he said. "So I had an interesting talk with Jackie on the way down."

"She know your victim?"

"Sure did. Billy Wofford was a regular at the dog park at the Landings. Apparently quite the ladies' man and, depending on what day it was, had different jobs and different girlfriends. He hit on Jackie but I guess he was not her type, even though in her words, he was, 'handsome as hell.'"

"'Was' being the operative word," Ryder said. "Keep going."

"You want to order first?" Janzek asked.

"Sure," Ryder said, taking another look at the menu, "I didn't realize this place was so expensive."

Janzek put his hands on hers. "You're worth it."

"Thank you, Nick, but I'll split it with you."

"Oh, no you won't," he said. "See, I want you to be beholden to me."

"I get it," she said, "so you get an extra long back rub, you mean."

"Exactly. Let's order so I can get tell you what else Jackie told me," he said, giving a little wave to their server.

They ordered and the server took their menus.

"Okay, let's hear," Ryder said, leaning into Janzek.

"The guy's got quite a history. At one point he was a bartender at a place called Vic's."

"Oh, yeah, over on the river."

"And the rumor was that he was dealing coke on the side."

"Really?"

"Yeah, but Jackie wasn't so sure that was true. I guess rumors fly around pretty good at the dog park. She said there were a lot of rumors about this guy. Then fact…or rumor number two is, he had a raging affair with the wife of a guy at the Landings who was the head of some labor union up in Michigan."

"Wonder what a Michigan labor union guy was doing at the Landings?"

"Apparently he spends a couple months there in the winter. Flying back and forth, I guess."

"Hmm, I'd think a labor union guy would be a guy you don't want to get on the wrong side of. Don't they have a reputation for being kind of rough customers?"

"Yeah, some of 'em, I guess."

"Sounds like Billy Wofford maybe liked to live a little recklessly?"

"I know. Dangerously, even," Janzek agreed. "Yet Jackie says, in person, he was the nicest guy in the world."

Ryder shrugged. "Hey, he loved dogs, what more do you need to know?"

Janzek nodded. "But hang on, listen to this. So one day he befriends this little old lady in the dog park, like twenty years older than him. Name was Helen Scotto. And I guess their 'friendship' gets pretty serious, but then, all of a sudden, she dies."

"Oh wow, was there any suspicion of foul play or anything?"

"Not by the detectives who investigated," Janzek said, "but definitely by the woman's son. Plus the son says that his father had a three-million-dollar baseball card collection, which his mother kept hidden in a safe place, which magically disappeared."

"And he suspects Wofford disappeared it?"

"Yup. That his mother told Wofford about it. And, get this, a month after she died, Billy showed up at the dog park in a brand new Bentley."

Ryder nodded. "So I guess that makes the son a prime suspect. 'Cause he thought Wofford maybe had something to do with his mothers death and the missing baseball cards."

"Bingo. Particularly after he heard about Wofford's Bentley," Janzek said. "That might jump him to the top of my list. I already called Delvin and asked him to try to track him down. The son, I mean. Jackie didn't know his name."

"Wow, she had some good info on this guy, Wofford. Anything else?"

"That's most of it. Oh, and one other thing. You ever heard of Wofford College?"

"Sure. It's up near you in South Carolina. Spartanburg, I think it is?"

Janzek pointed a finger at her. "Very good. Anyway Billy Wofford told Jackie once that his great grandfather was its benefactor, the guy who started the college. But Jackie was dubious and found out it was founded around 1850."

"So, you mean, the math didn't work if the college was, ah…over a hundred seventy years old."

Janzek smiled. "Yeah, exactly."

As the food arrived, Ryder said, "It would have had to have been like his…great, great, great, great grandfather."

Janzek nodded. "One other curious thing," he said, "and then let's talk less and eat more."

"Tell me."

"One of the women in the dog park said that when Wofford first came there, I guess like eight or ten years back, he introduced himself as Bobby Watson."

Ryder cocked her head. "That's pretty bizarre. You think maybe she just misheard it?"

"No, because he introduced himself as Bobby Watson to a few other people, too."

"Oh, man, this guy…. You know what, Nick? I think you might need some help on this case."

He laughed. "And I bet, it just so happens, you know the perfect women for the job."

*****

Ryder Farrell had five inches on her sister, Jackie, and dark brown hair and a nicely shaped body from vigorous daily workouts in her gym. As Jackie had once described her sister to a Savannah Investigations client: "She's got an amazing knack for sniffing things out and is persistent as hell. Plus, she can read people like nobody I ever met. I'm damn lucky to have her."

What Jackie was really thinking was that her sister had been nosey since the age of five and was outspoken to the point where folks often wanted to slap her. The "reading people" part was absolutely true and was, in fact, valuable as hell.

Ryder had been born Charlotte Ryder Farrell but didn't think Savannah was ready for a private investigator whose name sounded like a debutante or a lady who lunched. And besides, as Ryder said when Jackie questioned her new handle, "Half the women in the south have last names for first names anyway."

"Oh, yeah, like who?" Jackie had asked.

Ryder had to think for a moment but—English major that she was—came up with Harper Lee and Flannery O'Connor, the latter whom had grown up just down the street on East Charlton in Savannah.

Jacqueline Gardiner Farrell, five-foot-three, was a blonde with striking blue eyes, a dazzling smile and a gym-trim figure. She joked about her parentage, since her father was six-three and her mother was five-ten. Her clothes tended to run somewhat on the conservative side, but watch out: she'd surprise you once in a while with a slit skirt eight inches above the knee and a plunging neckline.

How and why she had started Savannah Investigation…well, that's a long story that can wait 'til later.

*****

It usually started with a back rub.

Janzek and Ryder were in her two-bedroom condo on West Jones Street in Savannah, which many considered to be the prettiest, most historic street in The Hostess City. It featured cobble stone streets, brick sidewalks and white moss- and vine-covered old buildings. Full canopied trees lined the street, keeping it cool and making it a strollers' paradise. Ryder had hit up her father and "mortgaged her soul" to pay for the new place but had never regretted it for a minute.

"Up a little higher," Janzek told her.

"Yes, boss," said Ryder.

"Just below my shoulders."

"I believe you're referring to your latissimus dorsi and trapezius muscles," Ryder said.

"Jesus, you're an anatomy expert in addition to all the rest of your vast knowledge?"

"Yup," Ryder said, "which is why I kick your ass at Jeopardy."

He chuckled. "I let you win 'cause I know you're a sore loser."

"Oh, I see," Ryder said. "Okay, so here's one… Foreign Countries for Two Hundred: what's the capital of…Monrovia?"

He laughed. "I'm not falling for that," he said, "That's a trick question because Monrovia's not a country, it's the capital of Liberia."

"Very good, I'm impressed. And the capital of Georgia is?"

He laughed. "Seriously?"

"Yeah, what is it?"

"Duh, Atlanta."

Aaahh-aahh, she made the wrong-answer Jeopardy glang. "I said the category was Foreign Countries and last time I checked the only Georgia that's a country, in case you didn't know, is the one sandwiched between Russia and Turkey. You'd get extra credit if you came up with the capital, which is Tbilisi, but, alas…you didn't."

Janzek chuckled and shook his head. "You know, you've gotten very cocky in your old age."

"Which, by the way, is thirty-one, and begs the question, 'What am I doing hanging around with an forty-year-old geezer?'"

"Um, correction, I'm only thirty-nine."

"But closing in on the big 4-0 fast."

A tad over six feet tall, Janzek had emerald green eyes and dark hair he wore a bit on the long side. A three-inch scar from below his left eye ran down the outside of his cheek and stopped at his chin. He was in good shape overall and hit the gym three days a week but could probably afford to lose eight to ten pounds. Which was why he didn't inhale bacon and cheddar croissants at Bad Bunnies seven days a week.

Slowly, he rolled over onto his back and reached up to Ryder, who was straddling him. He pulled her down and kissed her. And kissed her. And…

She pulled back. "Though I have to admit…you're a damn good kisser."

"And that's not all," he said, reaching around and unhooking her bra.

FOUR

It was a thirty-five-minute drive from Ryder's condo on West Jones Street to the dog park at the Landings on Skidaway Island. Jackie Farrell was already there when Janzek and Ryder arrived.

Janzek parked and he and Ryder walked into the park.

"Wow, this place is huge," Janzek said, waving to Jackie, who was sitting on a metal bench next to an older couple. "The ones in Charleston aren't half as big."

"Yeah, it is pretty big," Ryder said. "They take really good care of it too."

There were actually two sections of the park divided by six-foot fencing. The smaller rectangular space, Jackie had explained to her sister, was for small dogs, who sometimes got intimidated by the German Shepherds, Rhodesian Ridgebacks, and Rottweilers, the lords of the larger space. Jackie's dog, everyone conceded, was the fastest dog in the park and got along well with the others, which couldn't be said of some.

They walked over to Jackie, who gave Nick a smile and a nod, then introduced them to the couple next to her.

"You're lucky to have such a nice place," Janzek said to the couple. "I live in Charleston and the dog parks are much smaller."

"Yeah, well, this place gets a lot of use," said the husband, George.

"It's kind of social, too," said George's wife, Betsy, "and if you're not careful, it can get a little political."

"We try to steer clear of politics," George said with a wink. "I'm too old for fistfights."

Janzek and the sisters laughed.

It was time for Janzek to start mining for information.

"Did you tell them about what happened to Billy Wofford?" Janzek asked Jackie.

"Yes, she did," said George, "that's a terrible shame. Poor guy. He was actually murdered?"

"Yes, he sure was," Janzek said. "Did you know him pretty well?"

"Yup," Betsy said. "We knew him when he was Bobby Watson and later on when he became Billy Wofford."

"Ryder mentioned that. He actually went by two different names?"

George and Betsy nodded.

"It was very strange," Betsy said. "We wondered why but never came up with any good theories."

"Except maybe he was trying to hide from someone," George said with a shrug "Or hide his identity. Who knows?"

"By the way," Janzek said. "Jackie didn't mention it, but I'm a detective with the Charleston Police Department and I'm one of the lead detectives on Wofford's murder."

"Oh, are you really?" George said. "That must be an interesting job. Do you just do murders?"

"Yes, I do," Janzek said. "Unfortunately, we have enough to keep me pretty busy."

George leaned closer to Janzek. "How many do you have a year…ball park?" he asked.

"Um, usually between ten and fifteen," Janzek said, wanting to get back to being the interrogator instead of interrogatee. "Did Wofford, or Watson, ever talk about his personal life. Or mention other people? Family or friends? I'm trying to find people he knew to contact and ask questions."

"Understand," George said. "No, not that I can think of. No family that he ever mentioned…except that relative who supposedly started Wofford College."

Betsy laughed. "But nobody ever believed that."

Jackie's dog came up to them and licked Janzek's hand. "Nice pooch," he said, patting her, then to Jackie. "What's his name?"

"It's a her. Daisy."

"And what kind is she?"

"Well, that's a good question," Jackie said. "I got her at the local pound. I'm going with mutt… though she looks a lot like something called a Treeing Walker Coonhound."

"Wow, that's a mouthful," Janzek said, patting its head. "Beautiful face."

"There's a greyhound that comes here…. Daisy's faster than him," Jackie boasted.

Ryder laughed. "The proud mama."

"Well, she is," Jackie protested.

Ryder help up her hands. "Hey, I wasn't disagreeing."

"What kind of dog did Wofford have?" Janzek asked.

"This big old Great Pyrenees," George said, with a laugh. "It always liked to roll around in the mud."

"Got absolutely filthy," Betsy said, shaking her head.

"Well, listen, thanks for the info," Janzek said. "I think I'm gonna swing by Wofford's house on Priest Landing. See if anyone's there, by chance."

George nodded. "Guy used to have hot and cold running girls there."

Betsy laughed. "You sound kind of envious, George."

*****

Ryder and Jackie rode along with Janzek to the house on 1111 Priest Landing Drive.

Seeing no cars in front of the house, they drove in the driveway and simply observed for a few minutes.

No activity.

Janzek and Ryder got out first, then Jackie followed.

"No one's here," Janzek told them, pointing at a small pile newspapers on the front porch.

"So looks like he was up in Charleston for at least a few days," he said.

"Guys got a lot of security equipment," Jackie said, pointing at four cameras pointed in all directions.

"You don't suppose Billy might have left a door or a window open, do you?" Ryder asked slyly.

Janzek smiled. "Are you suggesting we enter the premises illegally? Shame on you."

Jackie shook her head. "There she goes again. Trying to get us in trouble."

"Oh, come on, why can't we have just a quick look-see?" Ryder said, then to Jackie, "You don't always have to be so damn by-the-book."

"Yeah, well, don't forget," Jackie said, "I live here. You two can go if you want."

"Let's have a look," Janzek said, observing the system with his binoculars, then pointing at a camera. "I know this system. It's the Rolls Royce of security. Made by this outfit called GW Security. It's got 24 hi-def cameras, 32 channels and this very sophisticated night vision feature. Goes for like 4 or 5 grand."

"32 channels, what's that even mean?" Ryder asked.

"You don't need to know," Janzek said. "All you need to know is the system's already made us."

'From this far away?" Ryder asked.

"Oh yeah, clear as day."

"But is it possible that someone's monitoring it?" Jackie asked. "Seeing us checking out the house right now?"

"Well, the owner's dead, so I don't know who that would be," Janzek said. "But who knows? Maybe. Could be that someone could monitor the system remotely. But I'm in favor of seeing if we can get in, take a quick look around."

"I second it," Ryder said, looking at her sister.

"But what if someone shows up?" Jackie asked. "Like the cops."

"So what if they do? I'm a cop, you're PIs," Janzek said. "It's not like we came here to steal the guy's stolen baseball cards, if he's actually got 'em."

"Sounded to me like he's already gone and sold 'em," Ryder said.

"Yeah, and with some of the money was ridin' around in a shiny, new Bentley," Jackie said.

Janzek nodded, assessing the house.

Jackie stepped back. "I can't do it. I live here. If I get caught I could get thrown out of the Landings, and I like it here."

Ryder glanced at Janzek.

"Guess it's just you and me," he told her.

Jackie stepped even farther back. "I'll be your look-out. Call you if someone shows up."

Janzek nodded and he and Ryder headed toward the house. First, Janzek tried the front door. No luck. Then they walked around to the back of the house. They peered in on what was apparently the master bedroom. It was clear Billy Wofford was not a hoarder; in fact, the opposite. The bedroom was sparsely furnished and an open walk-in closet had only a few shirts, one jacket, a pair of dress shoes, and two pairs of sneakers.

They walked a little further and found a back door, which had a dog door within it. Janzek tried the door but it too was locked. He looked down and saw Ryder crouching in front of the dog door. He knew what she was thinking

"Are you sure?" he asked.

She looked up at him. "Why not? I bet I'm not as big as a Great Pyrenees."

"All right, but before you do, I want to look around a second."

"What for?"

"Well, for one thing, I want to make sure the dog's not in there," Janzek said. "'Cause by now, he'd be pretty hungry."

Ryder smiled. "Good point."

"Don't want a big, hungry dog greeting you," Janzek said, going to a nearby window, shading his eyes and looking in. Then he went to another window and did the same. Then, satisfied, he came back to Ryder.

"No dog?" she said.

"No dog," he said with a shrug. "Hey, I just don't want to lose you."

"I know," she said. "'Cause who would rub your back?"

"Among other things."

"All right, here goes," she said and slipped through the doggie door easily, barely touching the sides. Once inside, she turned the lock and opened the door.

"Come on in," she said.

Janzek followed her in.

He went in one direction, she went in another.

Janzek's first reaction was the man lived a spartan existence. Like a priest, then he caught how appropriate the house's address was.

He started in the primary bedroom, glancing into the walk-in closet he had seen from afar. Everything looked as it had through the window…except for a loaded shotgun.

Not just loaded, but resting in a makeshift wooden stand pointing horizontally through a hole in the back of the closet at some unseen target. Half of the shotgun's barrel was not even visible. Janzek moved closer and crouched to study the rig. A plastic loop around the trigger connected to a small electronic box. He had heard about these mechanisms: they could be activated remotely to pull the trigger of a firearm, a rifle, and in this case, a shotgun.

Janzek took out his iPhone and clicked off a few shots. Then he walked out of the closet, then through the bedroom to where he suspected the shotgun would be aiming. He found a small landscape painting hanging on a wall…hanging lower than a normal painting would typically hang. He lifted the painting off of the picture hanger and saw a small circular hole in the wall with the barrel of the shotgun just sticking out.

"Ryder, come in here," he shouted, then took another picture with his iPhone.

He heard her footsteps. "What?"

She walked toward him. He put up his hand up as she was about to walk in front of the hole.

"Stop," he said, blocking her with his hand.

"What!"

"See that?" He pointed at the hole. "Don't get in front of it."

"What is it?" Ryder asked.

"Follow me," Janzek said, and he led her around to the bedroom closet where the shotgun was in the stand.

"Oh my God, what is that for?"

"It's aimed at the front door and my guess is that if someone shows up that Wofford doesn't want showing up, he might get his head blown off. See that plastic loop around the trigger connected to that black box?"

Ryder inched closer. "Yes?"

"That's a gizmo that can pull the trigger even if you're fifty miles away."

She side-eyed him. "Come on, really?"

"Yup, I've read about them."

"Oh my God, the man didn't fool around," Ryder said. "I was going through drawers and cabinets in the kitchen and you wouldn't believe all the guns and knives in there."

"Let's go take a look," he said.

He followed her into the kitchen. She opened one drawer and exposed three pistols.

Janzek started to pick one up, then stopped and pulled a pair of vinyl gloves out of his pocket and put them on. Then he picked up a pistol.

"A Ruger Mark IV," he said, then added, "fully loaded." He put it down and picked up another one. "Smith & Wesson Bodyguard 2.0…also fully loaded." He put it down and picked up the last handgun.

"That's a nasty looking one," Ryder said.

"An oldie but a goodie," Janzek said. "A Dardick 1100, also—"

"Fully loaded," Ryder said. "You trying to impress me with your knowledge of handguns, Nick?"

But Janzek was preoccupied and photographed the handguns with his iPhone. "Let's see the knives."

She took a few steps and opened a full length cabinet.

"Jesus," Janzek said. "Gotta be ten of 'em."

"Twelve, to be exact," said Ryder.

The knives, varying in length and size, were mounted on a pegboard at the back of the cabinet.

Janzek continued clicking off photos. "Anything else?"

"Not in here," Ryder said, "but we still have a bunch more rooms to cover."

In a broom closet they found four rifles and an AK-74, which Janzek explained came later than the AK-47 but, while essentially the same, used different ammunition. They, too, were loaded and ready for war.

The living room had been trashed. There were books and paintings all over the floor, along with cushions from couches, including ones that appeared to be cut open, as if someone had been searching for something.

"Looks like someone thought Wofford still had the baseball cards," Ryder said.

"Yeah, or something else," Janzek said. "I wonder if they found anything."

"When do you suppose this happened?" Ryder asked. "Before or after Wofford went up to Charleston?"

"Who knows…I'm guessing after," Janzek said. "But one thing's pretty clear. 'Ol Billy was ready for combat."

"Yeah, no kidding," Ryder said. "I'm surprised he didn't have a weapon on him when they found him."

"Maybe he did, but whoever killed him took it."

Ryder nodded. Then together they walked through the remainder of the house. A den, like the living room, was similarly trashed.

"Well," Janzek said. "I guess that about covers it. I've seen enough."

Ryder nodded. "Yeah, but I don't know about you, it poses a lot more question than answers."

"I agree," Janzek said. "Maybe what we get off the security camera will provide some answers."

Ryder nodded. "Let's hope so."

They walked back out the rear door and around the house to find Jackie on her phone.

"Okay, talk later," Jackie said, then clicked off. "So?" she asked, holding up her arms.

"So we got a houseful of guns and knives," Janzek said. "And a boobytrapped front door."

"It was like he was expecting someone to show up who wanted to kill him," Ryder said.

"Which, of course, eventually happened," Janzek said. "Check this out."

He held up his iPhone.

Jackie came closer and he clicked through all fifteen shots he had taken.

"Incredible...talk about being well-armed," Jackie said. "Unfortunately, it doesn't get you any closer to the killer, does it?"

Janzek nodded. "No, it doesn't," he said as his cell phone rang.

He glanced down at the caller. "Hang on, it's Delvin," he said. "Yeah, bro, what's up?"

"I located our vic's car not far from the lake," Delvin Rhett said. "It's a green Bentley. Big sucker with Georgia plates. It's been sitting here for a while, a neighbor told me. I ran the plate and his address is 1111 Priest Landing Drive, Savannah."

"Which, just so happens, is where I am right now," Janzek said.

"And his name is Barry Winston, right?"

Janzek laughed. "That's a new one. That's maybe the third name the guy went by. Around here he was also Bobby Watson and Billy Wofford."

"All similar names," Rhett said. "All BW initials."

"Yup, and the guy had an arsenal in his house. And someone tossed the place, searching for something."

"So where do we go from here?" Rhett said.

"That's a damn good question," Janzek said. "I'm coming back up there later in the afternoon. Let's sit down and I'll catch you up on what I've found out. You can do the same."

"Okay. And then we'll see how many more aliases we come up with for this joker."

COMING SOON...

Audio Books

Many of Tom's books are also available in Audio…

Listen to masterful narrator Frank Kearney and feel like you're right there in Palm Beach with Charlie, Mort and Dominica!

Audio books available include:

Palm Beach Nasty
Palm Beach Poison
Palm Beach Deadly
Palm Beach Bones
Palm Beach Pretenders
Palm Beach Predator
Palm Beach Broke
Palm Beach Bedlam
Palm Beach Blues
Palm Beach Taboo
Palm Beach Piranha
Palm Beach Perfidious
Palm Beach Betrayers

Charlie Crawford Box Set
(Books 1-3)

Killing Time in Charleston
Charleston Buzz Kill
Charleston Noir

The Savannah Madam
Savannah Road Kill
Dying for a Cocktail

Killers on the Doorstep

About the Author

A native New Englander, Tom Turner dropped out of college and ran a Vermont bar. Limping back a few years later to get his sheepskin, he went on to become an advertising copywriter, first in Boston, then New York. After ten years of post-Mad Men life, he made both a career and geography change and ended up in Palm Beach, renovating houses and collecting raw materials for his novels. After stints in Charleston, then Skidaway Island, outside of Savannah, Tom recently moved to Delray Beach, where he's busy writing about passion and murder among his neighbors. To date, Tom has written twenty-eight crime thrillers and mysteries and is probably best known for his Charlie Crawford series set in Palm Beach.

Learn more about Tom's books at:
www.tomturnerbooks.com

Made in the USA
Monee, IL
12 September 2025

25547594R00163